No Good Deed

by

C.D. Bennett

Dedication

To those of you who so readily lent their
support…Thank You!

Chapter 1

Kiya inhaled deeply as a breeze ruffled her hair and sent leaves scurrying across the ground. She lived for days like this. A late afternoon sun was shining bright and clear while a cool, crisp breeze rustled the newly colored leaves on the trees. Butterflies and birds took advantage of the warmth and beauty of the autumn landscape before the shorter days and colder weather of the coming winter took hold. Loosening her grip on the reins of her mount, Kiya allowed the horse to pick its own leisurely path along the woods line.

The surrounding hills and valleys were so still and tranquil that the only sounds to be heard were the footfalls of her horse, buzzing insects, and chirping birds. Occasionally, a crow would call out a loud cawing sound to its neighbors which was then echoed in the distance. She could almost convince herself that she was alone in the world and totally at peace.

Absolutely beautiful, she thought to herself with a satisfied smile on her face. "What do you think, Dax? Best day ever?" she asked, leaning forward in the saddle to pat her horse on the neck. The dark-gray gelding blew air out of his nostrils and tossed his head in apparent agreement. "Me too." Kiya sighed. Too bad it couldn't last. If she had her way, the world would be suspended in a state of perpetual autumn.

Kiya gathered in the reins to guide her horse

around some rocky areas and outcroppings. The loud crack of a rifle split the air somewhere nearby. Her horse danced nervously for a second before she calmed him with a soothing voice. "Easy Dax, easy. You're okay." So much for the peaceful part of her ride. It wasn't quite elk or deer hunting season yet. Who would be way out here firing a gun at this time of day she wondered.

A second shot that sounded even closer than the first, startled both her and the horse. She quickly dismounted to settle Dax and lead him behind some tall boulders before they would be able to move out into a more open area to get a look at who might be shooting, and at what.

As she rounded a large boulder, she froze at the sound of a male voice. "He's down."

"Are you sure?" a second voice inquired.

"I said, he's down. He will be lying there for a while before anyone finds him. Now let's get out of here."

"Shouldn't we check?"

"If you want to hike the whole way down there and check, you go right ahead. I'm getting out of here before the light starts to fade," came the gruff response.

"No, no, I'm with you. Let's go."

Kiya ran her palm down Dax's nose to keep him quiet but didn't move from her spot. Something about that exchange just didn't sound right. Didn't *feel* right. Goose bumps had risen on her arms, and her senses were tingling as if a predator were close. If those guys were hunting out of season, why would they just leave their kill for somebody else to find? And if they weren't hunting, just what exactly was *down?*

She was apprehensive enough to stay rooted in place for many long minutes until she heard the distant sound of an engine starting. Two distinct thuds of vehicle doors closing echoed faintly in the trees. Kiya looped her horse's reins over a branch and cautiously edged out from her position behind the rocks.

Off in the distance she spotted a dirty old blue pickup truck moving farther away down the hill until it finally passed out of her field of view. She released a breath she hadn't realized she was holding. *What was that all about?* She retrieved her horse while mulling over what she had seen and heard. They had to have been shooting down into the valley. It was the only direction that had a clear line of sight. She swung herself back into the saddle and made her way down to the wide grassy meadow below.

The quiet had returned, but the calm Kiya felt before her encounter with the unseen men was gone. There didn't seem to be any sign of whatever the men had been shooting at, yet the strange occurrence left her feeling uneasy. She nudged her horse into a faster pace. Right now, she just wanted to be safe at home enjoying a glass of wine while Dax munched happily on his dinner in the barn.

Something caught her eye off to her left. Was that movement? She narrowed her focus to scan the area to see what had grabbed her attention. An indistinct shape in the grass a short distance away had Kiya pulling Dax to a stop. She hopped to the ground. Knowing Dax would stay put, she left him to nuzzle through the grass as she moved closer to whatever was lying on the ground.

The shape shifted again in the grass before Kiya

realized it was a man. He had rolled partially onto his side and was currently aiming a pistol straight at her heart. Her blood ran cold; she stopped dead in her tracks. The man stared at her for one long tense moment before shifting onto his back and dropping his head to the ground.

Kiya instantly turned toward her horse, ready to flee. "Don't," called a low pain-filled voice. "Don't...leave. Help me." Once again Kiya froze where she was. Every instinct told her to run in the opposite direction as fast as possible, but she couldn't just leave an obviously wounded man lying on the ground. Especially after what she had witnessed.

Turning back toward the man, she warily moved closer. Hearing her approach, he shifted his head in her direction. He was obviously struggling to breathe and had an alarmingly gray cast to his skin. A large red stain soaked the front of his shirt. "Need help." He coughed.

"Toss the gun," she responded.

He glared at her in disbelief. "No."

"Then I'm leaving," she stated. "You were just pointing that thing at me."

The guy eyed her for another tense moment before he let out a wheezy grunt and tossed the handgun lightly in her direction. Kiya stepped forward and scooped up the weapon. She released the clip and saw that it was indeed loaded. She carefully checked the slide to make sure no rounds were in the chamber before shoving the clip back home. As she tucked the gun into the back of her waistband, she noticed the man watching her thoughtfully.

She ignored his questioning gaze and quickly

moved to his side. After dropping to her knees, Kiya placed her fingers in the bloody hole she found in his shirt and pulled. The fabric reluctantly gave way exposing a gaping hole in his side. He coughed again, spraying tiny droplets of blood around his mouth. With every labored breath, a gurgling sucking and blowing noise escaped through his chest while blood bubbled.

This is not good, she told herself as she popped up and dashed to her horse. She couldn't believe this was happening. Her blissful ride had turned into a nightmare. After quickly rummaging through her saddlebag and grabbing what she needed, Kiya hurried back to the injured man with a small first aid kit. It didn't contain much in the way of supplies, but it would have to do.

Pulling on a pair of thin vinyl gloves, she clamped a hand over the man's wound and pressed down. With the other hand, she gingerly felt under his back for an exit wound but didn't find one. That meant the bullet was still lodged somewhere in the man's chest. She visually searched for additional injuries but again found nothing obvious. Turning her full attention to the wound on his chest, Kiya opened a gauze patch and removed as much of the blood around the hole as she could. Then she ripped open a betadine swab and efficiently cleaned the wound and its surrounding area. Next, she grabbed a plastic zip lock bag containing a variety of loose band-aids and dumped it out on the ground. She tore the plastic bag along two seams before placing it over the hole and taping it securely in place on three sides.

Sitting back slightly on her heels, Kiya watched as the man's next inhalation sucked the plastic tight, sealing the hole then fluttered open on the exhale. She finally shifted her gaze to the man's pain-filled eyes. "Okay?" she asked.

"Better," he said after another breath.

"Good. I can't offer you anything for the pain, but that could mask complications anyway. Do you have a phone? Were you able to call for help?"

He gave a weak shake of his head. "Phone took off." When she raised an eyebrow, he added, "When my horse did."

"Well then," she said and rose to her feet. She gave a sharp whistle, and Dax started in their direction. She retrieved her phone from her bag. "How old are you?"

"Thirty," he replied incredulously.

"And where are we exactly?"

"Five M Ranch," he replied as comprehension dawned. "West field. Near Bareback..." He paused to suck in a ragged breath. "Ridge."

With her anxiety growing over his condition, Kiya punched nine-one-one into her phone and prayed for service. When the call finally connected, a somewhat bland voice asked about the nature of her emergency. She quickly interrupted to state in a very precise tone that she was reporting a thirty-year-old gunshot victim with a single bullet to the left chest resulting in a sucking chest wound. She added that she had been unable to locate an exit wound. "Victim states that we are on the Five M Ranch in the west field near Bareback Ridge." She turned slightly away from the man on the ground to add, "I'm new to the area so I don't know if you have the ability to do so, but if you do, this man's best chance for survival is if you can land medevac right in the middle of this field. There is plenty of space. No visible wires or power lines."

When she was sure the operator had all the information down correctly, Kiya disconnected the call and turned back to her patient. She knew she was supposed to stay on the line, but she also knew that in a location this remote, response time would be hindered. They needed help now. "Who else can I call?" she asked while checking his bandage and pulse. "Someone closer than E.M.S."

"Jake…brother." The words slurred as his eyes slid closed.

Kiya patted his cheek. "Hey, I need you to stay awake. Talk to me. Tell me your name."

"Dylan." He mustered enough will to force his eyes back open and focus on hers.

"Dylan," she repeated. "Give me Jake's number."

He painstakingly wheezed out a string of numbers that she tapped into her phone.

Two rings later the call was answered by a deep rich voice announcing, "Jake McCleary."

"Jake, my name is Kiya. I am with your brother Dylan, and we are in serious need of help." She quickly repeated the information she had given to the dispatch operator and Dylan's description of their location.

The man on the other end of the phone listened without interrupting, which Kiya appreciated. Most people would have bombarded her with a million questions that wasted precious time. She concluded her summary by adding, "I have him patched up the best I can with my limited supplies, but this isn't looking good."

"We have another brother named Cade that is out checking fence lines not far from the ridge. I will get him headed in your direction immediately, then put another call into emergency services to let them know that your call was legit and give them permission to land out there in case they had any doubt about sending in a chopper. I will be heading your way in the truck as soon as that is done. And Kiya?"

"Yes?"

"Thank you for making such an effort to assist my brother."

"You're welcome," she said before ending the call. She felt slightly better just knowing that his family was also on the way. She settled herself on the ground next to Dylan, taking his hand in hers, offering what little comfort she could. "Help is on the way, so hang in there for a little while longer, okay?" Instead of answering, he gave her fingers a gentle squeeze.

Now that there was nothing left to do but wait, Kiya found herself studying Dylan's features more closely. Under the ashen color and strained expression, he was quite handsome. His dark hair was cut into a long stylish crew cut where the lengthier hair on top arched artfully to one side. His nose was a little wide, but it balanced out his strong jawline which was covered in a short, well-groomed beard and mustache. His pain-filled eyes were a lovely shade of faded blue. The overall impression was one of masculine elegance, which considering their current situation, struck her as a little odd.

Kiya did everything she could to keep Dylan conscious, to keep his spirits up. She gently urged responses from him while talking quietly about anything that came to mind. Anything mundane enough to keep his mind off the dire consequence of each minute that slipped by. She kept a firm grip on his hand the entire time, not only to reassure him, but herself as well.

Time seemed to slow and drag on as they waited, but she urged him not to give up. Agonizing minutes later, Kiya gritted her teeth as she felt for Dylan's pulse. It was growing weaker; his forehead was beaded with sweat. Her own heart jumped at the sound of pounding hoofbeats as a rider galloped toward them. *Maybe the shooter decided to check up on his handiwork after all.* Kiya rose to her feet as a tall muscular man pulled his horse to a stop and swung to the ground.

Pulling the gun out of her waistband, she stepped farther away from Dylan, placing herself between him and the new arrival. "That's close enough," she called out. "Who are you?"

The man glanced at the gun in her hand, then at Dylan behind her before meeting her gaze. "Easy," he cautioned. He rotated his palms outward in a sign of nonaggression. "My name is Cade McCleary, and that—" He nodded in Dylan's direction. "—is my brother. Jake sent me. I would appreciate it if you would allow me to get a better look at our guy there."

Kiya returned the weapon to her waistband while taking a few steps backward giving him access to his sibling. On closer inspection, she could clearly see the resemblance between the two men. Both were tall and muscular, dark haired, and more than just casually handsome. Although Dylan's brother didn't have the same elegance to his look, and his face was slimmer, he had similar features but with more of an approachable *heartthrob next door* vibe.

Cade quickly assessed her handiwork and his

brother's overall condition. There wasn't much else he could do, he decided.

Dylan grabbed ahold of his brother's arm. "Good to…see you, man." His short speech ended in a violent coughing fit that left him exhausted and blood covering his mouth.

"You too, bro," Cade responded as he gripped Dylan's hand with his own. "You're going to make it, you hear me? Jake has mobilized half the county by now, and it is only a matter of minutes before they drop a bird right in the middle of this damn field," he vowed, referring to the medevac helicopter.

Dylan gazed into his brother's eyes and nodded once but said nothing. Cade kept talking encouragingly to his brother until he was distracted by an old Ford pickup truck that came barreling at them from across the field. It slid to a halt not far away. Dust swirled around the vehicle as yet another tall, dark, and strikingly handsome man jogged over. *There must be something special in the local water supply,* Kiya thought to herself just before Cade caught her attention.

"That's Jake," he stated, "and he won't like it if you pull a gun on him." Kiya gave the man a sardonic look. "Just saying," he told her with his hands raised.

Jake dropped to a knee on the ground beside Dylan, across from Cade. After a brief upward nod at Cade, Jake laid a hand on Dylan's shoulder. "Hey, man, you still with us?" Dylan tried to reply but couldn't get the words out, instead just shook his head and coughed weakly. As he struggled to take in a gurgling breath, Jake and Cade shared a worried look. It was obvious their brother was fading. "We are definitely going to have to discuss the sorry situations you get yourself into," Jake teased lightly to keep his brother focused.

The distinctive thumping sound of a low-flying helicopter filled the air. "Thank God!" Cade murmured. Jake continued to reassure Dylan as the medevac helicopter swung around and dropped slowly to the ground. Two men in medic uniforms hopped out of a side door and pulled a long backboard out with them prior to making their way over in a slightly crouched position.

As the medics arrived, they motioned both Cade and Jake aside and immediately went to work gaining a set of vitals and placing an I.V. The two brothers stepped a short distance away to keep a close watch and talk quietly. "He's struggling," Cade said as he watched the medic's work.

"But he's strong," Jake told him. "Not to mention bullheaded. He'll pull through even if it's just to spite whoever did this. Speaking of which," he said as he moved his intense gaze to Kiya. "What do we know about her, other than she seems to have a more than basic understanding of first aid and is cool under fire?"

"Well," Cade said as his focus zeroed in on her also. "I know she was willing to defend Dylan if necessary. She pulled a gun on me when I arrived and demanded to know who I was before she let me near him."

"She's armed?" Jake countered hotly.

"I think she has Dylan's gun."

"Could she have shot him?"

Cade shook his head. "Dylan was shot with a rifle not a handgun. It had to have been from a pretty good distance too. I haven't seen a rifle anywhere or any indication from either of them that would suggest she was involved."

The medical team finished stabilizing Dylan and strapped him securely onto the backboard then prepared to leave with their patient. Jake let them know that he and Cade would meet them at the hospital as soon as possible. As Dylan was loaded for takeoff, the two remaining brothers approached Kiya.

"I understand you have Dylan's gun. I'd like it back," Jake said.

"Not gonna happen," she replied.

Dylan's brother looked taken aback by her response. "I beg your pardon?" he almost growled.

Kiya took an involuntary step back at his tone but huffed out a defiant breath anyway. He had a tougher, more rugged, and chiseled appearance than his brothers. His body was harder, shoulders wider. He also had a definite edge to his demeanor. His smokey-blue eyes were intense as he watched her. "Look, I don't know you." She pointed at Cade. "I don't know him. And I sure as hell don't know what Dylan did to make those guys want to kill him, so I'm not giving the gun to anybody until the cops get here." She crossed her arms and waited for him to protest. It didn't take long.

"Explain!" he demanded.

Speaking in a manner that implied he was more than a little slow, Kiya tried again. "I don't think there is anything to explain. I don't feel comfortable turning the gun over to anyone except the police. I assume they are on their way also."

Jake made an impatient gesture. "You said the men that wanted to kill Dylan...*what men?*"

Just then the helicopter's engines roared. Its blades began to spin rapidly, drowning out any attempts at communicating. The three of them watched as it lifted gracefully into the air, made a wide arc, then sped off in the direction of the nearest trauma center.

Two vehicles, an SUV and a large black pickup, both emblazoned with the decal of the local sheriff's department, rumbled up as the helicopter made its exit. A man with wavy, light-colored hair, dressed in a brown uniform, stepped out of the truck and stood for a minute watching the helicopter disappear in the distance, then walked over to the small group still staring at the sky. "Jake," he said, extending a hand. He nodded to Cade.

"Mitch." Jake clasped the outstretched hand of the sheriff as another officer joined them. "Jenkins," he said to address the newcomer.

"How is he? Is he stable?" the sheriff wanted to know.

"Well, he is alive and still mostly coherent."

"What the hell happened?"

Jake pointed to Kiya. "That's exactly what she was about to tell us."

Kiya looked startled. "I'm sorry to disappoint you, but I don't know much of anything, and I really don't want to be involved in this any further than I absolutely have to be. I did my part; he's alive."

The sheriff turned his full attention to her for the first time since his arrival. "And you are?"

"Kiya James. I recently rented the Billings' place."

"I heard they had rented out the farm after they left to stay with their son in Seattle. What brought you out here?" Officer Jenkins asked, gesturing to the field they were standing in.

"I'd like to know the answer to that also," Jake

stated. "You crossed onto Five M land a good distance from here. How did you just happen to find my brother lying in the middle of nowhere?"

"That sounds more like an accusation than a question." She crossed her arms. "Maybe I should refrain from answering any questions until I can have a lawyer present."

The sheriff jumped in to smooth things over before they got out of hand. "Ma'am, I'm sure that won't be necessary."

Kiya turned a cool gaze in his direction. "My name is Kiya." It had always amazed her when that term was used to show so-called *respect* when to her it had always sounded so condescending.

"Kiya," the man conceded. "Why don't you just tell us what happened. Anything that might help."

"I was just out riding. It's a gorgeous day. I wanted to enjoy the landscape and get to know the area. I was originally up on the ridge beyond the outcropping." She pointed in that direction before looking back at Jake McCleary. "Which is on my side of the property line." She then explained to the sheriff about the two men, their odd exchange, where she thought the shots had been made from, how they had left the area, and in what direction. "The whole thing just felt...off. So, I stayed out of sight until they were gone. I thought they might be poachers, but why would they go through the effort only to leave the kill? Especially when they knew they hit something. I was curious, so I came down here to see if I could find what they had been shooting at as I circled back home. What I found was Dylan."

"And I, for one, am glad you did. That patch job you pulled off is why he was alive when they loaded him onto that chopper," Cade told her.

"You always ride with medical supplies?" Jake asked.

"As a matter of fact, yes. I used to be an EMT, so it's a habit. I usually carry at least a basic first aid kit with me. You should be grateful that I do, so…you're welcome." She didn't like feeling as if she needed to defend herself. She had just finished doing everything she could to save his brother's life for goodness' sake!

"I know, I'm sorry. We truly appreciate what you did for Dylan. This is just a bizarre situation. I can't make sense of it," Jake groused, running his fingers through his hair in agitation.

"Well, first thing we need to do is get a few men up on that ridgeline to see what evidence may have been left behind. Jenkins, call for some backup and head on up there. I also want someone out here combing through this immediate area where Dylan ended up," the sheriff instructed.

"On it," the deputy replied and jogged to his SUV.

"Cade, Jake, I'd like to follow you two to the hospital if you don't mind. I can officially check on Dylan's status and see if he can shed some light on what happened out here." When they had no objections, he turned back to Kiya. "I'll need you to come into the station tomorrow morning and make a formal statement."

"Can't we keep my name out of this? I already told you everything I know. And I really don't want to be associated with an attempted homicide investigation in my first few weeks in the area."

"Whether you want to be or not, you are already at the center of this investigation," he informed her.

"Other than Dylan himself, who may or may not have any additional information, *you* are the only person that saw or heard anything."

"That's the problem," she told him grudgingly. "We already know these people are dangerous. What happens when they find out someone saw what they did? This is a small town, people talk."

"I'll try to keep your name out of it as much as I can. Especially when it comes to any press coverage, but I need your formal statement on record to move forward. I'll make sure my guys include your place on their route for a drive-by when they're on duty."

"I would appreciate that," she told him. "I also need to give you Dylan's gun. He had it with him when I found him. He pointed it at me, so I made him hand it over." She cautiously removed the weapon from her waistband and passed it to the sheriff. "To my knowledge, it hasn't been fired. But like I told them"—she hitched a thumb at the two brothers—"I don't know anyone involved here or why it happened, so I just wanted to play it safe."

"And what about a rifle? Do you have one?"

Kiya gritted her teeth, but she knew he had to ask. "If you're asking if I have one with me, the answer is no. I own a .30-30 Winchester hunting rifle that belonged to my father and a legally registered Glock 42. Neither of which is a caliber that they are going to pull out of Dylan. Everything I own is locked up safe and sound at home. I have absolutely no reason to shoot a perfect stranger who lives near my home just to try and patch him up again."

"I agree that you would have no reasonable motive to be involved in harming Dylan, but I wouldn't be doing my job if I didn't ask."

"You have to do your job in order to help Dylan, I realize that." Resigned to her fate, Kiya agreed to meet the sheriff at his office the next day, then went to collect Dax as the rest of them headed to the hospital.

Chapter 2

Kiya smoothed down her dress as she climbed out of her Jeep Wrangler and stood gazing up at the multipurpose structure housing the police station. The small building contained not only the sheriff's office, but also the borough office and the fire department with its two bay doors for emergency vehicles. She made her way up the four concrete steps that led to the main door at the front of the building and pulled it open.

Inside the borough building was a small room immediately to her left with a sliding glass window cut into the wall. That single room housed the borough office. It currently appeared to be unoccupied. Directly in front of her, across a small square waiting area were two chairs pushed up against the wall. A short hallway was adorned with an arrow showing the fire department logo pointed straight ahead and to the right at the back of the building.

To her far right there were two more doors with a sign between them saying *Police*. Beyond that, in the back corner, was a larger room that appeared to be some sort of meeting room, which appeared mostly empty except for a single long table surrounded by chairs. Since the door marked *Sheriff Mitchell Patterson* was closed, and the other revealed a woman behind a desk carefully plucking away at a computer, Kiya moved toward what she assumed was the receptionist's office. Tapping lightly on the doorframe to gain attention, she addressed the woman. "Excuse me, I am looking for the sheriff. He asked me to stop by today."

After tapping two more keys, one with each index finger, the woman looked up with a bright smile. "Well, hi there." She all but chirped before popping out of her seat. "I'm Joni. Mitch's, I mean Sheriff Patterson's secretary." She paused and cocked her head to the side with a laugh. "Come to think of it, I'm everybody's secretary. But that is neither here nor there. Can I get you some coffee?"

Perky, Kiya thought to herself with a friendly smile for Joni. "No thanks. I just have some quick paperwork to deal with. Shouldn't take too long. Is he in?"

"Sure is. Might be on the phone if his door is closed. He's been mighty busy today, but I'll let him know you're here." She stepped around Kiya who was now standing slightly inside the doorway. Leaning over to the closed door, she rapped twice loudly, then called out, "Mitch? Someone to see ya!" Turning back to her office and Kiya, she smiled again. "He'll be right with you."

Trying to curb an amused smile, Kiya thanked her and glanced around the tiny office. The space was cheerfully decorated with pictures, plants, and a bounty of colorful knick-knacks. It appeared to reflect the personality of the woman that occupied it.

"You new in town?" Joni asked curiously.

"Yes. I'm renting the Billings' property. I've been told they are staying with their son."

"Oh, that's a lovely piece of property. You'll like it there. I know Bill and Edna were relieved to find a renter since it sat empty for a bit. The income will be a blessing, they have a new grandbaby due any day and were so excited to head out there. To Washington State, that is. I've never been, have you?"

"No. But I hear it is beautiful. I would like to visit someday," Kiya replied.

Sheriff Patterson stuck his head into the room. "Hello, Ms. James. I appreciate you coming in. We can talk in my office." He nodded back over his shoulder toward the room behind him. "Thanks for keeping her company, Joni."

"Sure thing, boss," the woman assured him. "You know I'd rather be catching up with the locals, old or new, rather than dealing with that infernal thing." She indicated the computer on her desk and winked at Kiya.

Once they were both inside the sheriff's office, he shut the door and gestured to the only chair facing his desk. "Have a seat. How are you holding up after yesterday's events?" he asked her.

"I'm okay," Kiya assured him. "I didn't get much sleep, but that is hardly a surprise. I would really like to hear how Dylan is doing. I am heading over to the hospital after we are done here with the hope that they will allow me to see him. How did things go last night?"

"The surgery took longer than expected. It was tricky with the amount of internal bleeding and the damage done to his lung. They also removed some bone fragments left behind from the bullet nicking his ribs, but he made it through surgery and was stable the last I heard."

"I am so relieved to hear that. What about the men who shot him? Did your guys find the area we were in when the shots were fired?"

"They did. Your description was dead on. We found a couple spent shell casings and an area that was trampled with quite a bit of foot traffic. Nothing distinctive or identifiable. The shot lines up too. Unfortunately, that's all we have at the moment. There is an overgrown hunting trail or access road where you saw the truck leave, but older model blue farm trucks are a dime a dozen around here, and sending those shells out for prints won't be a fast turnaround. Of course, we would need something to match them against to make them useful. I never got the chance to talk with Dylan last night. He was still in recovery when I left. Why don't we get your statement down on paper then head on over to the hospital to see how he's doing?"

****

Getting in to see Dylan turned out to be a breeze when accompanied by the town sheriff. After Kiya had followed his truck with her own vehicle to the hospital's main parking area, they walked straight through the hospital lobby without stopping and took the elevator to the third floor. Once there, he walked up to the ICU nurse's station and addressed an older lady behind the desk. "Hey, Marge, what room did they end up putting Dylan McCleary in last night? We need to speak with him."

"Room 308, Mitch. Nasty business, what happened to that boy. Gonna be a long while before he is right again."

"Nasty covers it," he agreed. "Is he awake this morning?"

"Not since I got here, but that is not unexpected.

An injury like that really knocks you flat."

"Sure does, but I am hoping he can give us some insight on how to find whoever did this."

"Could it have been nothing more than a horrible accident?" There was a slightly hopeful note to the question.

"Not looking that way, Marge, but we are just getting started on the investigation."

The woman shook her head sadly. "The McClearys, they are good people. It's just not right that this should happen to them. You be careful out there, Mitch, but make sure whoever pulled that trigger ends up behind bars."

"I'm working on it," he told her before he led Kiya down the hall toward room 308.

As they approached the partially closed door with the correct number, Kiya anxiously switched the items she held from one arm to the other. She had struggled over what might be considered an appropriate gift for an adult male that was hospitalized. Especially one that was a complete stranger. Showing up empty-handed, however, seemed rude. She had no idea what his likes or dislikes were. Flowers for a guy might be seen as odd, so she ruled those out. Plus, there could be allergy issues with that idea. If they were even allowed in this area of the hospital, that is. Balloons were too childlike and happy, in her opinion, for a gunshot victim. Eventually she had settled on a selection of men's magazines and a deck of cards. At least he would have options other than TV if he eventually felt up to them. The sheriff rapped on the door then pushed it open when someone inside called out, "Come on in."

Kiya lingered in the background once she realized

Dylan wasn't alone. Jake stood near his brother's bedside while Cade was sitting next to the window on a small, cushioned bench with his arm around a woman who had obviously been crying. The woman dabbed at her eyes with a soggy tissue before glancing at the sheriff then over at Kiya. Smiling tentatively, she rose to her feet with Cade following suit.

Jake was the first to speak. "Ms. James, I'm surprised to see you here. Yesterday you seemed adamant about not becoming more involved with our situation."

Kiya shifted uncomfortably. She shouldn't have come. What was she thinking? She was an outsider here, and what he had said was true. This wasn't a situation she wanted to be a part of. She simply hadn't been able to resist the need to make sure Dylan was all right. "I know, I'm sorry. I didn't mean to intrude. I just wanted to make sure Dylan was doing well. I'll, ah, I'll just leave this stuff here and go." She stepped forward to pass over her meager offerings.

"Jake, don't be rude," the woman next to Cade admonished quietly.

It looked like Jake was about to reply, but a raspy voice caught everyone's attention.

"My guardian angel returns." Dylan was awake. He smiled weakly at Kiya, drawing her closer. Without intending to, she found herself moving to his side and taking his hand in hers. She noted the clip on his finger monitoring his oxygen saturation levels, as the small nasal cannula in his nose supplemented his breathing. Wires attached to his chest recorded his heart rate and respirations which were displayed on a nearby monitor, while a blood pressure cuff periodically hummed to life around his bicep. She was relieved that everything seemed to be at acceptable levels. She brushed a lock of hair from his forehead with her free hand. "You look much better than the last time we met. How do you feel?"

"Like I've been shot," he grumbled.

"Don't worry, it won't be long before you're angling for a little extra TLC from some attractive nurse."

"Might be worth…a try," he replied brokenly.

Kiya smiled at him then grew serious. "I can't even tell you how glad I am that you were strong enough, determined enough, to pull through such an injury. You had me worried."

He rocked his head back and forth on his pillow. "Deck was stacked in my favor. I had you." He brought their linked hands to his lips to place a light kiss against her knuckles, then let his eyes droop closed again. The small exchange had sapped his energy.

Kiya's eyes glistened with unshed tears as she gently laid Dylan's hand back on the bed. Jake knew from watching their exchange that the woman in front of him had nothing to do with whatever happened out there in that field. He didn't know how, but she had been in the right place at the right time to save and protect Dylan. And even though she said she didn't want any further involvement, he was sure that she had, and would, do anything she could to help his brother.

"You're Kiya. You're the one that helped Dylan after he was left to die."

Kiya turned to look at the woman who spoke. She had almost forgotten the other woman's presence.

Tears rolled down an incredibly lovely face that

was remarkably similar to the others in the room. The woman was small like Kiya herself and had her family's dark natural beauty. Her hair was cut into a fashionable long pixie bob, or bixie, as some people call it. On her, Kiya would simply call it gorgeous. Her wide, expressive eyes reflected her emotions without any effort on her part. The woman approached Kiya and wrapped her in a tight hug. "Thank you. Thank you for saving my brother."

Kiya wasn't sure what to do as Dylan's sister cried. She patted the woman's shoulder soothingly. "I didn't do much. Dylan and the surgeon did the hard stuff."

"That's not true. If it weren't for you, he would have died alone out there, and we never would have known until it was too late," the woman said as she sniffed and pulled away to dab at her eyes. "I'm Hillary by the way. Hilly to most people, and I am very glad to meet you."

"She's right," Cade added, placing a comforting arm around his sister. "We will never be able to repay what you have done for our family."

"The only repayment I want is to see Dylan recover and leave here healthy," Kiya told him.

Cade smiled in acknowledgment of her comment then shifted his gaze to the sheriff. "Any news?"

"Not as much as we would like. I really need to get Dylan's take on things. Did he say anything last night or this morning?"

It was Jake who answered. "I stayed with him last night until he was moved here from recovery and for a couple hours afterward to make sure he remained stable. He opened his eyes once before I left, but never spoke. This morning he has woken up a few times and acknowledges our presence but hasn't said much. Not until he heard Kiya's voice, that is."

Kiya glanced at him to judge his thoughts on that matter, but his tone had been much softer when mentioning her name this time. He also didn't appear upset by his brother's reaction to her presence. He seemed encouraged by it.

"Well then, until he can talk to us, I will tell you what we've got," the sheriff said. "We were able to locate the area Kiya described. My guys were able to pick up her trail on the way in from the Billings' place and the location the shot came from just like she said. Her smaller prints led to a spot that was trampled down by at least two sets of larger booted prints that had arrived from the opposite direction." He glanced at Kiya to see how she responded to the knowledge that they had checked out her story. She returned the look calmly. "Like I told her," he continued, "nothing was very distinct or identifiable, but the line of fire fits. Not much in the way to obstruct a person's view, so it would be a hard sell for anyone to claim mistaken identity of the target. We also located the area where they parked a vehicle before walking in. Tire size would indicate a truck consistent with the one described as leaving the area, but once they got off that ridge, they could have gone anywhere. Any of you using the old logging road or trail up there where the truck was left?"

"That used to be the trail that led to Dad's old hunting cabin. It hasn't been used in years," Cade told him. "No one goes up there much anymore. That place turned to ruin a long time ago. It's mostly just the shell of a building. Not many people know a path existed at all."

"That's what has been bothering me," Mitch said. "Only a local could have known how to use that as an access to the area. It's not likely someone found it while out casually scouting around. Have you given permission for anyone to hunt out that way?"

"No. As you know, we have horses or cattle grazing the fields most of the time. We only move them closer to the main house when the weather changes. Local hunters know our land is off-limits—it's clearly marked. Still, it would seem more likely that someone was poaching rather than deliberately aiming for Dylan, right?" Cade asked.

The sheriff tipped his head. "I would agree with that if Kiya hadn't heard someone acknowledge that they had hit something and chose to leave the area without it. The shooter also said *he* was down, not it. I clarified that with her when she said it, just to make sure. And like I said, it would be hard to mis-identify the target from where they were. Unless they were shooting at anything that moved. Maybe if they were using live animals as nothing more than target practice, it could be an accident. I'm not saying they couldn't have used the word *he* to refer to an animal, but if they even suspected they might have hit anything other than an animal, they weren't too worried about it. Which doesn't bode well either. It was either deliberate or they just didn't care. What had you and Dylan that far out on the ranch yesterday?"

"We were checking separate fence lines for breaks. There have been a few of them that needed repairs lately," Cade supplied. He looked over at Kiya. His comment seemed to have caused a slight reaction in her. "Why does that interest you?"

She shook her head. "It's nothing really, just an odd coincidence. I have needed to patch the far side of my fence line a couple of times since I got here too, even though it doesn't seem overly worn or rusted. Of course, maintenance is always an ongoing thing."

There was a soft rap at the door as a nurse stepped in to check on her patient. Kiya thought that was a good time to make her exit. Being allowed to see that Dylan was improving alleviated her anxiety and filled her with happiness, but she was sure that his family would rather spend this harrowing time with him without a stranger present. She said goodbye, thanking them all, then headed for home with a lighter heart.

Chapter 3

A few days later, Kiya stood in her barn idly brushing Dax's glossy coat as he munched on grain. She had spent her morning cleaning out his stall and laying new bedding before putting him through his paces. Now he was enjoying a well-earned midday snack. He had already eaten his breakfast hours earlier, but a little extra treat wouldn't hurt him. Not with winter approaching.

She knew that lingering in the barn was only putting off her more mundane errands, but that didn't encourage her to get moving. If it involved town and people, she usually ended up finding ways to put it off. People were just so....taxing. Grocery shopping, going to the post office, or even the feed store, were just necessary evils. They weren't much fun. Especially when people she didn't even know stopped to talk and ask a bunch of questions. They were just being friendly, she supposed, and were curious about the newcomer, but she was much more comfortable on her own with her animals for company. That probably made her a little odd to most people, but she didn't really mind.

She gave Dax a final pat and moved out of his stall to latch the door. "Come on, Luna," she called to the black-and-white border collie keeping watch from her perch on top of some nearby hay bales. "Want to go for a ride?" The dog leaped to the ground with an excited bark and raced ahead. *At least someone is excited about going into town,* she thought. Then again, Luna loved everyone and was eternally happy, so going to town for her meant new friends, sights, sounds, and adventure.

Kiya found the dog waiting next to her Jeep. She chuckled and opened the door so the animal could jump in. "You wait. I need money before we can do anything." Leaving the dog with her head hanging out of the open window, she went inside to get her things.

Luna loved going to the feed store. She was allowed to tag along inside to pick out her own toys and treats as Kiya's order was filled. She was as spoiled as any small child and couldn't have been any happier as she trotted up to the counter with a brand-new grunting hedgehog toy clutched in her jaws. She had found the strange-looking thing in a sale bin and had been carrying it around ever since. Plopping her butt on the floor, she waited while the humans rang up her goods, which included kibble and a bag of her favorite treats. She entertained herself by giving the toy a tighter squeeze that resulted in a loud pig-like sound. Kiya ruffled the hair between the dog's ears and laughed at the silly doggie grin. "You are shameless, my friend."

The new playmate to cuddle and a tasty treat kept the dog busy as Kiya quickly finished the rest of her errands. She was congratulating herself on completing her tasks without interruption when an older lady stopped her outside of the market.

"You must be Kiya James. Hilly described you perfectly. I'm Margaret Hayes. I help the McClearys with cooking and cleaning a couple of days a week out at the Five M. Hilly told me what you did for Dylan, I just wanted to add my thanks to theirs. That family has been like my own since long before their parents passed away. Don't know how any of us could have stood to lose him. Thankfully, because of you, we don't have to find out."

Kiya was at a loss for words for a moment. She wasn't used to getting such heartfelt attention from strangers on the street. "No thanks are necessary. I'm just glad I was able to help. I have only met Hilly once, but I certainly remember her. The McClearys share an unusually strong family resemblance."

"Oh yes, they are an attractive lot, aren't they?" She chuckled. "It's so unfair, but you haven't even met them all yet. Gretchen—she's the eldest of the group—just flew in last night. I know she will want to meet you too."

"Oh but…surely, they will be more focused on taking care of Dylan. I am hoping he is well enough to go home soon. It has been my experience that patients tend to do better once they are strong enough to continue their recovery at home. The noise and constant activity of the hospital setting is hard to adjust to and is very disruptive. All the doctors and nurses coming and going for checkups and vitals every few hours, machines constantly making noise at the bedside, then there are the medications, blood work, and scans. It is amazing that people can get any rest at all."

"Good grief," Margaret said with a slight shudder. "You make me really glad I have never had to spend much time at a hospital. Luckily, Hilly said that Dylan is doing well. I went to visit him once but didn't stay long. He still tires easily. If he continues to improve and there is still no sign of infection, he could be released by the end of the week."

Only a few more days, Kiya thought. A loud bark rang out from her vehicle a short distance away. "Uh-oh, that's for me. Sounds like someone wants to get home for her dinner. It was nice to meet you, Margaret, and I am so glad Dylan is improving." They shared goodbyes before Kiya jogged to her Jeep with her bag.

The light was starting to fade as she pulled into the driveway. There was just enough time to put away her few groceries then feed Dax before she could settle in for the night to relax. Kiya hurried through her outdoor evening routine effortlessly. The repetition of the nightly chores settled her nerves after a long day. Once she was inside for the night, she kicked off her shoes by the door and padded through the kitchen in her fluffy socks. The extra layer of protection added a welcome barrier against the chilly hardwood floors. The sensations and freedom of being barefoot in the summer were fun, but now that the weather was changing fast, she preferred the homey comfort of an extra layer.

She moved around the kitchen preparing a light dinner and mixing Luna's kibble with a spoonful of canned food for a special flavor boost. She bent to place the dog's meal on the spill-proof mat covering a section of floor next to the island. She smoothed a hand down the dog's back, giving her a soft pat. The sound of breaking glass caused her to jump. Luna barked in agitation. Looking around to find where the sound had come from, Kiya saw that the window on the opposite wall from her was broken and jagged.

What in the world? She moved cautiously across the kitchen toward the window and the glass that now littered the floor. She couldn't imagine what could have caused the window to break. No trees or loose objects were located on that side of the house. A glass bowl on the counter shattered just before there was a low thud of impact against the wall to her left. Luna started barking wildly, interspersed with high-pitched whines. "Luna, stay," she instructed the dog as she herself inched closer to the side of the room where the window was broken. Something had to have come through the window to break the bowl.

A small object whizzed past her arm leaving fire in its wake. She hissed in pain as she dropped to the floor to avoid the wood chips exploding out of the kitchen island. *Gunfire!* Someone was shooting into the house! On her hands and knees, Kiya scrambled over to Luna and grabbed her collar. "Down," she commanded. The dog immediately dropped to the floor and waited for another command. "Stay!"

After making sure the dog would hold her position under such circumstances, Kiya inched across the floor to the wooden stand beside the door. Bullets seemed to be coming from different angles as she moved. She remained on the floor and reached an arm up to the tabletop to feel around for her cell phone. Luna whined in distress from her position on the floor. Her body shivered with fear and worry. "Good girl, Luna. Stay," Kiya reassured her in a strained voice.

Finally locating and grasping the phone, she punched nine-one-one into the device for the second time in merely a week. Plaster and wood chips continued to rain down from the bullets hitting the walls and furniture.

"Nine-one-one, what is the location of your emergency?"

Shaking with adrenaline and fear, Kiya rattled off

her address. "Someone is shooting at my house!" She let out a small yelp when a window in the door above her exploded and came flying inward. Scooting back over to her dog, she pulled the animal close as she relayed information to the dispatcher on the other end of the call. Kiya pressed her face into her dog's neck as the woman spoke to her calmly and assured her that all available units were en route. Time slowed to a crawl as she waited for help amid the ongoing assault.

In an instant, the commotion stopped, and stillness prevailed around them. The silence was almost as unnerving as the chaos. *Are they gone, or is someone busy reloading? They could also be sneaking closer right now to enter the house.* Kiya held her breath and listened for any noise coming from outside. She waited without moving. Dust and debris settled to the floor around her. Everything remained quiet as she crouched on the floor curled around Luna's quaking form. She wasn't sure how long it was before the dog whimpered again in response to the sound of sirens in the distance. Her whines turned to barks when tires crunched in the driveway. Loud voices and a flurry of activity could be heard as people approached, but Kiya remained where she was.

Someone knocked on the door then called out through the broken window frame in the middle. "Kiya? It's Sheriff Patterson. I'm coming in." The door groaned as it was shoved open over the mess on the floor.

Mitch spotted Kiya and the dog huddled on the floor next to the sink and hurried over. He placed a hand gently on her shoulder. Tremors racked her entire body as he bent down and spoke in a soothing tone.

"Kiya? It's over now. You're going to be okay." He surveyed the destruction around him. There were bullet holes everywhere he looked. It was hard to take it all in. Things like this just didn't happen in this quiet little community. He turned his attention back to the woman beside him. "Let's get you out of here."

Kiya released the dog and climbed to her feet. She felt almost numb as she followed the sheriff outside. Luna was unusually subdued, not greeting anyone, and wouldn't leave her side. "Dax! I need to check on my horse," Kiya cried trying to veer off in the direction of the barn.

Mitch caught her arm and pulled her up short. "I will make sure someone checks on your horse. All the damage seems to have been focused on the house. Right now, I'm more concerned about you…you're bleeding." He nodded to her other arm.

Looking down at her throbbing right arm, she saw the crimson color staining her shirt sleeve and the droplets of blood dripping from her fingertips. Her face stung from nicks caused by flying wood chips and bits of glass. She sighed and allowed the sheriff to steer her in the direction of a waiting ambulance.

Men in police uniforms seemed to be everywhere. They had positioned their vehicles in such a way that their headlights illuminated the dark around them. The sheriff moved among them directing their search for evidence and answering questions or asking his own. Seated at the end of a stretcher in the back of the ambulance, Kiya watched their movements with detached interest while an EMT took her vitals and asked her a series of health questions. When she had given him all her pertinent medical information, he cut the thin sleeve off her shirt to view the extent of the injury there. The wound was deeper than it was wide and spanned a little more than three inches across the outer portion of her bicep. He flushed the wound with a saline solution to clear away the blood and pieces of fabric stuck to the damaged flesh. Next, he lightly patted the area dry, then covered it with a few layers of nonstick gauze patches and secured it to control the bleeding. Moving on, he quickly checked the knicks and cuts dotting her face. Once he was satisfied that most of those injuries were superficial, he called the sheriff over. "Mitch, we are good to go, over here."

"Thanks, Zach. What's the verdict?"

The EMT shook his head. "That's for the docs to decide, but my guess would be that she ends up with some stitches and a tetanus booster. That arm will be sore for a while, but she'll live." He smiled and winked at Kiya to lighten the tone of his pronouncement.

"Give me a few minutes here, and you can be on your way," Mitch said. He laid a hand on Kiya's shoulder. "Your horse is fine. A little antsy, but unharmed."

"Thank you," she said with relief. The knot in her stomach loosened slightly. Luna stood on her hind legs and braced her front paws on the vehicle's bumper to push her nose under Kiya's hand offering comfort. Or maybe seeking it. The dog had remained near the back of the ambulance while Kiya was being treated.

"That's a devoted friend you have there," Mitch commented as Kiya stroked the animal's head. "She wasn't harmed, was she?"

"No, she's okay. Just shaken up."

"That's to be expected for both of you under the

circumstances. Did you see who did this?"

"No. One minute I was feeding Luna her dinner, and the next, bullets were flying. I spent most of the time on the floor and couldn't see anything."

"You did the right thing," he assured her. "I'm going to finish up here, then I'll check in on you at the hospital. We will go over things then."

"I can't go to the hospital. I'm not leaving Luna in a house that is missing windows and full of things she can get hurt on. And then there's Dax…no way. I have to stay here."

"Kiya, I will make sure your animals are safe and taken care of. You are the one that's injured and needs medical attention. This place isn't fit for anyone right now. Go, I'll handle things here, I promise."

She looked over at the house riddled with bullet holes. He was right, the place wasn't fit to stay in. "How am I ever going to explain this to Bill and Edna?" Kiya asked, referring to the property owners.

"Don't worry about that now. They carry insurance, and if I know the Billings at all, they will be more concerned about your safety than they are about property damage that can be fixed." Mitch signaled the EMT that his patient was ready to go then glanced down at the dog still hovering near the back of the ambulance. "Will she come with me?" he asked Kiya.

"Once I am gone, she will do what you tell her. But to be safe, there is a leash hanging on the wall just inside the door. She won't like that I am leaving her behind."

Moments later, Kiya watched as her home grew smaller and smaller outside the tiny windows at the back of the ambulance as they left for the hospital.

Chapter 4

Seated on an examining table, Kiya waited patiently for the nurse to return with her discharge papers. As predicted by the EMT who had treated her on scene, she now had eight stitches in her arm closing the bullet graze she had sustained, and three additional ones in her right cheek where splinters of either glass or wood had struck her face. She had been given a tetanus booster as a precaution, some mild pain killers, and was declared fit to leave the hospital.

A deputy had stopped by at the sheriff's request to take her statement a short time ago. Now all she had to do was wait. She wasn't sure where she was supposed to go when she was released, or how she would get there, but she would worry about that in a minute or two. Now that the adrenaline was no longer coursing through her system, and the pain meds were dulling the burning ache in her arm, she was fading fast. Exhaustion was weighing her down. She moved to sit in a chair next to the wall and leaned her head against it before closing her eyes. *I just need a minute,* she told herself.

Jake came to an abrupt stop in the doorway when he spotted her. He was reluctant to disturb her after what she had been through tonight. He still couldn't wrap his head around it. She looked a little worse for the wear, and probably needed the rest. He studied the unusual paleness of her skin and the dark lines of stitches marring her arm and face. Dusky shadows were forming under her eyes confirming her fatigue. None of those things took away from her natural beauty, he decided. Her heart-shaped face had a porcelain-like quality that made it look smooth and flawless. When open, he knew her eyes were wide and a rich, warm amber color. A small straight nose led to softly bowed lips that needed little enhancement. Long, dark mahogany-colored tresses flowed in soft layered waves well past her delicate collarbones. With an internal cringe, he shook his head to clear his thoughts. He had never caught himself admiring a woman's collarbones before. *Maybe I'm the one that needs to rest.*

Jake was at a total loss as to what was going on lately, but it couldn't be a coincidence that two shooting events happened within miles of each other in the same week. It bothered him that Kiya saving his brother's life could have led to this.

When Kiya opened her eyes, she was startled to see Jake watching her from the doorway. She quickly pushed herself upright. *Why is he here, and how long has he been standing there?* He must have been visiting Dylan upstairs.

"Jake," she said as she brushed back a few strands of hair that had fallen into her eyes as she changed position. "Is Dylan doing all right?"

He wasn't really surprised that she immediately asked about Dylan even under the current circumstances, but he wasn't sure if it impressed him or annoyed him. "Dylan is healing very well. Although I had to practically sit on him to stop him from commandeering a wheelchair and coming down here himself, when he heard what happened. I had to promise I would make sure you were receiving top-notch care and report straight back to him before he would agree to stay in his bed."

That explained his presence. He wasn't here for her per se but out of concern for his brother's wellbeing. That was only natural she assumed. As an only child, she had never experienced the close bond of a sibling. "I'm fine," she said as both the sheriff and her nurse walked into the room.

"All patched up I see," Mitch said with a smile.

"I'm fine," Kiya repeated. "Where's Luna?"

The sheriff glanced at the man next to him then back to Kiya. "Jake had her and your horse moved to the ranch for the time being. I had your doors and windows covered temporarily with plywood to secure the house when we left, but you are going to need a place to stay until the proper repairs can be made."

"That's easy," Jake interjected. "She'll stay at the ranch."

"No I won't," Kiya said in disbelief.

"Yes you will."

"I can't do that," she insisted.

"Yes, you can," he responded.

"I'll find a hotel, or motel"—she gave a little shrug—"or something."

Jake ignored her and addressed the nurse who was watching them curiously. "Any special instructions?"

"Well…" The woman couldn't seem to decide who she should give the answer to. She settled her gaze on Kiya since she was the patient and said, "Those sutures should stay dry for a couple days to allow them to start to heal properly. After that, showers are okay as long as you carefully pat the stitches dry afterward. It's better to leave them open to the air, so no bandages are needed, unless you are doing something where dirt could get into the wound. A thin coating of antibiotic ointment can be used if the area starts to feel overly tight or starts to tug. Other than that, it isn't necessary. The doctor wants you to fill a prescription for some antibiotics to ward off any possible infection. You can come back in about a week to have the stitches on your face removed, but the ones on your arm will probably stay in for a little while longer. If you have any questions or concerns, you can always give us a call." She handed Kiya a clipboard and indicated where she should sign, then passed over a small batch of papers for her to keep. She wished Kiya luck, then hurried on her way.

Mitch cleared his throat as silence lingered in the room following the nurse's departure. "Okay, I guess I will leave the two of you to figure out any further details. If either of you need anything from me in the meantime, just let me know. Oh, I almost forgot your keys." He handed them to Kiya. "I grabbed them off your counter and made sure the doors were locked when I left your place. I will be sure to keep you both up to date if anything new turns up while we sort through all of this."

Jake nodded. "Thanks, Mitch."

The sheriff briefly clapped a hand on his friend's shoulder then sent a two-finger salute in Kiya's direction as he left the room.

"I'm not going to your ranch," she told Jake when the sheriff was gone.

"Don't start that again."

"I don't want to impose like that, and you can't possibly want a total stranger living at your home. It would be better if I found somewhere else to stay."

"So, you are going to leave your animals at my place, but you're not willing to take the same offer of help for yourself?"

"I just found out a couple of minutes ago that they had been moved there," she insisted, "and I had no idea the sheriff would ask you to take them in. I will, of course, cover their boarding expenses."

"You will do no such thing. Taking them to the ranch was the most logical solution. We *are* neighbors. The distance of a few miles between the houses doesn't matter. We look out for each other around here. You're new in the area and probably haven't even met many people other than us right now. We have plenty of room at the ranch to take in a couple of animals in need. People too, for that matter. It's likely that you wouldn't even be in this situation if it hadn't been for what happened to Dylan, so of course we offered our help. The closest hotel is about twenty miles from here, and staying there alone right now doesn't make much sense."

"You're used to taking charge of everything, aren't you?"

"Comes with the territory, I run a multifaceted ranching operation. Now can we stop debating this? If it makes a difference, you won't be the only female. My sisters will be staying at the ranch, and a family friend pops in all the time to help out with household chores. Plus, we have a couple small cabins on the property that serve as housing for seasonal workers and hired hands. If you refuse to stay in the main house, you can use one of those. Besides, Dylan will skin me alive if I let you end up anywhere else."

There really wasn't much else she could do, so she relented. "Okay, you win…if Luna is allowed to stay inside with me."

"Of course. I expected that."

"I've met Margaret by the way," she told him, referring to his "family friend" comment. "She introduced herself at the market, thanked me for helping Dylan."

"You've…" He shook his head. When he stopped to think about it, it made perfect sense that Margaret would have been on the lookout for Kiya and make it a point to introduce herself. "She must have been talking to Hilly. My sister is incapable of keeping things to herself. Secrets churn and bubble inside her until they just come spewing out of her mouth completely unhindered. Remember that before ever telling her something you don't want others to know," he warned gravely.

"Thanks for the tip," Kiya quipped.

"I know you will need to collect some things from your place, but I would much rather do that in full daylight. So, if you can get by until tomorrow with a few necessities from the market, I think we should head there first. Then you can crash for the rest of the night in one of our guest rooms."

She nodded her agreement. Everything could wait. All she wanted right now was a hot bath and some rest.

****

It was eerie pulling into her driveway again after the events of last night. The small wooden barn with its attached paddock and open field behind sat desolate ahead of them. To their left, her once pretty little home looked more like the backdrop for a horror film. The grass around the house had been trampled flat by the feet of officers. Holes and chipped wood were scattered along the outside walls. Wood panels now covered the spaces that once held windows. *What a mess,* Kiya thought as she walked up the stone pathway to the door. She stopped for a moment before entering the house and scanned the surrounding area. She couldn't help but feel uneasy about being here. She hoped the feeling would eventually fade, but right now she wasn't sure if she would ever feel completely safe here after this. It was a sobering thought.

She turned to Jake who was standing near his truck. "I need to drive my own vehicle back to the ranch, but I would appreciate it if you would hang around long enough for me to grab some things and load them up."

"I have no intention of leaving you here alone. Go, do what you need to do. I'll be here," he assured her softly.

She thanked him and went inside for her things. The interior of the house was even worse than the outside. Glass and splinters littered the room. Many items had been damaged or destroyed, their pieces scattered across the counters and floor haphazardly. She was glad she didn't have to deal with sorting through everything and cleaning it up right now. Just looking at the damage was overwhelming. She collected her spare keys and Luna's bowls and food, which she piled near the door, then headed to her bedroom for clothes and toiletries. She noticed that the destruction lessened as soon as she left the kitchen area. The living room had minor damage, as did the other rooms. The rooms at the back of the house were untouched. Whoever was firing the shots last night had focused on the room she occupied at the time. They must have seen the lights on in there and directed their efforts where they would be most effective. It's possible that the person had even seen her moving about through the windows. The thought of some unseen observer watching her while she went about her nightly routine made her blood run cold. She shivered and hurried through the rest of her packing.

Outside, she tossed her belongings into the back of her Jeep then went looking for Jake. She found him around the backside of the house, where the worst of the gunfire had been focused. It was on the opposite side from the road so that it looked out over the barn and the field behind it. An ideal way to approach the house and remain out of sight from anyone passing by. Jake stood facing the kitchen window where the first bullet had entered, shattering the glass and her illusions of safety. He was quiet as she approached. She stopped beside him and surveyed the damage in silence.

Jake couldn't believe what he was seeing or that the woman beside him had been inside while it took place. Things like this only happened in movies, or maybe in large cities that were prone to gang violence. That it had happened here, in their rural community, was mind-boggling. His face was tense when he turned to face Kiya. "You were lucky."

"I know," she said, still looking at the house. "Just being back here makes me uneasy. Thank you for staying. I wouldn't have liked being here alone just yet."

Her tone was self-deprecating, as if she were ashamed to feel that way, and it irritated him. He took her shoulders and turned her to face him. "Of course, you feel that way. It's a perfectly normal reaction to what happened here. No one could go through something like this and not be affected by it. And nobody, least of all me, expects anything else."

Kiya's eyes glistened. Her emotions kept swinging from one extreme to another and back again. It was as if the enormity of recent events were just now catching up with her. In a matter of days, she had experienced not one but two traumatic life-altering events, been forced out of her home with violence, and into the care of strangers while she tried to piece things back together. She was feeling hunted and scared. Mad, and desperate all at the same time. Not to mention a little lost, confused. The ache in her arm was a constant reminder of the horror she couldn't escape. How would she get past this? How did anyone return to normal life when things like this happened? Just thinking about it was overwhelming…and exhausting. She had always thought of herself as a strong and independent person, but now she couldn't stand the thought of being alone. Kiya rubbed her palms on her thighs to stop their trembling.

Jake watched as one emotion after another flashed across Kiya's face. For a moment or two, her every thought was displayed like an open book. Growing up with two sisters, he had seen his fair share of tears and raging emotions, but watching Kiya struggle to remain strong and composed while dealing with the aftermath of this attack tugged at him. He did the only thing he could think of to help her. He stepped forward and wrapped his arms around her and pulled her close. He was careful not to hurt any of her injuries as he settled her against his chest. "It's going to be okay. We will figure all this out. You don't have to handle any of it alone, all right?"

Kiya nodded against his chest but said nothing. She remained where she was for a little while, simply listening to the steady rhythm of his heartbeat. His calm manner and strong embrace soothed her frayed nerves. It annoyed her that she wanted to stay tucked up against him, that she sought his strength when hers was so low, but she couldn't bring herself to pull away. Having someone lend support when it was needed was a unique but welcome feeling.

"You ready to leave this mess?" he wanted to know.

She moved away and nodded her head, feeling a little foolish.

"Then let's get you out of here and back to the ranch." He placed a hand on her lower back and guided her to their waiting vehicles.

Chapter 5

After he had left Kiya at the main house, Jake went to the hospital to check in with his brothers. Getting Kiya settled in her new location would go much smoother if he wasn't underfoot, or so he was told by his sisters.

"And you're sure she's all right? She's good with all this?" Dylan asked as he watched his brother pace near the window of his hospital room.

"Physically, she will be fine. The doctor stitched her up and made sure there wouldn't be any secondary complications. At most, she'll end up with a couple scars and a story her grandkids will never believe. Not bad, considering what could have happened. I think she's struggling a little with it emotionally, but that's to be expected. That house looked like something out of a TV crime drama. When I dropped her off at the ranch, Hilly and Margaret were all too ready to fuss over her and help her get settled in. She wanted to stay at the Ridgeway Inn, but I thought the ranch would be the best option. Plus, I didn't think you would like it if I let her end up alone at some low budget motel."

"No, you're right, I wouldn't. She's better off at the ranch where we can all keep an eye on her. Keep her as safe as possible. She shouldn't have to fear for her life because she chose to save mine. I owe it to her to make sure she is protected until we find out what is happening." He rubbed lightly at his healing wound. "Thanks, Jake. I know taking in a stranger wouldn't be your first choice, but I appreciate it."

"I didn't do it just because I thought it was what you would want. I don't want anything to happen to her either."

"Okay, so we all agree that Kiya stays with us for the time being. That's the easy part," Cade said from his position in the chair next to the bed. "It's obvious that someone got wind of the fact that Kiya was there when they went after Dylan. They are sure to hear that they failed again. What's Mitch's take on all this? We really need to get together with him to go over everything and come up with a plan of action. A way to make sure nobody else gets hurt."

"I just wish I had seen something useful that day, or at least had an idea about who would do this and why. But all I remember is riding across the field then getting hit by something that felt like a freight train. I didn't even hear the shot until I was falling off my horse from the impact. I think the second shot was to scare the horse off," Dylan said.

Their conversation shifted to the investigation and plans for Dylan's upcoming release from the hospital.

****

While the McCleary brothers were busy talking strategy and safety measures, Kiya was getting a crash course in what family life with women was like. After succumbing to exhaustion in an empty guest room for the night, Kiya had chosen to move to one of the small cottages on the property rather than stay in the main house. She felt the situation was stressful enough without the whole family tripping over her, a virtual stranger, every time they turned around in their own home.

Margaret was currently bustling around the small cottage Kiya had selected, cleaning and straightening everything in sight while Hilly happily chatted nonstop as she found the best places to put her new friend's belongings. She had insisted that she be allowed to unpack Kiya's things so the other woman could rest her arm.

Gretchen was more reserved than the other two, but Kiya found her composed and efficient manner reassuring. Her task had been to make sure the heater and phones were working properly and that Kiya had enough blankets and towels. All Kiya had been allowed to do was sit on her newly made bed and pet Luna as she watched the other women prep her new temporary home.

Luna was in heaven with all the new people around to give her attention. She made occasional rounds going from one person to the next, sitting at their feet until they reached down to rub her ears or head before moving on. She was having no trouble adjusting to her new environment. Kiya wished she was as at ease as her pet. Everyone had been so welcoming, but it was a little disconcerting to have so many people wanting to do everything for her. She continued to observe their interactions with a bemused expression.

"Well, you should be all set on linens and towels," Gretchen told her. "Extras are in the tiny closet just outside the bathroom. There is an apartment-size washer and dryer in the larger utility closet at the back of the cabin. It's warming up nicely in here with the heater back on, but you can always start a fire in the fireplace if you need to. The woodshed is around back. You are of course welcome to meals at the main house, but there are some basic supplies in the kitchenette along with coffee, tea, things like that. We can make a supply run if you would feel more comfortable making your meals here. The phone is pretty straightforward once you get used to it."

She showed Kiya how to operate the different modes on the system. The first button was a dedicated line that connected directly to the main house. The second was an outside line for normal calls, and the third was a private answering machine for the cabin.

Gretchen smiled. "Now, why don't we give you some time alone to rest and get acquainted with everything. I'm sure this move is stressful for you. If you need us, all you have to do is call."

"You have all been so kind. Thank you for this," Kiya said, as everyone moved toward the door.

Margaret patted her shoulder. "You'll be safe here, honey. Get some rest."

"I'm so glad you agreed to stay here," Hilly told her as she hugged Kiya tightly.

Once she was alone, the silence Kiya was used to returned. Slowly, she felt herself starting to relax. While exploring her new accommodations, Kiya came to the conclusion that if she had to leave home for some unknown location, she could do a lot worse. The cabin was small but not cramped. It felt spacious with its distinctive space-saving design features and appliances. In the living area, a love seat faced a set of built-in recessed bookcases with wide shelves that held a smattering of paperback books and a radio-CD player. Between them was a lovely little fireplace with a flat-screen TV high on the wall above it.

Next to the window was a perfect place for curling up with a book or viewing the scenery. A comfortable-looking chair sat next to a tiny coffee table and lamp. On the opposite side of the open space was the kitchen and dining area. The mini-size appliances reminded Kiya of her childhood dollhouse. She had spent many happy hours rearranging the furniture and decorating the rooms. She had loved imagining the types of families that would live inside its walls. The toy house had been her favorite possession. Running her hand over the island prepping area, she noticed the stools hiding underneath. It was meant to serve double duty as a dining table. The bathroom was located just outside of the bedroom and held a tub and shower combo. Knowing she would still be able to soak in a relaxing bath made her smile with anticipation. Her bedroom held a small, comfortable bed with thick, luxurious blankets, an antique dresser, and a bedside table holding the match to the lamp in the living area. The way the entire cabin was put together could be summed up as cozy, homey even.

Poking her head into the utility closet, she noted the stacked apartment-size washer and dryer Gretchen had mentioned, in addition to the hot water heater, furnace, and a variety of cleaning supplies. Luna lost interest in following her master from room to room and went off to find a more interesting pastime.

Kiya busied herself setting out Luna's bowls and hanging a leash on a wooden peg near the door. Since Hillary had already done the rest of her unpacking, which hadn't been much to begin with, she found herself at a loss for something to do. Her arm was starting to throb again, so after downing some ibuprofen, she took Luna outside to get a better picture of her new surroundings.

The Five M ranch was impressive. Beautiful and expansive. Nestled between two ridges covered in aspen trees and evergreens, the ranch itself occupied a wide green valley. It sat at the end of a long, tree-shaded lane that began under an arched wooden sign proudly displaying its family logo. Horses grazed contentedly in many of the lush fields surrounding the property. A small herd of cattle dotted the pasture farther in the distance. The main house was a sprawling multi-level log structure that seemed to blend harmoniously into its environment. A large, covered porch ran the entire length of the front of the building, framing the double, solid wood doors at its entrance. The porch displayed a multitude of bench-style swings, and comfortable-looking chairs for outdoor entertaining. Another entryway was located at the side of the house facing a huge modern barn and the tiny, scattered cabins like the one Kiya now inhabited. Her overall impression of the place was one of prosperous grandeur. The McCleary family had created a gorgeous and welcoming homestead. What a joy it must be to call a place like this your home. And for now, Kiya got to enjoy it as well.

She called Luna back to her side, then returned to the cabin. After a light meal, Kiya selected an interesting-looking novel from one of the bookshelves and settled into a chair to relax.

She was startled awake a while later by someone knocking on the door. *Must be more tired than I thought*. Rubbing at her eyes, Kiya walked to the door and eased it open. Cade stood on the other side holding a small box.

"I have been sent to tell you that dinner is ready if you feel up to joining us," he said, eyeing her disheveled state. "Everyone will understand if you would rather rest."

"I appreciate the invitation, and I really don't want to be rude after you all have taken me in so graciously, but I would rather take Luna on a short stroll and turn in early. I'm just not sure I'm ready for the whole group dinner thing."

"I get it, don't worry. We understand that this is a stressful situation." He gestured to her injured arm. "You feeling all right? Need anything before I go?"

Kiya shook her head. "You have all done enough, I'm fine. I just need a little time to adjust."

He nodded his understanding. "Oh, I almost forgot…Jake wanted me to make sure you got this back." He handed her the small first aid kit she had used to treat Dylan. She had forgotten it in the field after all the commotion. When she reached out and took it from him, he said, "One of the deputies found it when they were searching the area. It's amazing to think that you, and that tiny box, made such a significant impact on our lives. Get some rest, Kiya. We will see you in the morning."

****

The early night had Kiya up bright and early the next morning. Once she had let Luna out for her morning run, she set about making coffee and dropping toast into the toaster. She was surprised at how at home she felt in her new accommodations and how easy it was to keep her normal routine. After eating a light breakfast and downing a second cup of coffee, she headed out to the barn to check on Dax.

She found the gelding in a freshly cleaned box stall near the barn entrance. He was happily pulling hay from a feeder rack on the side of his stall. Kiya opened the latch on the door and walked over to stroke his neck. "Good morning, handsome. How are you feeling today?"

"Are you talking to the horse or me?"

Startled, Kiya quickly turned toward the voice and saw Jake standing at the stall entrance with his arms draped over the door. "You scared me," she said mildly.

"Sorry, didn't mean to. You're up early."

"I'm just checking on Dax here, seeing if he is settling in okay. I needed to make sure he'd calmed down and reassure myself that he didn't have any injuries."

"I figured you would be concerned about that. That's why I had the vet give him a quick once-over this morning before he left. Doc gave him a clean bill of health. He met Luna too while she was out exploring. He said to tell you there is nothing to worry about. They are both in good health and seem to have weathered their ordeal without any ill effects."

Kiya was surprised but touched that he would think to ease her mind about her animals. "Thank you. You didn't have to do that, but I appreciate it. You can have the vet bill sent to me when it arrives."

"No need. Doc Higgins was here for a scheduled appointment anyway. He was examining a couple of mares that are new arrivals. Taking a quick look at Dax and the dog wasn't a problem."

Kiya patted her horse, thankful that he hadn't been

harmed by either flying bullets or his own frantic actions in his stall that night. "What do you say, big guy, now that we know you're doing well, you up for some exercise? Might do us both some good."

Jake watched as she ran her hands over the horse's neck and withers. He wasn't comfortable with the idea of her leaving the ranch alone on horseback. Not after what happened to his brother, or her. "I know I can't force you to stay here, but I am concerned about you riding alone. Would you be open to a suggestion?" he asked.

"What's the suggestion?"

"Until we know that you are safe venturing out on your own, I would feel better if you would use the exercise arena off the back side of the barn. It has plenty of room to put him through his paces, nobody will get in your way so you can do what you want, but you will be close to the house and everyone here."

She continued to stroke Dax's neck but turned her head to look at Jake. She watched him quietly for a moment. She thought of Dylan also and Jake's understandable concern. She didn't want a repeat of that experience either. She nodded. "I can do that."

"Thank you." He turned to leave.

"Oh, but could I borrow…"

Jake cut her off with a wave of his hand. "When I had Dax brought over, I figured you would want your own things available. Your tack is hanging in the room just past the last stall on the left."

Kiya was impressed. When he took charge of a situation, he did it efficiently.

"Wow, you thought of everything didn't you? Even on such short notice."

"I try to keep things as well organized as possible. They tend to run more smoothly that way."

"Well thank you…again."

"You're welcome. Before I go, I should tell you that the hospital has decided to release Dylan later today. We are having a welcome home dinner at the house. It would be nice if you could join us. I know Dylan will want to see you—see for himself that you are still in one piece, and we haven't mistreated you."

She smiled. "You all have been more than kind, and I would love to see Dylan. What time should I arrive?"

"I'll have one of the girls ring the cabin when we go to pick him up," he told her, referring to his sisters.

"I'll see everyone later tonight then." She watched as Jake strode out of the barn, then went off to find the tack room.

Chapter 6

Kiya knocked lightly on the door to the main house and waited while footsteps approached from the other side. Hilly answered the door with a wide smile.

"Why are you knocking?" she asked while pulling Kiya into the kitchen by grabbing her hand. "No one expects you to knock. While you are here, you can make yourself at home and visit any time you want. Just come on in. If you can't find one of us, just give a shout; someone will hear you." She went back to work setting the table, while calling out to Gretchen that Kiya had arrived.

When Gretchen entered the room, she too greeted Kiya warmly and asked how she was feeling.

"A little sore, and the stitches feel tight, but nothing to complain about," she answered, flexing her arm. "I even took Dax out to stretch his legs a little. It kept my mind off things for a while."

Hilly looked surprised. "Jake let you leave the ranch?"

When Kiya turned to her with a startled expression, the other woman chuckled. "I didn't mean it like that. You're not a prisoner or anything. It's just that Jake has been understandably edgy lately. He is very protective, and I know he would be worried if he knew you went out riding alone."

"Actually, he suggested I stay on the ranch and use

the arena behind the barn."

Hilly nodded. "Yep, *that* sounds like Jake. Just be warned that it will only get worse once Dylan is home too. They will have us moving around in pairs, so we are never alone. Not that it is a bad idea, considering."

"What about Cade? Is he the most reasonable?" Kiya asked.

"Reasonable? I'm not sure that is the word I would use," Gretchen told her. "Cade likes to at least give the people closest to him the impression that they have a choice in what they do. That they can go about doing their own thing. All the while he is hovering silently in the background watching everything and ready to spring into action. He *is* more willing to hear people out. Cade is simply more laid back in his approach than the other two, who will just tell you how they think it should be. Jake's the worst though, always wants things his way. Always has, even when he was little." She finished in an exasperated voice that belied the soft smile on her face. Her love for her brothers was clear. Kiya envied their family bond. She had always wondered what it would be like to have a large family, always active in each other's lives. Bossy siblings and all.

As Hilly and Gretchen went about setting out the things they would need for dinner and Dylan's arrival, Kiya admired the enormous, homey kitchen. Its center was dominated by a solid wood table large enough to seat eight people. To her left, a coffee and tea bar was set up near the door and looked as if it was always stocked and ready to go as people were coming or going. Counter and cabinet space ran almost the entire length of that wall, only interrupted by the sink and slightly farther down, the stove. A huge double-door refrigerator with freezer drawers was against the wall at the opposite end of the room. The space was well lit and wide open, giving everyone plenty of leeway to move around. To her right, a doorway opened into an open-shelved pantry. The functional but welcoming layout made it obvious that this room was the heart of their large, busy family. "Can I help with anything? I feel kind of useless just standing here watching you both."

"You can stir the stew and make sure it doesn't burn. Everything else is pretty much done. Now, we just need the guys to get here. I hope they didn't run into any trouble at the hospital," Hilly said as she took a pitcher of iced tea out of the refrigerator.

"I'm sure everything is fine," Kiya assured her as she picked up a wooden spoon and stirred the fragrant beef stew simmering on the stove. "Sometimes it seems to take forever to get all the paperwork ready."

The sound of vehicles caught Gretchen's attention. "That sounds like them now." She hurried over to the window to look outside. A happy smile and nod confirmed the arrival of her brothers.

Moments later the door swung open, and Jake walked in carrying some of Dylan's belongings. "This door should be locked when we're not here with you," he stated before turning to see if his brother needed any help making it inside.

Hillary rolled her eyes, then spotted Dylan. He was walking cautiously but under his own power. She let out a small squeal before rushing over to wrap him in a gentle hug. "I'm so glad you're home," she informed him with damp eyes.

Gretchen waited until her sister had released him and he moved slightly farther into the room, allowing Cade to follow them inside and close the door. Then she too wrapped her brother in a hug saying softly, "Welcome home, baby brother."

"I can't tell you how good it feels to be here," Dylan told them both. He spotted Kiya hovering near the stove trying to stay out of everyone's way. He carefully made his way over to her and placed his hands on either side of her face before placing a light kiss upon her lips. "Hello, angel."

Touched by the show of affection, Kiya brought her hands up to rest lightly on his forearms and looked up at him. "It is *really* good to see you again, and on your feet, but you can drop the angel part. I don't come close to that title."

"You will always be an angel to me," he informed her while lightly running his thumb under the stitches in her cheek. "It's nice to see you all in one piece too. You good?"

She nodded. "I'm good."

Dylan searched her face for a moment more, then nodded and moved away to ease himself into a nearby chair. Kiya glanced over at Jake who hadn't moved from his position near the door. He appeared tense and was watching her closely. She quickly switched her gaze to Cade who had finished greeting his sisters and was moving toward her. Like he had with his sisters, he gave her a quick peck on the forehead.

"Glad you decided to join us." He bent over the pot on the stove and inhaled deeply. "Mmmm…looks like Gretchen decided to pamper Dylan. She made his favorite."

Feeling embarrassed by all the attention, Kiya hurried to turn off the stove and move the steaming pot of stew onto a cast iron trivet located at the center of the table.

Jake cleared his throat. "I guess if we plan on eating before Dylan keels over, we better get to it."

"Funny," the man responded.

"Just let me dump this stuff in the living room, then we can eat," Jake added.

Once they had all gathered around the table with bowls filled and bread passed, conversation remained light for Dylan's first night back home. Everyone made sure Kiya felt included by entertaining her with funny stories of their childhood and the many adventures of growing up on the ranch.

As time passed, Kiya noticed that Dylan was growing quieter and seemed to shift more often in discomfort. He had stopped eating after half a bowl of stew. She reached over to place her hand on top of his as it rested on the table.

"You doing okay?" she questioned softly.

He patted her hand with his free one. "I'm all right, just tired."

The conversation around the table had come to a halt, and everyone was watching them.

"You've barely eaten," Gretchen noted in concern.

"It was delicious as usual, far superior to the stuff they served in the hospital. I just don't have much of an appetite yet. I really enjoyed all of this, but I think I've used up my limited energy reserves for the evening. Never thought I would say it after so long in that hospital bed, but I think I just need to lie down for a while."

"Of course, we should have been more careful not to tire you out. We are just so glad to have you with us again," Gretchen told him. She helped him get to his feet while the others gathered around to collect Dylan's things and get him settled into his room to rest.

When they left the room as a group, Kiya stayed behind to start cleaning up. She would let the family have some alone time with their brother. She put away the leftovers, gathered the empty dishes, and loaded them into the dishwasher. She was wiping down the counters when Hilly and Cade reappeared.

"You didn't have to clean this up," Hilly exclaimed.

"You told me to make myself at home," Kiya reminded her while finishing.

"I'm so sorry we abandoned you," the woman added sheepishly. "We didn't mean to leave you out here to do this on your own. You should have at least waited for us to help."

Kiya assured her that it was no trouble at all, and she was glad to help. "But now, I think it is time I let you all have your family time and head back to the cabin. Luna will be wondering where *her* dinner is by now. Thank you for including me tonight."

"If you remembered to make yourself at home, you should remember that you are welcome at any time." Hilly gave her a tight hug.

"Give me a sec to get ready, and I'll walk you back," Cade told her.

Jake spoke from the doorway to the living room. "I'm ready. I'll walk her back."

****

Outside, the air had turned chilly causing Kiya to

shiver slightly when the wind blew across the yard. Jake immediately wrapped his jacket around her shoulders. He had snagged it from a peg hanging inside the door as they were leaving. "What are you doing running around out here without a jacket?"

"Thanks, I didn't need one on my way over, and I wasn't expecting it to get so cold. The temperature changes fast around here," she said as she snuggled farther into the jacket.

They made the short walk to the cabin in relative silence, but as they entered the glow given off by the light near the front door, Kiya stopped and turned toward Jake. "Thank you for inviting me tonight. It was great getting to see Dylan that way. Even if he still tires easily."

"It's surprising how effortless it is for you to tune in to how he's feeling. You noticed his change in energy quicker than any of the rest of us."

Jake's words were spoken lightly, but his eyes appeared guarded. Kiya shrugged. "I know what to look for, that's all."

"I suppose that could be it," he allowed.

The wind picked up again causing Kiya's hair to flutter across her cheeks. Without thinking, Jake reached over and smoothed the silky strands away from her face, but the mental image of his brother's interaction with her earlier in the evening had him pulling his hand back and shoving it into his pocket. He had been unprepared for his reaction to their almost instant and very obvious bond. He was struggling with the fact that he didn't like it.

"Lock the door when you get inside. Good night, Kiya." He turned on his heel and headed back to the main house.

Chapter 7

Kiya finished her morning chores early the next day. She noticed that Dax's stall maintenance and feeding were being done along with the ranch's other horses, so she didn't have a lot to do. She rubbed Luna's ears and asked if she wanted to take a walk. The dog danced in a happy circle then raced over to the door. Taking that as a resounding *yes*, Kiya grabbed Jake's jacket from the counter, where she had placed it so she wouldn't forget to return it, and headed to the house.

Luna ran ahead sniffing here and there when she found something interesting but never strayed more than a few yards from her owner. It didn't take them long to reach the house. Kiya rapped on the door, but it opened almost instantly.

"What did I tell you about knocking?" Hilly admonished in a teasing voice.

"Sorry, I'll have to get used to that one." Kiya told Luna to go play, so the dog would know she was allowed to entertain herself nearby, then followed the woman inside.

"Want coffee?" Hilly asked, pouring herself a cup.

"Thanks, but no. I think I've reached my caffeine limit for the day," Kiya said as she hung the jacket she was holding back on its peg near the door. Walking farther into the room, she noticed that Hillary wasn't alone in the kitchen. Jake leaned casually against the counter, and Dylan was seated at the table. Both held steaming cups of coffee.

"I'm sorry I interrupted your morning. I just wanted to return the jacket before I left."

"Left?" Jake and Dylan asked in unison. They glanced at each other then back to Kiya.

"I am heading into town today. I need to pick up some supplies, and the doctor wanted me to stop by so he can look at my stitches and make sure my arm is healing as it should."

"Take Hilly with you," Jake said. "It's safer if you girls double up whenever you can and not travel around alone."

"I agree. You should stay together while you're in town too. No splitting up," Dylan added.

Hilly snorted into her coffee cup in a muffled laugh. She looked at Kiya and cocked an eyebrow. "See, I told you they would be bossing you around and have us moving in pairs."

"Shut up, brat," Jake chided her in a teasing voice as he chucked a nearby dish towel at her head. "It's not being bossy; it's keeping everyone safe."

"Bossy," his sister insisted, tossing the towel back.

"I'm sure Hilly has better things to do than follow me around town. It is broad daylight; I really don't mind going alone."

Dylan and Jake were both shaking their heads before she had even finished talking, but Dylan was the first to speak.

"Kiya, do this for *me*. We have no idea who or what to be watching for. So far, all we *do* know is that both times the intended target was alone. It is simply safer if Hilly goes too. She was saying she needed to do some shopping, so it just makes sense. Besides, if you go alone, I will worry, and probably end up back in the hospital when I reinjure myself by trying to follow you around all day."

Kiya stared at him in disbelief. "Wow, you fight dirty."

An impish grin spread across the man's face. "Did I win?"

"You win," she said laughing. "Hilly, it looks like you're spending the day with me whether you like it or not."

"If it gets me away from these two…I'm in."

****

After a day of errands, eating, shopping, and bonding, Kiya and Hilly were pleasantly exhausted. They had picked up a few pizzas, so after quickly unloading their purchases, they found themselves calling everyone together around the table in the main house for the second night in a row.

"So how was shopping?" Gretchen asked.

"We had fun. You should have come too," Hilly told her.

"Next time. We can make it a complete girl's day out thing. Today, I really needed to get some work done on the books. I've been putting it off too long. Besides, with Cade and Jake working away from the house today, I wanted to be close by if Dylan needed anything."

"Now that we're done training those cutting horses and have started getting them delivered, we can stick closer to home for a while. Get things around here ready for the winter season. I have one more delivery scheduled tomorrow, then Cade and I will be available to check in on Dylan during the day too. Having someone around won't be a concern when we are all popping in and out of the house all day," Jake said.

"Where is Dylan?" Kiya asked as the others started in on the pizza.

"He was sleeping, but I let him know dinner is here. He will join us soon," Gretchen replied.

Kiya was instantly concerned. "Is he not feeling well?"

"He's fine, just stubborn. Tries doing too much and ends up overdoing it," she assured her.

"I'm not stubborn; I'm determined," Dylan corrected as he walked into the room. He planted a loud smacking kiss on Gretchen's cheek. Stopping beside Kiya, he looped an arm around her shoulders and briefly hugged her against his uninjured side. "Did you ladies get a lot done today?"

Hillary launched into a detailed description of their day, while everyone enjoyed their dinner. As they were cleaning up afterward, the discussion turned to what they wanted to get accomplished the next day.

"Well, I for one need to finish getting the ranch's books in order. I won't have time to do it when I return home. I will be playing catch up for weeks as it is. Sometimes I wonder what I was thinking when I decided to become an accountant," Gretchen grumbled.

"I've always wondered that too." Hilly laughed.

"Ha ha. I'm not creative enough to be a freelance writer like you. I prefer things that are clear cut, and more structured. Speaking of which, have you gotten your latest article turned in?"

"Not yet, but I can easily have it done by the

deadline tomorrow night. What about you, Kiya? What do you have planned for tomorrow?" Hilly wanted to know.

Kiya told them that she had been in touch with the owners of her house and had gotten the go-ahead to schedule someone to come out and assess the damage so they could get an estimate for repairs. She had someone lined up for an inspection tomorrow. She had offered to help cover costs, but the couple had flatly refused. They insisted that they were only concerned about her welfare. The least she could do for them is handle all the arrangements.

"While I'm there, I might as well clean the place up as much as I can. Can't say I'm looking forward to it though."

"You can't go alone," Jake told her, concerned that whoever was involved might be keeping an eye on the place in case she returned. When he voiced his concern, Dylan seconded the objection.

"I can take her over and stay with her," Cade suggested. "Since Jake is handling the last horse delivery, all I had planned on doing was picking up a feed order and repairing some fencing. That's easy enough to put off."

"I can't take you away from your own work to play babysitter," Kiya insisted. "You have all disrupted your lives enough for me already."

"The work isn't going anywhere; it will still be there when I can get to it. It won't be a problem. Besides, you are not a disruption. You were there when Dylan needed you, and now, we will be here for you. End of story," Cade informed her.

"If she doesn't agree, we could always threaten

Dylan with bodily harm, and she'll cave," Jake suggested.

"Hey, I don't think I like the sound of that," Dylan complained.

The siblings all laughed and enjoyed coming up with ideas on how to torture their brother, but Kiya was unsure how to take Jake's comment since she was certain there had been a slight edge to Jake's joking tone.

Darkness was settling in fast, and Kiya decided to call it a night. She bid everyone a good night and headed to the door to collect her jacket. She was starting to anticipate the rapid temperature drop after the sun went down.

"I'll walk you back."

She turned to see Jake donning his own jacket. She started to say that it wasn't necessary, but she figured that was an argument she wouldn't win anyway. Kiya waved to the rest of the group and stepped out into the night. The crispness of the air could be felt even through the protective layer she wore. The stars overhead shone brightly and sparkled like jewels. The fact that there was no light pollution to obscure the beauty of the night delighted her. That's what she loved the most about Colorado, and what had drawn her here. The vast expanses of unspoiled natural beauty and how connected to it you felt.

They walked at a casual pace enjoying their surroundings, but Kiya didn't feel up to making small talk.

"You're awfully quiet. Everything okay?"

"Yes, I'm fine."

Jake took ahold of her good arm and gently pulled

her to a stop. "Kiya, what's bothering you?"

"This whole situation is getting to me. You're always kind, but sometimes you seem to have a problem with me, and I don't want to intrude into your lives. I don't want anyone to think they owe me anything. I helped Dylan because he needed help, and I was able to supply it. I don't expect anything from any of you."

"I know you don't expect anything from us. We want to be here for you. All of us. It's not such a hardship to have you around, you know. You blend well with my family. Everyone likes you for you. I think you like them just as much if I'm not mistaken."

"No, you're right. I really enjoy spending time with them. They just make it so easy, don't they?"

He smiled. "Yes, they do." She tried to turn and resume walking, but he didn't release her. "I don't have a problem with you."

She studied him quietly without answering.

He laughed softly. "I *don't* have a problem with you. At least not the way you mean. So, you're stuck with the lot of us. Okay?"

Kiya wasn't sure what he meant, but she nodded. "Okay."

"You know, when you and Hilly were talking about your day in town, you forgot to mention the fact that you were able to do away with some of your stitches," he said skimming the back of a finger lightly down her injured cheek.

She raised a hand to her face. "I forgot, and nobody seemed to notice."

"I noticed," he told her in a low voice.

He turned, and they finished the short walk to

Kiya's door. When it was opened, Luna waited for permission then raced outside. The dog pranced happily around their legs in an excited greeting. When Jake bent down to ruffle the dog's fur, she sat and held out a paw.

"Hey there, cutie, you keeping an eye on things around here?" he asked, holding her paw lightly. Luna barked then headed off to make her nightly rounds. Jake stood to watch the dog as she moved off. "She's well trained. Maybe we should find her a fun job to do around the ranch."

"I don't know if it is her training or if she is secretly part human," Kiya joked. "She has tons of personality and learns almost effortlessly. When she was younger, it was hard to keep ahead of her learning curve. I prefer her company over most people."

"I can see why. Make sure you bring her to the house with you when you can. It has been a while since we have had a dog around here. She will be a welcome addition."

"Thanks, I will." It was nice knowing that her companion was so warmly accepted.

Jake wished her good night then returned to the house.

Chapter 8

Before the sun was even tickling the horizon, Jake was out feeding, separating, and loading horses for transport to their new homes. This final shipment and the resulting paychecks would set them up nicely for the winter months. He rubbed his hands together to warm them. Winter was approaching fast this year. The air was cold enough to see his breath this morning, and he was looking forward to a rejuvenating hot cup of coffee. He finished his last few preparations as the sun finally made an appearance and brightened the morning sky. He headed inside to get his coffee and fill a thermos for the road. It was going to be a long day. After he grabbed what he needed, he would let everyone know he was heading out. It never struck him as odd that when he thought of the family, he automatically included Kiya.

Jake opened the kitchen door, pulled off his outer layer, and hung it up. He moved farther into the kitchen only to stop mid-stride. Dylan sat in a chair in the middle of the room bare-chested with his head bent toward Kiya who knelt on the floor beside him with her hands on his rib cage. All thoughts of coffee were forgotten.

Kiya glanced over her shoulder and smiled. "Good morning, Jake."

He had to unclench his jaw to respond. "Uh,

morning. What's with the Chippendale impression?"

Dylan grinned at Kiya. "Hey, good idea. Next time you should bring dollar bills."

She stood up and playfully swatted Dylan on the back of the head. "Idiot." Turning to Jake, she told him that the wound on Dylan's side had been seeping. Probably from him moving around more freely. "I cleaned it up, so he is good as new. Well almost, but I don't see any signs of infection."

"You all set with the horses?" Dylan asked while pulling on his shirt.

Kiya filled a mug with coffee and handed it to Jake.

"Thanks, I've been wanting that." He took a sip before answering his brother. "Yeah, I'm loaded and ready. I'll finish this then get going. I wanted to let you guys know I am pulling out." He finished his coffee, filled a thermos, went out to his waiting truck, and climbed inside. As he put it into gear, he glanced at the house. Kiya was standing near the kitchen door. She raised a hand in farewell. He returned the gesture, thinking that it felt good to have her see him off.

****

Cade carried another heavy bag loaded with debris and broken household items out to the garbage tote behind the house. He had spent most of the day helping Kiya clean up her battered home and talking with the carpenter hired to complete the repairs of the walls and windows. He was still having trouble coming to terms with what had taken place here. When he had surveyed the damage with the man handling the repairs, Cade's level of disbelief and anger rose. Who would resort to this level of violence against a woman because of what she *might* have seen? Or because of her selfless actions to help another. It was mind-boggling. He had no idea what could have started all this in motion.

The sound of a vehicle pulling into the driveway had him instantly on alert. The carpenter had left for the day to finish drawing up a contract and finalizing ideas on how best to complete the work. Only he and Kiya remained at the house. Luna barked from inside. Cade made a beeline for the front door, only to breathe a sigh of relief when he spotted the sheriff getting out of his truck.

"Mitch, I'm glad to see you. What brings you by? Please tell me it's because you figured out who is behind all this, and you have them sitting in a jail cell."

"I wish I could, my friend. A couple of my guys noted the activity over here during a routine drive-by and let me know you were here. I'm assuming Ms. James is here also?"

"Yeah, Kiya's inside. We were just finishing up. Come on in, and we can talk."

Kiya greeted the sheriff warmly and poured him some coffee as he and Cade settled into chairs at the table. Mitch told her he was glad she appeared to be healing well and was able to start getting her place put back to rights. When Kiya asked how the investigation was going, his response was not as optimistic.

"I wish I had better news for the two of you, but unfortunately, we still have very little to go on. No suspects, no motive. Given the secluded nature of the two crimes, the opportunity is there…but that doesn't help us much, especially when no one believes these two acts are random attacks of opportunity. There is a reason behind this. We just haven't discovered it yet."

He assured them that his department was still pushing forward with what they did have. A list had been compiled of registered vehicles in the area that matched Kiya's description of the truck present at Dylan's shooting. However, that list wouldn't be much help until they could narrow it down with possible suspects. The ballistics on the gun used on Dylan came back as a thirty-ought-six, a common hunting rifle among the local hunters. Half the hunters in the entire state probably own one. Mitch and Cade themselves owned guns of the same caliber for deer season. The only interesting thing about the ballistics was that a weapon of the same caliber was identified as one of the weapons used in Kiya's attack. The bullets pulled from the walls of Kiya's house and the one that had hit Dylan were rather mangled, but there was a possibility that if the rifle used was recovered, it could be matched to one or both crime scenes.

"You said, *one of the weapons* used in Kiya's attack. Meaning there was more than one gun used? More than one person involved?" Cade wanted to know.

"There were at least two weapons used that we have identified. The thirty-ought-six and a five-five-six. Probably semi-automatic. That type of gun is popular with coyote hunters." Mitch looked at Kiya. "You did say that there were two men present when Dylan was shot. It's possible that the same two men were involved here."

"Okay, I can see how in some twisted way someone might want to scare or harm me because I saw something they didn't want anyone to see. I unwittingly thwarted whatever plan they were acting out when I stepped in to save Dylan, but why on earth would anyone have shot him in the first place? What could have started the whole thing? It doesn't make sense," Kiya said exasperated.

"I agree," Mitch responded. "That is the question we are currently focusing on. Trying to find out what started the ball rolling so to speak. I'm also wondering if and how they knew Dylan would be in that field, or if it was just a chance encounter. If he just happened to be riding through, why shoot at all?"

"Good questions," Cade told him. "Dylan was well within Five M land. That can't be disputed. Why shoot a man riding through his own pastureland? My mind keeps going in circles. Nothing adds up. I'll talk with Jake and Dylan, see what we can come up with. For now, I think it's time to pack it in for the night. It has been a long day."

****

A few days later, everyone at the Five M was gathered in the kitchen sharing morning coffee, as was their habit. Kiya found that she liked the ritual even though she had previously preferred to be more solitary. There was something to be said for family gatherings, even if she had to keep reminding herself that she wasn't truly part of this family group. It made her hopeful that she might one day have a family of her own to gather with and share her life with. Luna, of course, liked having the extra company too. She spent most mornings curled at Kiya's feet watching to see who the next person would be to offer her a morsel of this or drop a bit of that.

Life was settling into a new but comfortable routine. Kiya spent the mornings in the barn helping

Jake with the horses which freed Cade up to accomplish other tasks. Work on her house was progressing smoothly now and wouldn't take much longer to complete. The investigation into both her and Dylan's shootings had hit a dead end. Now the question she would soon be facing was whether to move back into her place when the work was done. She couldn't hide out in the McClearys' cabin forever. Especially if there were no leads to keep an investigation going. She was going to have to get back to her normal life sometime. The only problem was that she wasn't sure what that looked like anymore.

She had plenty of time recently to work on her web designs and keep up with her workload. As a professional website and graphic designer, she may never be rich, but she made a good living and could work from home and follow her own schedule. She loved the creativity and flexibility of her chosen career. She wasn't confined to a traditional crowded, stuffy office setting, and that usually suited her very well. In this case, however, it meant that she spent most of her time home alone and it made her an easy target. She would have plenty of time to worry about that later, she reminded herself. For now, she would focus on helping with morning chores in the barn, and this afternoon she would have her remaining stitches removed. Overall, things were looking up. She snagged an apple for later, thinking she would share it with Dax. Everyone finished their coffee or breakfast and prepared to get started on the day ahead.

As Kiya, Cade, and Jake left the house for the barn, Luna raced ahead until she spotted something and stopped to bark excitedly. An expensive looking car rolled to a stop next to the house.

"Nice car," Cade said. "Not very practical for this area. Any idea who that is?"

Jake shook his head as a man wearing an equally expensive and impractical suit climbed out of the vehicle. The man secured a single button on his long, dark-gray overcoat while approaching. It couldn't be more obvious that this guy was not a local. He dressed to impress, not fit in. Which in other words meant that he stuck out like a sore thumb. His dapper style coat was paired with a slightly lighter gray suit with a pale blue-gray button-down shirt, a gray-and-white dotted tie, and a stylish gray-and-black striped scarf draped around his neck. Thin brows framed a lean face with deep-set eyes. He had a long, thin, slightly hooked nose, and a cleft chin. Not a single hair was out of place.

Kiya was aware that this man's goal was to project the polished and wealthy air of a businessman, but the word that instantly popped into her mind was…smarmy. He had the look of a smug, unscrupulous, big city lawyer. He gave Kiya the creeps.

The new arrival glanced warily at the dog now sitting at Kiya's feet, but his voice when he greeted them was smooth and controlled. "Good morning, I am Preston Kennedy. I'm assuming you are the McClearys."

"I'm Cade McCleary. This is my brother Jake," Cade said as he shook the guy's outstretched hand.

"A pleasure to meet you both. And who might you be?" the man asked shifting in Kiya's direction to shake her hand also. His eyes held hers with unusually direct interest. Almost as if he was sizing up an opponent.

"Kiya James," she responded, trying to withdraw her hand from his perfectly manicured one, but he appeared to be in no hurry to release her.

"Kiya. What a beautiful name for a beautiful lady. You live here also?"

"Live here? Not exactly."

Picking up on Kiya's discomfort when the man still seemed reluctant to relinquish her hand, Jake stepped forward and thrust his own forward making it impossible for the guy to not drop Kiya's hand and take his. "What can we do for you, Mr. Kennedy, was it?"

"Yes, I thought you might be familiar with my name. I spoke with a Dylan McCleary not too long ago about a business proposition. I was told he is your business manager, but seeing as how this is a family run business, I was hoping he would have had the chance to discuss my proposal with you."

The door to the house opened, and Dylan stepped out. The look on his face wasn't exactly welcoming.

"Ah, here he is now. Speak of the devil, as they say. Maybe we could go inside and talk over my offer?" His words might have been presented as a question, but his manner implied that he expected to be accommodated.

"That won't be necessary, Mr. Kennedy. As I told you before, we are not interested in selling any portion of the Five M," Dylan informed him.

"If I could have only a few minutes of your time, I'm sure you and your brothers would see that what I propose is a sound and lucrative offer for land that isn't being utilized. The sale would have no negative effect on your day-to-day operations but would have a sizable impact on your bottom line. It wouldn't be prudent to dismiss this out of hand without proper consideration."

Jake was getting a little tired of this guy's domineering attitude. Dylan hadn't mentioned this offer before, but if it involved selling off pieces of land, he wouldn't have needed to. So, it was time to cut this visit short and get to work. "Mr. Kennedy, I'm sorry you drove all the way out here for nothing, but if you're looking for land to buy, I'm afraid you're wasting your time."

"Surely as fellow businessmen you are open to entertaining new opportunities," the man insisted.

Cade held up a hand to stop any further arguments. "Opportunities yes, but on this we agree. If your offer involves selling Five M land, I'm afraid the answer is no."

A muscle twitched in Kennedy's jaw as if he were holding back another rebuttal. Instead, he reached into a pocket inside his coat and pulled out a slim silver case. Opening it, he removed a card and handed it to Cade. "It appears that your minds are made up on the matter. I have to say that I am disappointed with your unwillingness to hear me out. If you change your minds, you have my card." He turned on the heel of his shiny oxford shoes and strode back to his car.

They watched the car drive away leaving a trail of dust in its wake.

"What was that all about?" Cade wanted to know.

"You know that guy?" Jake asked Dylan.

"I don't know him, but he showed up a few weeks ago out of the blue while I was in town, said he was interested in buying the tract of land on the backside of the property, up by the old hunting cabin. I would have mentioned it, but it didn't seem important. I knew none of us would be willing to sell. Not only that, but the guy just rubbed me the wrong way. That hasn't changed. Then later, I forgot all about it with what has happened around here."

Jake nodded. "You're right about us having enough going on around here already without throwing that guy into the mix. I think he got the message this time. Now, how about we get some work done?"

Chapter 9

The next morning when Kiya entered the main house, Margaret was bustling around the kitchen humming a tune under her breath. When she saw Kiya come in, she dropped what she was doing and hurried over.

"There she is. It's good to see you again, honey." The woman wrapped her in a hug and rocked back and forth happily. "How are you feeling? Better, I hope. I heard you're healing fast. You look good, this place seems to agree with you."

Kiya smiled at Margaret's enthusiasm. "Thanks, I feel good. I had the last of my stitches removed, so I'm practically back to normal. All I need now is some coffee." She looked around the empty kitchen as she poured herself a mug of the fragrant brew waiting in its usual place on the counter. "You have the house to yourself today, Margaret?"

"No, no, you just have a seat, honey. Fresh muffins are on the table. The others will be down in a minute. Mitch called to say he is on his way over too, or maybe I should say Sheriff Patterson. Calling him by that title is still hard, when I can remember those boys running wild all over town causing all sorts of trouble." She laughed.

Wondering what kinds of trouble a bunch of rowdy country kids could get into, Kiya said she would be interested in hearing some of those stories.

"What stories?" Hilly asked as she walked into the kitchen with her sister in tow.

"Stories of your brothers and Mitch getting into trouble and causing a ruckus around town when they were younger," Margaret told them while pouring their coffee.

"Oh, like the time they decided to light a bonfire behind old man Jenkins's place so they could have a party and accidently caught the barn on fire?" Gretchen asked, grabbing a muffin to go with her coffee.

"Or the time they caught Sally Masterson and her friends skinny dipping at the creek, then made off with their clothes? There were pieces of girls' clothing hanging in the trees for at least a mile alongside the road by the time they were done. When Sally's brother caught up with them at the diner, all hell broke loose," Hilly added.

"Hey, Sally brought that on herself," Jake said, picking up the thread of conversation as he and his brothers filed into the room. "She was going steady with Mitch at the time but agreed to go to the spring dance with that loser Brad Warner, just because his daddy had a lot of money. We were defending a friend's honor."

"Hooligans, the lot of you," Margaret said fondly.

"You guys actually set someone's barn on fire?" Kiya couldn't wrap her head around that one.

"Oh, don't worry, it was falling down and empty at the time," Gretchen told her, as if that changed things. "Old man Jenkins thanked them later, saying he hadn't had the money to have the derelict thing taken down."

When Cade said he had no idea what everyone was

going on about since he was never a troublemaker, that it was Jake and Mitch that were always stirring things up, his siblings all erupted into laughter.

"So, when principal Matthews got locked into his office for an entire day after giving you detention, it was a total accident?" Gretchen wondered, rubbing her chin thoughtfully.

"Exactly!" Cade said with a decisive nod.

The sound of a vehicle pulling in only distracted them for an instant before Dylan came up with another childhood escapade involving Cade and Mitch wrapping a box of live chickens as a gag gift at a friend's birthday party. He could still picture the pair doubled over in laughter as party goers were chased all over the yard by an angry flock of birds. Moments later, when Mitch walked in, Margaret was still shaking her head. She pointed a finger in his direction and doubled down on her hooligan declaration.

Mitch looked from one person to the next in utter confusion as the older woman left the room.

"What did I do?" he asked, watching her leave.

The room filled with laughter once again. "Just reminiscing about old times, my friend," Jake informed him.

"In that case...I plead the fifth," Mitch said and joined the others at the table. "If anyone ever brings up our antics as kids, I simply blame you all. Everyone knows what a bad influence the bunch of you were back then." He managed to keep a solemn look on his face, barely.

They bantered back and forth for a bit before Hillary excused herself to get started on a new project. Gretchen sighed. She had a conference call starting soon that she wanted to prep for. She wished everyone a good day, then headed to the home office. She passed Margaret on her way back into the kitchen. The woman had come this morning to drive Dylan to a doctor's appointment, insisting that until he was fully recovered, he had no business driving himself all over the county. Margaret pretended she was just the helpful neighbor, but in reality, she was as protective and loving as a mother hen looking after her chicks. She didn't fool anyone.

Margaret half sweet-talked, half bullied Dylan into grabbing his wallet and jacket, saying she wasn't about to let him be late for his checkup. Once they were out the door, the conversation turned to more serious topics.

"It's good to be able to talk about the good ol' days, but I doubt that is what brought you out here this morning. What's on your mind, Mitch?" Cade watched his friend shift back into work mode.

"I was hoping I could get the two of you to ride out to the west field with me. My guys have been over the area, but I want to get a better feel for it myself. I would like to get a look at the place the shot was fired from, explore a wider radius. I'm not entirely sure what I hope to get out of it, but it can't hurt to have a clearer picture of how things went down. Maybe the three of us can come up with some ideas on how and why someone was out there that day. We are obviously missing something; I just can't fathom what that could be. Has anyone noticed anything out of the ordinary lately?"

Cade shook his head and said that things had been quiet and almost normal. If it wasn't for an underlying feeling of tension hovering just under the surface.

Jake agreed that things were almost too normal. As

if nothing had happened. "Unless you count that entitled jackass insisting we consider his offer to buy Five M land. But according to Dylan that guy approached him before anything had even happened."

That piqued Mitch's interest. "What guy and what offer? Nobody mentioned anything about it."

They discussed the visit from Preston Kennedy and how he had made a point of tracking Dylan down in town a while ago about his interest in acquiring a tract of land.

"He gave us his business card. I tossed it on the desk in the office. It's still there if you want to see it," Cade offered.

"Could just be a coincidence, but I can do some checking around and see what I come up with. I'm curious to find out why he is interested in Five M land. Even if nothing comes of it, it's good to know who is coming and going in our area. And at least you will know who you are dealing with."

"We won't be dealing with him; he didn't strike any of us as the type of person we would want to do business with," Jake told him. "And there is no way he is getting his hands on our property. But you're right— it would be smart to know exactly who the guy is and what his interest is in our land." He left to retrieve the card then handed it to Mitch when he returned.

As the men made plans to saddle some horses and ride out to the west pasture, Kiya asked to join them. "I could be useful in walking you through what I saw, and from where. Maybe going through it again would jog something from my memory that I didn't think of before. Besides, Dax could use a real ride. He's getting bored with the riding ring for exercise."

"You don't need to convince us, Kiya. If you want to ride along, you're welcome to do so. You are the only one of us that was actually there," Jake told her. "Just promise me you will always stay within sight of at least one of us. I doubt we have anything to worry about going out there as a group, but I would rather not take the chance of inviting trouble."

Kiya had no problem agreeing to that. In fact, she was only going because she trusted them to be there for her no matter what happened. She found that she liked having people around that she knew she could count on, people that knew they could count on her. Maybe they hadn't known each other long, and the reason they had come together was unusual, but they had formed a bond that they were all willing to adhere to.

****

The air was brisk, the clouds low and heavy. The trees waving from the hills were starting to drop their leaves in response to the rapidly changing seasons. Kiya could all but smell winter approaching as the wind blew through the wide grass-covered fields. She pulled in a deep breath and shivered with delight. Being out here, surrounded by the beauty of nature, doing something she loved doing, was pure bliss. She hadn't realized until this very moment how cooped up and tense she had been feeling. Never one to stay inside or sit still for long, Kiya had always preferred setting out on some kind of fun adventure, filling her free time with as many engaging outdoor activities as she possibly could.

She patted Dax as he kept up a quick prancing step. He was clearly enjoying today's outing as well. Occasionally, Kiya could feel the animal's muscles bunch and tighten as if he wanted to lengthen his stride and run, but overall, he appeared happy to keep pace with his companions and have fun. Luna jogged along at Dax's side with her usual joyful doggy smile.

Jake and Cade were using this opportunity to check some of the intermittent fence lines for damage as they rode along. No one seemed to be worried about trying to keep up a conversation for the time being, which pleased Kiya. They traveled along, content with each other's company.

When they crossed into the back fields, everyone moved closer together and increased their pace. Finally allowed to work off some of his pent-up energy, Dax cantered confidently across the open land. His long stride ate up the distance with effortless ease.

It wasn't hard for Kiya to lead everyone back to the path she had taken while out riding the day she had found Dylan. Even though she hadn't been familiar with the area, everything about that day was now embedded deep in her memory. She retraced her movements showing Mitch and the others her exact trail, where she first heard a shot and the male voices. She climbed off Dax to explain where she had left him previously and took them to the exact spot the men had fired from. She pointed to the distant location the truck had occupied.

The men explored the hillside and discussed the line of fire and range. Dylan's location could still be seen from their position thanks to the markers left by Mitch's deputies. When they had gotten all the information they could from that area, they gathered the horses and moved to the old overgrown track leading higher up into the hills and to the old hunting cabin.

It was obvious that the pathway had been used a lot more recently than either Cade or Jake said it should have been. They dismounted again to look around the site where the truck had been parked. While the guys searched the immediate area surrounding the tire tracks and then moved down the trail in the direction the truck had originally taken, Kiya moved farther uphill. She glanced over her shoulder to make sure she didn't get too far away from the rest of the group. Luna had her nose to the ground and continued moving upward.

There were tire marks in this direction also, but they stopped at a rocky runoff where a tree limb partially blocked the path. From there, much smaller tread marks continued over the hill. It looked as if a truck had backed up to this location and unloaded some kind of four-wheeler or utility vehicle.

Kiya called out and waved the men over. "It looks like your visitors off-loaded something smaller and kept going."

Mitch bent down and looked at the marks on the other side of the tree limb. "She's right. Someone has been up here more than once. Maybe what happened to Dylan wasn't random chance at all."

"The entire ranch is clearly posted and marked with no trespassing signs. Looks like that isn't much of a deterrent to these people," Cade muttered with a scowl.

"I say we go up top and check out the meadow near the cabin. See if we can get an idea of where they were going," Jake suggested.

When Kiya crested the ridge, she pulled her horse to a stop. "Oh, it's lovely," she breathed. How could anyone own such a beautiful place and not use it? The meadow Jake had mentioned was a flat, open hilltop full of tall grass and wildflowers, still holding out against the cooler weather. Trees sheltered the hidden oasis on all sides giving it a secluded, magical feel. Kiya could imagine what the area would look like bathed in the colorful new growth of spring, thick leaves blocking the wind, a plethora of flowers scattered like carpet across the hilltop. She smiled at the mental image.

Off to her left at the far end of the open expanse, sat an old log structure with a rusted metal roof. As they rode closer, following the tire tracks, Kiya could see moss and weeds growing on its outer walls. The chinking connecting the logs had deteriorated in some spots to the point that she could see small gaps between them. Contradicting its abandoned nature, it appeared as if the structure had recently undergone some minor repairs to the roof and door. Nothing overtly obvious, but noticeable on closer inspection. The ATV tracks led straight to the structure along with what looked like dirt bike paths leading up to and beyond the cabin into the woods.

"What the hell?" Jake jumped down from his horse and strode over to the door that sported a shiny new padlock. He gave it a sharp tug and found that it was very securely attached to both the door and its frame.

"Why would anyone drive all the way out here on private land and put a padlock on a rundown building they don't own?" Cade looked over at Mitch before he continued, "You think this could be because someone is staying out here?"

"I don't know of any homeless people around town or transients passing through. Especially none that would be familiar enough with the area to know about or be able to locate this place."

Jake peered through a crack in the logs. "Nothing inside. No sleeping bag, no blankets, no lantern, no trash. It's completely empty. Nobody's staying here."

Luna made a circuit around the outside of the building sniffing at any crevice she could reach. She ended up back at the door where she scratched at the wood wanting in.

"The dog is interested in something. Too bad she can't tell us how long it's been since someone was here," Jake complained in frustration. "How is this related to Dylan being shot? The possibility of getting caught trespassing isn't a reason to try and kill someone. It doesn't make sense for anyone to resort to that level of violence just to keep their use of this place secret."

"I don't suppose either of you have any tools with you that will get that lock open?" Mitch asked hopefully.

"I have a small pair of fencing pliers in my saddlebag but nothing that is getting through that lock," Jake responded.

Cade shook his head and gestured back at Mitch. "You're the one with a gun on your hip, my friend. Why don't you shoot it off?"

"That only works in the movies. In real life it takes a whole lot of up close and personal fire power to accomplish that, which produces dangerous amounts of shrapnel," the man replied seriously.

Kiya looked at him warily. "It's kinda scary that you know that."

Jake chuckled softly. "There's nothing in there

worth shooting the place up for anyway. We can come back up here and cut it off some other time. What I'm wondering is how there has been this amount of traffic in and out of here with no one noticing. Yeah, it's a bit out of the way, but we have been in the general vicinity and never saw or heard anything."

"Except that the last person that came out this far ended up in the hospital," Mitch reminded him. "Besides, they could be using electric ATVs. That type of machine is catching on with both hunters and nature or environmental enthusiasts. They operate almost silently, leave little impact on the landscape, and have decent battery life if you're not out running hard all day. The good ones are on the pricey side for locals though. It would also indicate a deliberate and calculating level of subterfuge, which only compounds the questions…for what reason and why here?"

None of them could come up with any viable answers for now, so they returned to the house with more questions than answers.

****

Adjusting the focus on his binoculars, a lone sentinel watched as the small group of people milled around the cabin before finally following their route back the way they had arrived. The McClearys and that nosy neighbor of theirs were becoming a real problem. Not to mention that they had brought the cop with them. This place was getting way too much attention lately, and the boss wasn't going to like that. There had scarcely been time to get to cover before being seen when they had arrived. Guess they hadn't gotten the message yet to mind their own business. Nope, the boss sure wasn't going to like this, and things were about to get interesting.

Chapter 10

After returning from their morning ride, Kiya received a call from her carpenter saying that the repairs on her house had been completed. She agreed to meet him later in the day to retrieve the spare keys he had been using during the restoration. Once she had completed the final paperwork signing off on the project, she would be free to move back into her place. She had mixed feelings on the matter. On one hand, nothing out of the ordinary had happened for a while now and she was eager to get back to her normal life. She missed her home and the pleasant niche she had created for herself there. On the other hand, she had to admit that going back there when the person or people responsible for her attack were still unknown, and still out there somewhere, filled her with apprehension.

Maybe whoever it was had moved past the urge to punish her for getting in the way of their plans. If that was indeed what had initiated the attack. She couldn't think of any other reason, but that didn't mean someone else didn't perceive her presence here in town as a threat or a slight in some way. Maybe they just didn't like outsiders. Or maybe someone else had wanted the Billings' place before the couple had rented the property to her. She was unsure how that could trigger such a violent response, but you just never knew what could set someone off. No matter what, there *had* been an attack, and she really didn't want to endure another. Next time she might not be as lucky.

The best and undisputedly positive news was that Dylan had been given the green light to gradually return to his usual routine and had gotten a clean bill of health from his doctor. Margaret was beaming with happiness upon returning from Dylan's appointment. She delivered the news that Dylan's injury had healed well enough for him to ease back into normal activities with her customary enthusiasm and before the man himself could even open his mouth.

Kiya gave Dylan a warm congratulatory hug upon hearing his prognosis. "Glad to hear that you didn't waste all my hard work on your behalf," she joked. "I guess you showed those would-be assassins a thing or two, but no more getting shot, okay? I've decided that the world is a much better place with you in it."

Dylan kissed the top of her head. "I feel the same way about you, so we better make sure the good guys prevail, huh?"

"We already have," she told him relinquishing her hold on him so that his family could gather around him.

It looked like the time had come for her to try and move on from this experience also. These people, her new friends, would be better off not feeling as if they had to look after her. She wanted them to be able to focus on the good in their lives and wanted that for herself also. She knew Mitch wouldn't give up on finding answers. Until then, it would be best for everyone to move forward. She would move back home and reclaim her life.

Margaret prepared a picnic style lunch and served it on the porch. The meal had a celebratory feel to it as everyone settled into chairs around the small coffee-style tables. Dylan perched on the railing to enjoy the midday sun. Jake took the opportunity to claim the seat next to Kiya on one of the swings. Everyone ate, chatted, and laughed. It was a pleasant way to spend the afternoon.

When they were both done eating, Jake set the swing he and Kiya occupied into motion with a push of his foot. He leaned back and enjoyed the feeling of having his family around him happy and healthy. Kiya tucked her feet up under her and allowed him to control their motion. It amazed her how at home and comfortable she felt with these people. They had become one of the most important pieces of her life in such a short time. Her usual preference of solitude didn't apply to them. She smiled to herself because it still seemed to apply to anyone but them, but she was okay with that. She only hoped they would all still want to be a part of her life once she went back home.

A small sigh escaped her and drew Jake's attention. "I hope that was a happy sigh," he told her as he gently brushed a lock of hair off her shoulder.

"It was. Today is a good day. In fact, I have some good news of my own." She spoke up to include the others. "I will be moving back home again soon. The repairs are done, and I pick up my keys later today. That means I will be out of your hair in no time." She made her voice as upbeat as she could muster.

Everyone grew quiet at her pronouncement. The swing came to an abrupt halt beneath her. Hillary looked distressed. "You can't just leave." Her gaze moved to the others in search of support. "Tell her she can't leave."

"You don't need to go just because the work on the Billings' place is complete. The house isn't going anywhere," Gretchen told her.

"I can't hide out here forever," Kiya insisted.

"I think you should stay," Dylan told her. Cade nodded in agreement.

"Honey, I may not live here, but I think you're better off staying with the rest of the family," Margaret urged.

"Margaret, you may not live here, but you *are* family, and I agree that Kiya needs to be with us," Jake told the older woman then turned to Kiya. "There is no reason to rush your decision. There are still too many unknown variables at play. You can see where we all stand on this. Promise me you will think this through."

Kiya agreed to spend some more time thinking it over. She didn't want to spoil the mood for the day, so she moved the conversation back to Dylan's recovery and how she was more than happy to allow him to reclaim his portion of the barn duties as soon as he was up to it.

They finished their lunch, then one by one, they left to get back to their own schedules, but not before agreeing that they would all have dinner in the main house.

When Cade asked what time Kiya was going to get her keys, she told him that she would be leaving shortly.

Jake opened his mouth, but Dylan held up a hand to stop him. "Don't worry, I will go with her. It feels good to be able to get out and about a little bit." Cade's brows drew together. He pulled in a breath, but before he could speak, he was cut off as well. "Yes, I will still take it easy. You two are as bad as a couple of old women."

Cade looked at Jake. "I didn't say a thing, did you?" he asked, trying to look perplexed rather than amused that their brother knew them so well.

"Nope, not a word," Jake assured him.

"Cute," Dylan told them. "But I stand by what I said."

The ride to pick up her keys was quick and pleasant with Dylan's company. Kiya signed papers saying that she was satisfied with the work and thanked the carpenter for his help. They dropped a copy of the forms in the mail for the Billings, and they made their way back to the ranch.

Dinner was as boisterous as usual. Kiya watched in amusement as the people around the table carried on multiple conversations at once and still managed to eat and poke fun at each other. Topics ranged from ranch business dealings to old boyfriends, and Gretchen's eventual return to the city. Kiya found it hard to keep up. Things quieted down when Cade and Jake went to the barn to check on a gelding that had gotten himself injured after picking a fight with another horse. Gretchen had cooked, so she happily retired to her room while Hilly was on cleanup duty. Kiya offered to help, but Hilly shooed her away.

"It's my turn tonight. I've got this. Go unwind a bit. I know this rowdy bunch isn't what you are used to."

"I don't mind. It's fun to see how the other half lives so to speak. Dinners at my house when I was growing up were small and almost silent. Just the usual 'how was school' type of thing. Now that I am on my own, I usually find myself talking to Luna as if she might answer me."

Luna perked up at her name. The dog had waited patiently for the humans to finish their meal and was now anticipating her evening playtime. She wiggled in joy when Kiya told Hilly that getting some air would be a good idea.

Outside, the atmosphere was still and peaceful. Kiya breathed in deep and felt herself begin to relax. She sank into a chair while watching Luna pounce on a stick as if it was a long-lost friend and trot off with it.

The door to the house opened again, and Dylan stepped out. "Hey there, angel, you mind some company?"

Kiya looked up with a happy smile. "I will never mind having company if that company is you."

"My feelings exactly." Easing himself into a chair, Dylan leaned back and sighed. They sat in companionable silence for a few minutes, simply enjoying the evening in each other's presence.

When Dylan shifted trying to find a more comfortable position, Kiya watched him with empathy. "I'm surprised you are still up and around after your busy day today. You shouldn't overdo it." She was relieved to see that he appeared tired but content. There wasn't any pain reflecting in his expression.

"I have to admit, I'm starting to feel the effects of it, but it was nice to be *able* to do it. Getting out helped ease the tension of being relatively housebound for a while. I'm not used to having so much downtime. It tends to drive me crazy." His smile grew as she continued to study him. "I will turn in soon, I promise. But I wanted to see how you're feeling about getting your house back."

"To tell you the truth, I'm not sure what to feel yet." She sighed. "It changes minute by minute."

"I would be surprised if you weren't conflicted about it. I would be too. I can understand you wanting to get back to normal and have your own space, your own routine, but I can also see how unsettling being there alone would be after what happened. I just wanted to make sure you knew that every one of us meant it when we said that there was no hurry for you to go back. You don't need to make that decision yet. Take whatever time you need to think it through. You are a welcome addition around here. It's not just a matter of safety anymore. You fit in so well, it's like you have always been here. But even if you feel the need to get back to your own place, just know that you are welcome here anytime. We would expect you back…often. And be prepared to have us drop by for visits too." He leaned over to cover her hand with his. "When you saved my life, you made a lifelong commitment. You're stuck with me."

"Now, he tells me," Kiya joked, rolling her eyes.

When Jake entered the house a short time later, he found Hilly alone finishing up her evening chores. Cade followed his brother inside but kept going through the kitchen into the great room where they heard the TV turned on to some sports channel.

"Where's Kiya?" Jake asked. "I didn't see her leave for the cabin yet."

"She and Dylan are out on the porch."

When he didn't respond, Hilly glanced at her brother. "You all right?"

"Yeah, why wouldn't I be?"

She smiled. "Oh, I don't know, maybe because Kiya is out on the porch with Dylan."

Jake shot her a disgruntled look.

"You can join them if you want. I'm not quite done here," she told him.

He leaned against the counter and frowned. "I'm not sure they would appreciate the intrusion. Just make sure he walks her back to the cabin." He turned and left the room.

****

The next morning, Kiya skipped having her morning coffee at the main house in favor of a quiet morning to herself. She needed to think over her options and to start gathering up her belongings. It had been easier than she thought it would be to make herself at home here. Her personal items were spread out all over the tiny cabin. She had to admit that the thought of leaving the ranch made her feel more than a little melancholy. Luna sensed her mistress's mood and leaned against Kiya's leg offering her own version of reassurance.

A knock at the door pulled Kiya from her musings. She opened it to find Jake leaning against the doorjamb on the other side. "I am here to inform you that you have been summoned to the house."

"I…what?"

"Hilly wants you to come up to the house. She was going to ring down but got sucked into a conference call with a magazine editor. I told her I would stop by and send you up." He spotted the pile of items she had deposited on the couch. A muscle twitched at his jawline. His eyes were concerned when they met hers. "I thought you agreed to not rush your decision."

"I'm not. I was just getting things together and more organized just in case. I seem to have spread out and taken over the place." She laughed.

He bent down to rub Luna's chin while addressing her comment. "That's what you were supposed to do. It's good that you feel comfortable here."

"Too comfortable maybe. It is going to be hard to regain that feeling back at my place."

"Perhaps that's a sign that you should wait. Give yourself more time to adapt. Give Mitch and the rest of us the chance to remove the reason for your anxiety about the place. We *will* figure this out."

"Maybe you're right," she relented.

"I'm always right." His teasing pronouncement lightened the mood.

"Of course you are." Smiling, she followed him out the door.

****

"We're what?" Kiya inquired when Hilly filled her in on the plan she and Gretchen had come up with for the afternoon.

"Playing hooky. From work, from chores, hovering males, and worrying about anything. We grab lunch at the diner, visit all the best shops, maybe get a facial or a manicure, then dinner and drinks at the best restaurant we can find." She winked at Kiya and in an exaggerated whisper stated, "Lots of drinks."

Amused with her sister's antics, Gretchen seconded the motion by adding that they all deserved a break. Especially since her stay would soon come to an end. "I say we live it up while we can. I won't get the chance to have a girl's night with you two again until my next visit home. I need some fun to remember and look forward to until next time."

Kiya felt a rush of pleasure at the mention of future outings with these two women. It felt wonderful knowing that they were looking forward to continuing a friendship with her just as she was with them.

"In that case, I'm all for it. What should I wear? I didn't bring the right kind clothes for an outing like that."

Hilly assured her that between Gretchen and herself, they could find something suitable for Kiya to wear.

As it turned out, closet surfing with them and trying on outfits was just as fun as the day itself. They spent a leisurely day palling around town doing whatever struck their fancy. For Kiya it was a day like none other. She learned what it was like to have sisters. They cajoled her into trying new things and looks she never would have tried for herself, argued good naturedly over who had the best tastes, and pampered themselves without remorse.

Seafood was chosen for dinner, and they settled in at a table located in a trendy upscale restaurant in a nearby town with happy sighs. Kiya rubbed at her tired feet. "I don't think I have ever walked so much in heels in my entire life."

"Yeah, but they look fantastic on you," Gretchen told her.

"They really do. They give your legs some great definition," Hilly added. "I also love that new color of lipstick. Not a bad find if I do say so myself." She breathed on her newly manicured nails and rubbed them on her blouse.

Gretchen tilted her head to the side and studied

Kiya thoughtfully. "You were right," she agreed. "I changed my mind. It suits her skin tone beautifully."

Her sister's mouth fell open in exaggerated shock. Holding a cupped hand to her ear she leaned closer to Gretchen. "What did you say? I didn't quite catch that. Did you say…I was right?"

Kiya broke out in laughter when Gretchen informed her sister that there are firsts for everything, and she had been long overdue for hers.

"Don't laugh. She will start to think she's amusing," Hilly chided Kiya with a haughty look in her sister's direction.

They placed an order for calamari and wine to start and reminisced about their day. The evening passed swiftly and pleasantly. When they selected main dishes, Hilly and Gretchen debated the merits of the items listed on the specialty drink menu.

"What do you think, Kiya? Sweet, salty, spicy, or sophisticated?" Hilly inquired.

"I'm going to be boring and stick to my wine. I am driving after all, but I would say the Tahitian sunrise for you. It's sweet and sassy. And the espresso martini for Gretchen. Rich and sophisticated."

"Oh, you're good," Hilly told Kiya with a broad smile. "And an incredibly delightful companion." She turned to her sister. "I say we adopt her."

"Agreed." Gretchen raised her glass. "Here's to our newest sister and finally not being outnumbered by overbearing brothers."

Kiya said she was honored, and they clinked their glasses together in solidarity.

All too soon, the evening came to an end. They paid their bill, gathered their bags, and headed for the parking lot lugging the spoils of the day. They chatted happily as they piled everything into the back of Kiya's Jeep and climbed into their seats. Hilly sat in the middle of the back seat then leaned forward to talk and lend her opinion on driving routes.

"The back roads are better. Not as much traffic and more importantly, less chance of Mitch pulling us over and lecturing us on the perils of driving after a day…and night, of revelry."

Kiya turned her head to look over her shoulder at the woman. "I've only had a glass and a half of wine you know. There is nothing for him to lecture about."

"It's Mitch. He can lecture about anything and everything. He's been practicing on Gretchen and me since childhood," Hilly told her.

"Back roads it is," Kiya agreed.

They cranked up the radio and sang along as they traversed the dirt roads leading back to the ranch. Kiya's fingers tapped the steering wheel in time with the music. She glanced at her rearview mirror. A truck had appeared out of nowhere and was coming up on them fast.

"Wow, this guy is in a hurry. And you were worried about our driving," she told Hilly.

Hillary looked behind them at the approaching truck. She couldn't make out the color or model of the vehicle; the headlights were too bright.

"Maybe you should slow down and let them pass," Gretchen advised as the truck moved even closer.

Kiya reduced her speed then glanced at her mirror again. The vehicle showed no indication that it would pass them by. In fact, it edged right up behind their bumper and blinded Kiya with its high beams.

"Seriously?" Kiya demanded of the unknown driver. "Just go around already."

"I don't like this," Hilly told them in a quivering voice. "Where's Mitch and his endless lectures when you need them?"

"He lectures you because he has always been sweet on you," Gretchen told her sister, trying to distract her.

"He has not."

"Has so."

Before Hilly could form a comeback, the truck following them sped up and pushed against the rear of Kiya's Jeep. It fishtailed slightly before regaining its grip on the road. Gretchen cursed then looked at her terrified sister. "I'm calling Jake. This isn't just some yahoo out for a joyride."

Kiya sped up again to avoid another impact as Gretchen grabbed her phone. She pressed a speed dial number and mentally urged her brother to pick up.

"You guys planning on staying out all night?" he asked as a greeting.

"Jake, we have a problem."

His tone immediately turned serious. "What's wrong?"

Gretchen rapidly explained what was happening. As she finished, the Jeep took another hit from behind. Hilly screamed as their vehicle swerved from one side of the road to the other.

"I got it, I got it, I got it," Kiya chanted as she righted the Jeep and punched the gas.

"Where are you?" Jake demanded.

"We are on…um…Hollow Mill Road. Just past the old quarry," Gretchen replied as she clutched the handle above her head near the door in a death grip.

"I'm calling Mitch then we'll head your way. Don't try anything risky. We're coming."

The call disconnected just as the truck behind them pressed its front bumper against Kiya's back bumper and increased its speed to a terrifying level. The tires beneath them started to lose traction from the added force. They skidded sideways with the truck still pushing against the rear of the Jeep. Kiya fought to keep them pointed in the right direction. Just as she thought she might be able to regain control, a final shove from behind sent them flying into a dizzying high-speed spin.

Hilly screamed and pressed her hands firmly against the roof above her head. Kiya's head bounced off the driver's side window as they whirled. The last thing she heard was Gretchen's terrified shriek as their tires hit the edge of the road and flipped them onto their roof. The Jeep came to rest upside down facing the opposite direction in a wide shallow ditch next to the road.

****

Jake shouted for his brothers before he even hit the end button on his phone. He punched in Mitch's personal cell number. He held up a finger to the men that rushed to his side and waited until Mitch picked up the phone before explaining the situation to everyone at once. That done, he and his brothers hit the front door of the ranch at a run.

The three men flew down the road at speeds that didn't exactly match the posted limit, but Jake handled the truck expertly. His hands clutched the wheel so tightly that his knuckles turned white with the pressure. At a juncture about a mile from the last known location of the women, two sets of flashing lights slid into position behind them with sirens blaring. Jake crested a small rise, and the accident scene spread out before them.

"Oh my God," Cade breathed as they took in the long stretch of torn-up gravel, skid marks, and debris littering the roadway leading to the upside-down vehicle.

Jake stomped on the brakes near the wreck and was climbing out of the truck before it had even come to a complete stop. His brothers were close on his heels. Together, they rushed to either side of the vehicle while Mitch and a couple of deputies swung in behind them.

Dropping to his knees beside the driver's side window, Jake brushed aside the shattered glass and leaned down to peer inside. Kiya was unconscious, hanging from her belt. Blood covered the entire left side of her face. Hilly was crying in the back seat struggling frantically with the seat belt that held her suspended.

"Hilly, honey, calm down. We're here now, and we're going to get you out. Just hold on a little while longer. I need to get Kiya out so we can reach you, okay?" He saw Cade and Dylan crouching next to Gretchen's window. "Can you get her out?" he asked.

Cade shook his head. "The seat belt is jammed with the force of her weight against it."

"I can fix that," Mitch said, nudging Dylan aside. He bent and cut through Gretchen's restraint with a seat belt cutter. With Cade helping to break her fall, they pulled her from the wreckage. One of the deputies wrapped her in a protective blanket as she came around enough to stumble away from the ditch with Cade's help. The other deputy was on the radio with dispatch reporting multiple victims in need of medical assistance. Dylan sat beside Gretchen on the ground a short distance away and ran a soothing hand over her back while they watched the others trying to get Kiya and Hilly out of the wreckage.

Mitch handed Jake the car escape tool then focused on getting to Hillary. He shimmied his way into the vehicle on his stomach to reach the back seat.

At the same time, Jake positioned his arm under Kiya's shoulders to support her and sliced through her seat belt. She landed against him with a groan. He tossed the instrument in his hand back inside to Mitch and backed away from the window pulling Kiya along with him until they had cleared the jagged edge of the glass. Jake tugged until she rested between his outstretched legs and leaned against his thigh.

"Kiya? Can you hear me? Open your eyes, baby," he coaxed gently. "Come on, Kiya, wake up." Her eyes fluttered then opened. Jake stroked his knuckles along her cheek. "There you are. Stay with me."

Inside the mangled wreck, Mitch gingerly maneuvered himself underneath Hilly then rolled onto his back. He grabbed for the cutting tool and looked up at the woman suspended above him. When their gazes met, Hillary's eyes welled up with tears again.

"Are they okay? They wouldn't answer me. I called to them over and over, but they wouldn't answer me," she sobbed.

"They're going to be fine, honey, and so are you. Your brothers are taking good care of them. Now, how about we get you down from there, huh?"

Hilly nodded and reached for his shoulders. She braced herself against him and tried to shift her weight off the strap so he could cut through it. A moment later, she dropped onto his chest. Instantly, she wrapped her arms around his neck and clung to him. Mitch folded his arms around her quaking form and held her against him.

"Are you hurt?" he asked anxiously.

She shook her head against his neck but didn't let go.

"Honey, I know you're upset, but I would really like to get you out of this damn Jeep."

Hilly scrambled off him the best she could. "I'm sorry. I really want to get out of here too."

Turning back onto his stomach, Mitch inched his way backward out the window. Once free, he reached inside to help Hilly crawl out. Cade waited nearby until she was on her feet, then pulled her into a tight hug. He kept an arm around her while they skirted the vehicle. Their siblings joined them and huddled together as they moved to where Jake still cradled Kiya next to the road. Gretchen held on to her sister's hand, and they sank to the ground beside their friend. "How's she doing?" she asked.

Jake lifted the bloody, matted hair off Kiya's forehead to get a better look at the injury beneath.

"She's coming around more now," he reassured them. "Are you two all right?"

Hilly nodded. "A little lightheaded from hanging upside down, but it's fading. Gretchen was out for a while too. It was terrible when I couldn't get loose to help."

"We are all safe now," Gretchen assured her, patting her hand in comfort.

Everyone turned in the direction of the sound of

vehicles approaching. Two ambulances eased to a stop on the shoulder of the road. Cade and Dylan helped their sisters into the back of one ambulance while Kiya was placed onto a stretcher and loaded into another. Jake saw the pale color of Dylan's skin as they waited for the medics to get their patients prepped for transport. Worried that tonight's events were overtaxing him, Jake laid a hand on Dylan's shoulder.

"This has been a lot for you too. Why don't you ride to the hospital with Kiya and keep an eye on her while Cade and I stay here and help Mitch finish up? Hilly and Gretchen will be fine together for now. We will meet you there in a little while."

By the time the ambulances made it to the hospital, Kiya was fully awake and irritated with the fact that she was once again being carted off for treatment. The doctors in the ER were kept busy running back and forth between the three women with test results and treating minor injuries. Hilly was cleared pretty quickly when it became evident that her only injury was a sprained wrist. Following x-rays, a Velcro brace was all she needed to be released from care.

Gretchen thankfully had no signs of any head trauma, but she and Kiya, who received three stitches to close the laceration to her forehead, were told that due to the fact that they had lost consciousness, they would be kept overnight for observation. They would be released the next day if no complications presented themselves.

Hilly and Dylan switched places back and forth visiting Kiya and Gretchen in their rooms while they waited for the others to arrive. Dylan remembered Kiya's comment about getting attention from the nurses when he was in the hospital, so he returned the sentiment by pointing out that at least she and Gretchen had the opportunity to meet eligible doctors or nurses during their stay at the hospital.

"I wonder if doctors have a friends and family discount plan. I might need one if I keep ending up in here," she told him with a laugh.

"I'm sorry that you have. I never would have wanted this for you after what you did for me. It tears me up that you got sucked into such a perilous mess."

She squeezed his hand as he sat next to her. "This isn't your fault. And I was only teasing. It helps to be able to keep things in perspective. We are all alive and well. I for one feel that I have gained some amazing friends out of this mess, and that's pretty darn great. I hate that you got shot in order for it to happen, but I am very happy with what has come out of it."

"And we got you. So, you're right, we have many things to be grateful for."

A couple hours later, Kiya woke from a light doze to see Jake sitting in the chair that Dylan had occupied.

"Jake, I didn't hear you come in. I thought Dylan was here."

"He was, I sent him home to get some rest," he replied calmly.

She nodded in approval. "Good, he was looking a little peaked."

"How are *you* feeling?"

"I feel fine. I have a bit of a headache, but nothing that should have warranted an overnight stay," she told him with a huff.

"It's better to play it safe. Gretchen was complaining about the same thing when I stopped by her room a few minutes ago."

"Great minds and all that," Kiya quipped.

He moved to sit at the edge of her bed and lifted some hair away from her face. "I see you gained a new set of stitches. That wound looks a lot better than I thought it would."

"Yeah, and just after I was able to get rid of the last ones too," she grumbled. "But head wounds tend to bleed a lot so they can look worse than they are." She reached for a Styrofoam cup sitting on the stand next to the bed, but Jake snagged it first and handed it to her.

"Thanks. Was someone able to haul my Jeep off the side of the road?"

"We got everything taken care of for now. All you need to do is rest. You will have plenty of time to deal with that stuff later."

"I guess my vehicle will be a total loss." A frown marred her brow for a moment before it was replaced by a light smile. "But on the bright side, that means I get a brand new one."

He chuckled at her optimistic tone. "That's one way of looking at it."

"Well, like I told Dylan, it's a matter of perspective. Good things have come from all this too."

Chapter 11

Late the next morning, Gretchen and Kiya were escorted home by Cade and Hilly. Both women had spent the night resting comfortably with no residual problems and were happy to say goodbye to their temporary accommodations.

They entered the house to find it filled with the aromatic scent of the homemade chicken noodle soup that Margaret had prepared for their lunch. She was bustling about making sure that neither they, nor Hilly, would have to lift a finger for the day.

Luna came running when she heard Kiya's voice and greeted everyone in turn.

"Well, she seems happy and unfazed after spending the night at the big house," Kiya claimed, ruffling the dog's fur and warding off enthusiastic kisses.

"She was a perfect lady and kept me company all night," Dylan informed her.

Everyone allowed Margaret to herd them into the kitchen for a bowl of hot soup before she left for home. The feel-good classic was a major hit with the entire family.

"I don't know about you," Gretchen told Kiya when she had finished, "but I am dying for a hot shower."

When Kiya agreed that a shower sounded like heaven, Hilly offered Kiya the use of hers.

"It has a detachable showerhead. That will make it easier to wash your hair without soaking your stitches."

The trio left the room and filed upstairs. Gretchen went to her room to clean up while Hilly led Kiya to her own room and waited for her to finish. When Hilly heard the water shut off, she tapped on the door and handed Kiya a set of well-worn sweats.

"I thought you could use these. It's the most comfortable thing I own, and sisters share," she told Kiya cheerfully. She perched on the edge of the tub and kept up a flow of conversation while the other woman blew her hair dry.

When the three women came back downstairs, they were laughing and chatting as if they had known each other forever.

"Well, I'm glad to see that you are all feeling better after your ordeal," Mitch greeted them when they entered the great room. "I hate to break the mood, but do you ladies feel up to talking us through everything that happened last night?"

The women sat side by side on the couch while the men took seats nearby. They recounted the events of the previous day as thoroughly as possible and filled in pieces of each other's descriptions where they could. When they had finished, Mitch was quiet for a moment before saying that it was obvious that the ranch and the people on it were being watched somehow.

"No one could have guessed the girls would decide on a night out last night, and it wasn't a chance encounter either. They are receiving information on your whereabouts."

Cade got to his feet and paced the floor. "So, what do we do? It's not even safe for them to leave the ranch as a group anymore. They can't live in lockdown on the ranch and under guard."

The women wholeheartedly agreed.

"It may not be any safer for the rest of you either," Mitch told them. "If they know where the girls are, they know where you are too."

They spent some time discussing safety measures they could take to reduce the likelihood of further incidents. Mitch prepared to return to his office to file his official report and make some phone calls to arrange some extra protection for the ranch.

"On a different note, I did a quick check into that guy on the business card you gave me. There doesn't seem to be anything overly remarkable about him. No record, operates a rather ordinary business, has expensive taste but doesn't necessarily live outside of his means. He has made offers on some small pieces of land scattered around the area. Just isolated tracts with no real development opportunities. They seem to be more along the lines of investment purchases than anything else. In fact, when I spoke to the Billings about their property damages and sent them a copy of the official report, they mentioned getting a written offer on the place a while back. They didn't want to sell and decided to rent the place out instead. That's how Kiya ended up getting the place." He rose and turned toward the door. "I'll let you all know if I hear anything else or get any new leads. Hilly, you want to walk me out?"

She looked confused but agreed. She pulled her sweater closer around her body as they walked to Mitch's truck. "Did you need something?" she asked when he didn't speak.

He opened his door and turned toward her. His eyes moved over her face, studying her. "No, I just wanted to make sure you are doing all right."

"Of course. I'm not the one that had to spend the night in the hospital."

"Maybe not, but you experienced the same thing they did. You just happened to be in the safer seating position. You were the one awake and trapped, not knowing the condition of the other two and being unable to help. That takes an emotional toll that the others didn't feel. You were very upset when we got to the scene."

Hilly scuffed the toe of her shoe at a pebble on the ground by her feet, embarrassed by her actions the day before. She had bordered on the verge of hysterics and wasn't proud of it.

"I appreciate the concern, but everything turned out well, and I'm fine," she replied.

Mitch nodded, but the concern didn't leave his eyes. He reached out, carefully lifted her braced wrist, and held it gently.

"No tennis for you for a while, huh?" he teased.

"Yeah, and I'm such the sporty type too," she scoffed back.

"You're the beautiful and kind type," he told her, then seemed to realize what he had said and hastily released her to climb into his truck. "Stay safe, Hilly. Don't take any unnecessary chances."

As he drove off, Hillary remained where she was, wondering how to interpret his words. Then she chided herself for overthinking it. He was probably just being nice to the sister of his best friends. He hadn't meant anything at all by it. She turned and retraced her steps to the house.

****

Following an unusually subdued dinner and helping with some light evening chores, Dylan walked into the kitchen to find Hillary sitting at the table vacantly staring into a cup of tea. He tapped on the table to get her attention as he sat down and leaned his elbows on the table.

"How's it going, Hill?" he asked. "How's my favorite sister?"

"Oh, now I'm your favorite sister? This afternoon you called Gretchen your favorite sister."

"That was this afternoon. You're my favorite tonight," he vowed with a grin.

She laughed and waved away his comment, calling him a suck-up. They all knew his so-called favorite flip flopped every few hours and depended on which sister he was with. It had been his way of making them both feel special ever since he was a kid. "But to answer your question, I am doing fine. Just enjoying the lack of chaos."

"It *is* awfully quiet around here. Where is everybody?"

"I'm not sure about Jake and Cade, but Gretchen is taking one of her marathon bubble baths, and Kiya decided to call it an early night."

"She didn't go back to the cabin, did she? We agreed she should move into the house for the time being. If someone is watching the ranch, she needs to be here with us. Not alone out there."

"Calm down, papa bear. She's upstairs in a spare room. I swear, I don't know which of you is more protective of her…you, or Jake."

"It's not a competition. We both care about what happens to her. We do the same with you and Gretchen."

"Are you sure that's all it is?" she inquired in a soft tone.

"What do you mean?"

"Jake seems to be under the impression that you have feelings for her."

"Of course, I have feelings for her. She saved my life…literally. She was there for me during a traumatic time when I needed someone. She could have turned her back on the whole crazy scenario, but she didn't. She chose to stay with me and give me hope when I desperately needed it. But besides that, she's kind, and smart, and fun to be around. It's like she has become a part of the family. A slightly sarcastic family member that isn't quite sure what to do with us yet, but family nonetheless."

"That's perfect," Hilly claimed.

"It is? I mean, *it is*, but why do you say that?"

"Because Gretchen and I have already somewhat officially adopted her, and she agreed. We toasted to it and everything," she told him happily.

"Well, that settles it then, doesn't it?" He chuckled at her obvious delight.

"Yes, it does."

****

"Maybe I should stay," Gretchen hedged, dropping another shirt into the open suitcase on the bed. "I hate leaving all of you when things are so crazy around here. What if something happens after I leave?"

"Then we will call you and handle the situation like we have everything else," Hilly reassured her sister.

"You being here isn't going to stop anything from happening. We have already seen that. It would only give them an additional target. I say if you have the chance to get away from all this and be safe...do it. It will be better for us to know that you are far away from it. Give us less to worry about. Not to mention the fact that you have used up all of your emergency leave time anyway. Don't risk your career over this."

"It might not be my place to say, but I agree with your sister. The fewer people we have to worry about, the better. I know I would prefer knowing you are safe, and if something were to happen, you can always come back," Kiya supplied cautiously.

"Of course, you have a say," Gretchen told Kiya. She looked at the two women sitting on either side of her luggage and sighed. "I know you are both right, and I do have a bunch of clients waiting on me. It just *feels* so wrong to pick up and go."

Hillary rose and gave her sister a squeeze. "Don't worry. The next time you get an opportunity to come home, this will all be behind us, and we will be able to relax, have fun, and enjoy the visit," she promised.

Kiya and Hilly helped Gretchen complete her preflight to-do list then joined the rest of the family in seeing her off to the airport for her flight home to Denver.

****

Meanwhile at another location on the ranch, different preparations were being made and carried out. To date, there hadn't been any major interruptions to their schedule or plans, and the boss wanted to keep it that way.

Radio confirmation had come through that the

McClearys were otherwise occupied for the evening, and there had been no further visits from the cop or interest in the hunting cabin. Things continued to run smoothly for now.

A vibrating phone alerted him to the incoming call he had been waiting for. He answered the call and listened to the instructions being given.

"Yeah, I understand. When do you want this done?"

"As soon as you can arrange it. The sooner the better. If their attention is focused elsewhere, they will be less inclined to stick their noses where they aren't wanted," came the reply.

"This isn't going to be as easy as shooting a lone rider from afar or running some defenseless broads off a deserted public road. We still don't know what that bitch saw when McCleary was hit. This ups the chances of getting seen or causing problems. You sure this is how you want to play it?"

"It isn't your job to question my decisions. It's your job to carry out my instructions. I am aware that this plan has its risks, and you will be compensated accordingly, but it *will* be done. Do I make myself clear?"

"Consider it done."

"Good, now finish what you need to do tonight, then get on this. I will expect to hear from you soon."

****

Kiya was bored. Her workload had slacked off to nothing more than a couple small routine projects that were not at all challenging. Nothing in depth enough to keep her interest or focus. She was not used to having all this free time with nothing to do. Normally if her schedule got slow or she needed a change of scenery, she would saddle Dax for a nice long ride, or take Luna on a hiking excursion. It was getting late in the year for kayaking or paddle boarding, but anything to keep her busy at this point would be welcome. She had taken Luna up and down the long drive leading to the main house, cleaned stalls in the barn, and helped Hilly prepare her garden beds for winter. Now, she was at a loss. Suddenly, she had an idea. She quickly logged on to the internet to do some research.

By the time dinner was served, Kiya had formulated a plan. It would not only give her something worthwhile to do, but it could boost the profits of the ranch as well. It would be nice to give something back after they had so graciously taken her and her animals in.

It was Cade's turn to cook so Kiya volunteered to set the table. At first, she had been surprised that all the siblings took turns preparing meals and doing clean-up after. However, Dylan told her that their mother wouldn't stand for the old adage that men handled the barn and livestock, while the women took care of the house. She believed in the equal division of labor, and all of her children were taught to pitch in wherever they could. She was adamant that they would all be able to fend for themselves but still work well as a team. Kiya could find no fault with the philosophy.

After the goulash was passed and the usual dinner conversation slowed, Kiya presented them with her idea. "I looked at your company website today. I have to say I'm impressed with the scope and breadth of your brand."

"Checking us out, are ya?" Cade asked with a

wink.

"Why do I have the feeling that there was a 'but' coming on the heels of that statement?" Jake wondered aloud.

"You heard that too, huh?" Dylan laughed.

"Just hear me out," Kiya urged. "You have a good setup. It provides a lot of detail and has a functional design. It's a little wordy and outdated, but that is easily fixed. However, I could do wonders with a whole new interactive, multi-page, service specific design. Right now, you have one main page and concept as a backdrop that covers your entire operation. Visitors must read or search through a lot of information on the ranch as a whole in order to find information on the services they need. Then they call one number for the primary office and leave a message to receive specific details on accommodations, fees, available dates, things of that nature. From what I can tell, the three of you each have your specialty or niche within the whole. Dylan's degree and background function as an overall business manager, with ranch operations, client outreach, contracts, billing, holdings, etcetera. Cade deals with the cattle, land usage and rotation, bloodlines, sales, feeding, and that kind of thing. Whereas Jake handles the horses. Training specific to the client's needs, buying, selling, breeding, and transport. You collaborate on all of it but have your areas of interest and expertise. Am I right?"

At their nods of agreement, Kiya went on to explain how they could use that to their advantage. Draw new clients in and streamline the information for their specific field of interest. She laid out a homepage that would capture the attention of the casual browser or searcher with beautiful imagery and give an overview of the ranch's history and goals. From there, they could divide the different sections or areas of operation into three separate link buttons leading to another page for each brother and his particular division of the ranch. On their own pages, they would provide a more detailed overview of their specialty with tabs for information on services offered, references, general sales and price info, and listing separate contact names, numbers, and email links for the person in charge of those interactions. They could each personalize their own pages and sections, making them distinctive and unique. Interactive schedules could be posted with available dates for distinct types of services or meeting appointments where interested parties could then reserve times and services. All of which they would be notified about immediately via email and/or text. Secure deposits and payments could be done online at the click of a mouse, and all the pages would be easy to navigate between.

"When Dylan does outreach promotions, he can focus mailings to specific groups of people who use different individual services and direct them to the exact page that pertains to their interests, but they can always access any other division of the ranch's site from there. That can also be done when you hand out business cards or have interactions with customers, simply point them to your personal page and voila, all the information they need in one convenient stop. And of course, all the different functions available could be modified at any time once you see what works for you or if you have ideas on things that would be helpful. Message boards, virtual meeting rooms, automated phone responses, and things like that." Kiya finished talking then held her breath as she waited for their reaction.

Hillary was looking at her with surprised approval. "I have told them many times that they need to move with the times and update that site. Your ideas sound wonderful to me. Efficiency breeds prosperity, as I always say."

"I'm not trying to butt into your business or tell you how to run things. I am only offering my help if you want it," Kiya told them earnestly.

"Your offer is appreciated, but hiring a professional to overhaul our entire website wasn't exactly included in the current budget," Cade worried. "And it is a lot of work for you to take on."

"The work would be a welcome distraction, and I wasn't suggesting this to score a big paycheck. I'm not worried about that."

"You don't work for free Kiya, and we wouldn't let you anyway," Dylan told her.

"Agreed. We won't take advantage of you, your talent, or your generosity," Jake added.

"You wouldn't be taking advantage," she insisted. "I offered. Okay, how about this…I work up something to show you, so you can determine if you think it would benefit you. If you decide to accept my ideas and designs, once they go live, and *if* they generate new business or result in a profit for the ranch, then we can discuss if it warrants payment. Agreed?"

The siblings pondered the idea and shared looks around the table. "I gave my opinion, and I think it would be foolish to refuse, but this type of decision is up to the three of you," Hillary remarked.

"Cade, Dylan?" Jake prompted.

"I'm game," Cade decided.

"Let's see what she's got," Dylan seconded.

"Looks like you got a deal," Jake told her.

Chapter 12

A tap at the door to her room pulled Kiya out of her task and back into the real world. She scrubbed at her eyes and noted that she had been lost in her work for much longer than she had thought.

"Come on in," she called out to whoever was on the other side of the door.

Hilly popped her head in far enough to see Kiya sitting cross-legged on the bed with her computer on her lap. "Sorry to interrupt. You got a minute?"

"Because it's you," Kiya said with a smile and patted the bed. "What's up?"

"I accepted a new writing assignment today, and get this...it's on how small-town police departments with limited resources deal with violent crime."

Kiya made a sound that could have been either a cough or a snort. "You're kidding?"

"Nope. So, I am headed into town to put Mitch and his propensity for lectures on crime and safety to good use. I am dropping Cade off at the feed store, and I thought I would ask if you wanted to ride along or if you needed anything while I'm out."

"I would, but I really want to finish this portion of the new website. I tend to get tunnel vision when I'm in the middle of a project and hate to leave a promising idea for later."

"I hear ya. I'm the same way when I get an idea

and start researching or drafting an article. Any requests?"

Kiya grabbed her wallet and a piece of paper. She scribbled something on the paper then pulled some money out of her wallet and handed both to Hilly. "If you would ask Cade to pick up this food for Luna while he's at the feed store, I would appreciate it."

"No problem. We will be home in time for dinner." She hopped off the bed and disappeared out the door, closing it behind her.

****

Mitch was at his desk with his door open when Hillary walked into the municipal building. Taking that as a good sign, she went straight to his office and rapped her knuckles against the doorframe. "Hey, Mitch, are you super busy, or could you help me with some information for an article?"

He looked up in surprise. "Hilly. What are you doing here?"

She raised an eyebrow. "I need some information for an article."

"Yeah, you said that already, didn't you?" His lips twitched with a rueful smile. "Sorry. Come on in. It's just that you've never showed up in my office before."

She cocked her head in thought. *Is that true? In all the years I've known him, I have never visited him at work?* She shrugged. "I never had a reason to."

"Do you need a reason?" He gestured to the chair in front of his desk.

Hillary considered the question as she sat down. "No, I guess not. But it seems silly to show up unexpectedly for no reason, doesn't it?" She laughed.

His gaze skimmed over her face before he replied

in a neutral tone. "I suppose so." Then he seemed to draw himself up and in a more "official" manner asked, "Since work brought you here, what is it that you need from me?"

She blinked. The abrupt shift in attitude gave her pause, but she followed his lead and explained her current assignment. She laid out the type of material she needed to meet the article's requirements, then tried to coax him back to a more friendly vibe. "I thought that maybe I could kill two birds with one stone and pick your brain on official procedure but also maybe wheedle some more relevant tidbits out of you as one of the friends involved in your most recent case." She phrased the last part of her sentence as a hopeful question and flashed him an enticing smile. Her ploy didn't work.

"I am happy to go over basic investigative procedures and give you an idea of what resources are and are not available to us as a small jurisdiction, but you realize that officially, we don't give out specific details of any ongoing investigation or division policies to the press."

Hilly's smile faltered. Confused by his overly formal response, she caught her bottom lip between her teeth and nodded. "Okay." She self-consciously closed her notebook and pocketed her phone. "You know what…I shouldn't have bothered you with this here. You have enough going on already. I'm sorry, I wasn't thinking. I don't like getting interrupted when I'm in the middle of something either. I can come back…maybe talk to one of your officers?" She stood up. "I'll schedule something through Joni."

"Hillary, wait."

"No, really," she said, trying to sound upbeat. "I can get what I need from a deputy when they have some free time. It's not a problem."

Mitch closed his eyes and shook his head. He hadn't meant to chase her off, but her continued refusal to see him as anything other than her brothers' friend, and therefore hers, if only by default, annoyed him. Climbing to his feet, he made a conscious effort to relax.

"Hilly, please. I'm obviously not at my best today, but I'm glad you came to me. Sit down, and I will give you whatever information I can, okay?"

Hillary paused but didn't return to her seat.

He took on a playful tone. "Besides, Jake will kick my butt if he hears that I was short with you, and that is one particular brand of trouble that I just don't want to deal with right now."

"You're sure?"

"I'm sure."

Hillary sat back down, and they spent the next hour going over police procedure, the pros and cons of small-town jurisdictions, available resources and funding options, and any other question Hillary could come up with to make her article more interesting. When he had answered all her questions to the best of his ability, Mitch filled her in on the leads and procedures his office was following up on with the cases involving her family.

She listened carefully as he described how he was tracking down vehicle registrations, models and their paint colors, in addition to the years they were used, ballistics, possible suspects based on priors, and examining trace evidence to narrow down their focus and give them new directions to explore.

Impressed with his tenacity to explore any and all possibilities, Hillary complimented his efforts on her family's behalf. She knew his job wasn't easy based on the limited information they had been able to provide.

Hilly snapped her notebook shut with a satisfied smile and stood up, saying she had taken up enough of his time. On impulse, she rounded his desk and stood on her toes to plant a kiss on his cheek.

"Thanks, Mitch, you're the best!"

Mitch caught her arm as she turned to go. His brows drew together in contemplation. He seemed to waver for a second or two before his expression cleared. He drew her closer. "Do that again. But do it right this time."

Hilly saw the challenge glinting in his eyes. *Maybe Gretchen hadn't been so far off the mark after all,* she thought to herself. She considered her options, then slowly stepped forward, placed a hand on his chest for support, and raised up to place a soft lingering kiss on his lips.

The hand on her arm released, but only to snake under her hair and grasp the back of her neck before he slanted his mouth hungrily across hers. His other arm curled around her waist, molding her to his body. His low sound of approval sent a shiver racing up the length of her spine. Hillary allowed her arms to circle around his waist as he continued to explore her mouth with his. He glided his tongue along her lower lip then kissed it softly. He eased back slightly and breathed her name.

The sound of the outer doors opening to male voices had Hillary hastily extracting herself from his embrace. Mitch saw her discomfort and tried to reassure her. "Hilly, it's okay," he said, reaching for her hand.

She shook her head and moved out of reach. "I-I need to go. Thank you for the help, Mitch, I appreciate it. I'll see you later."

Frustrated, Mitch watched as she whirled and practically ran from the building.

****

Hillary put the finishing touches on her article and hit send. She had to admit, the insight Mitch had given her made it possible for her to submit an informative, thought-provoking piece. She knew the editor was going to love it. It was exactly what he had asked for.

She reached her arms above her head and stretched her stiff muscles. She had spent the better part of the day hunched over her notes and computer, writing and rewriting the article, until she had come up with a version she was proud of. Now it was time to get some fresh air and ease the tension out of her neck and back.

Feeling more chipper by the moment, she exited the house humming a little tune. Since Kiya was still tied up with her web designs, maybe she would find Luna and toss a few balls for the dog to chase. Happy with the idea, she strode out into the yard, only to pull up short. Jake stood next to Mitch's truck talking to his friend. Her brother raised a hand in greeting and waved her over. She grudgingly held up her own hand in response. There was no avoiding it—she would have to go over and say hello just to be polite. Anxiety bubbled within her. What should she say to Mitch? She was still processing what had occurred between them and didn't feel ready to deal with the man in person yet.

She took her time and ambled over just as the two

men seemed to finish their conversation. "I haven't seen you all day. Did you get your article finished?" Jake asked.

"Just finished. My muscles were starting to complain, so I thought I would get up and move around a little," she replied, glancing at Mitch then away.

"Does that mean you're free to talk for a few minutes?" Mitch wanted to know.

Hilly hated the trapped feeling that had her stomach burning with apprehension. This was Mitch. She shouldn't feel so panicky around him. Nevertheless, she found herself making up an excuse. "Actually, I have a few more things to do before I can knock off for the day. I should probably…" She twisted to the side and hitched a thumb in the direction of the house.

Mitch's firm voice stopped her. "Hillary, I need to speak to you."

Jake's curious gaze shifted from the man beside him back to her. She knew the only way to avoid making a scene was to agree.

Mitch let Jake know that he would stop back in soon. Taking that as his cue to shove off, Jake nodded then walked to the barn.

Hillary watched until Jake had crossed the threshold into the barn before turning her gaze to Mitch. He was studying her closely.

"What?" she asked, sounding mildly defensive.

He didn't react to her tone. Instead, he leaned back against the side of his vehicle, acting casual but determined. "You know what," he told her.

She raised her hands and let them fall helplessly. "What do you want me to say, Mitch?"

A self-deprecating look crossed his face. "I want you to say you're not mad at me. That we're okay."

She sighed. "I'm not mad at you."

"I don't want this to cause a problem between us, Hilly. You mean too much to me, but I also don't want to be forced back into the friend zone. I will if you give me no other choice, but it's not what I want."

Her voice trembled. "What is it that you *do* want?"

He paused long enough for his gaze to lock with hers. "You, Hillary. I want you. All of you, for as long as I can possibly have you."

The earnest answer shook her. *How could I not have known how he felt?* She closed the distance between them and wrapped her arms around his waist, laying her head on his chest. His arms closed around her to hold her tight. He rubbed a hand over her back then shifted her slightly away from his body. He tilted her face up with a finger under her chin. His eyes searched hers before he lowered his head and kissed her.

Warmth spread through her system, and she returned his kiss freely. All her apprehensions dissolved away. Being in Mitch's arms felt right. It felt natural and as easy as breathing. Together, they would figure out how to move forward with this new aspect of their relationship. For now, she leaned into him, allowing herself to revel in the multitude of feelings his kiss pulled from deep within her.

****

Still floating on a cloud of euphoria, Hillary walked into the kitchen a short time later feeling mildly dazed. Which, truth be told, she was. She spotted Jake leaning against the counter with a smug look plastered across his face. Pausing mid-stride, she narrowed her eyes at his expression. Knowing she was busted, she placed one hand on her hip and cocked her head to the side. "Go ahead," she told him. "Let's hear it."

"Hear what?"

"That innocent act means nothing when you're practically bursting at the seams with self-satisfaction," she informed him in a haughty manner.

"Okay, fine. I'm just surprised that Mitch finally worked up enough gumption to act on his feelings, and that you managed to pick up on it when he did."

"Well, he made it rather hard to miss." Annoyance tickled her senses. The fact that Jake knew of Mitch's interest, also, bothered her. It proved that Gretchen wasn't the only one that had been able to see the man's attraction, while it had completely escaped her own attention. "How is it that everyone seems to know how he felt except me?" she demanded in frustration.

"Well, first of all, it is hard for a guy to miss the fact that his best friend is hung up on his sister," he stated matter-of-factly. "As for how you missed it, I personally concluded that you automatically overlooked him because you lumped him together with the rest of us. You saw him as just another brother figure since he was so tightly woven into our group. Cade, myself, Dylan…and Mitch. You seemed unable to separate him from us, and for the most part, he accepted that. I guess he got tired of waiting for you to really *see* him."

It was hard to believe that she had been so clueless. She had always thought of Mitch as a vital, necessary piece of her life, her family. She relied on him. He was the first person she thought of when she needed help or support. She never doubted the fact that he would always be there for her when she needed him, or that she would do the same for him. It had just taken her a while to see that while he was just as important as her brothers, his role was much different. She knew the closeness she felt toward him was not the same as with her brothers. She had always known it, but she had never stopped to consider why it went so deep that she couldn't imagine her life without him. The thought of losing him, or watching him walk away, was unimaginable. Now she understood why. He had a hold on her heart that no one else ever had, or ever would, and it didn't have anything to do with his relationship with her brothers.

Chapter 13

"This is impressive," Jake admitted as he clicked through Kiya's work. The site she had envisioned and produced was well thought out, easy to use, and streamlined their operation in a way that had not been achieved by the previous version. Not that any of them had been all that efficient in, or overly concerned with for that matter, the impact of their digital footprint. This proved that they should have been. If this reflected the reasons why Hilly had called their current website inefficient and out of date, he had to agree. This website would function much more efficiently than the current site. It would garner a lot more interest and restructure each portion of their enterprise in a way that could vastly improve the outreach of the ranch, scheduling, time management, and therefore their bottom line.

Jake moved his attention away from his computer screen and onto Kiya's anxious face. "I will need to get Cade and Dylan's approval, but I'm in. You have done a phenomenal job. I don't see how this site could be a detriment to the Five M. It can only move us forward. I will have them go over it after dinner." Jake stood to move away from the desk where Kiya had placed her laptop.

"I'm so glad you think so." Kiya rocked onto the balls of her feet and silently clapped her hands as he stood. When he had reached his full height, Kiya latched onto Jake in excitement. She wrapped her arms around his neck and hugged him. "Thank you for being open to this."

Never one to let such an opportunity pass him by, Jake caught her close. He dropped a light kiss on her startled mouth. "Don't thank me yet," he told her mildly. "But getting your hopes up wouldn't be out of the question. We tend to notice when progress is staring us in the face."

****

Kiya set the swing in motion as Luna raced down the steps for her nightly romp. Hillary had wanted to review Kiya's handiwork with her brothers, so that left Kiya free to enjoy the evening alone as darkness descended across the ranch. Insects and birds still sent calls into the night before the cold of winter could silence them. Kiya listened to their varied sounds and marveled at the feeling of belonging and of peace that lodged within her. The ranch had become her home, her oasis from the world. She found it increasingly hard to picture her world without this place and these people within it. The realization should scare her, but it didn't.

She rocked contentedly back and forth until a pale glow in the nighttime landscape captured her attention. The muted pastels of mauve and purple that had painted the sunset sky were long past, and the flickering cadence of the hazy atmosphere struck Kiya as unusual. Luna barked from her position at the edge of the house. The normally happy animal sounded tense and fearful rather than playful. Intrigued, Kiya made her way to the end of the porch and gazed in the direction of the odd glow and Luna's growing interest. The dog's barks turned frantic as Kiya's eyes came to rest on the barn.

Disbelief froze her mind and body. Flames rose from the side of the building in an eerie, unnatural dancing glow. Dark smoke billowed into the air like a cloud. The frightened whinnies of the horses trapped inside were beginning to echo across the yard. The thunderous sound of frenzied hooves pounding against the walls of the stalls galvanized her into action. Kiya spun on her heel and sprinted into the house.

"Jake!" she shouted desperately the instant she burst through the door. "Fire!"

Inside, Jake reacted to the panic in her voice before the words even had a chance to register. He whirled toward the sound of her voice and ran. His siblings followed closely behind him. They charged into the great room as Kiya was racing out.

"The barn is on fire," she shouted as she disappeared out the door. "*We have to get the horses out*," she chanted to herself over and over as she raced toward the barn. Fear gripped her as she rushed into the smoke-filled building and tried to get her bearings in the disorienting vapor. She tried to draw in a calming breath but ended up choking on the thick plumes of noxious fumes saturating the air. Kiya tucked her mouth and nose into the fabric covering the crook of her bent elbow to shield her next breath.

Jake and the others came to an abrupt halt at her side while they took in the chaos unfolding around them. "Cade, help Kiya and Hilly get the horses to the paddock out back. Dylan and I will call fire rescue, grab the hoses, and buy you as much time as we can," Jake shouted over the din of the raging fire. Coughing with almost every breath, Kiya hurried to a stall that was deep into the thick smoke. She would start there and work her way back to the horses farther away from the flames. Using her sleeve to open the hot latch on the door, she stepped into the stall and tried to grab the horse's halter. The spooked animal reared onto its back legs, striking at the air with its front hooves. Talking as calmly as she could, Kiya quieted the huge gelding and moved him toward the exit. Sensing freedom from his confinement, the gelding stopped resisting her efforts and jogged at her side out of the side door and into the enclosed riding arena behind it. On her way back to the barn, Cade and Hilly passed her with two more horses in tow. Working together, they ushered the remaining frightened horses to safety, then joined the battle against the flames. They fought until most of the fire subsided into a smoldering hiss. Sirens wailed, reassuring them that the end of this ordeal was in sight. They watched the last of the flames die away under the cold spray of water launched in its direction.

Jake tossed his hose aside as the firetrucks rolled to a stop next to the charred, smoking walls of the barn. Men in fire gear took over the scene and worked to douse hot spots and ensure that the fire could not reignite. Dylan was comforting his distraught sister while Cade stood staring at the damaged barn in shock.

Kiya couldn't stop shaking. With nothing physical left for her to do, emotion was taking over. She hugged her arms around herself tightly. Even though the worst of this nightmare was over, the shivering could not be controlled. They could have lost everything. All the horses, including her beautiful Dax, the tack, riding and training supplies, along with most of the hay and grain that had been stockpiled for the winter. Tears blurred her vision.

She jumped when a hand circled her upper arm. "I'm okay," she said automatically. Then, admitting to herself that she wasn't, turned and buried her head against Jake's shoulder. His arms folded around her instantly, offering comfort. Like she had done before when she had been attacked, Kiya allowed herself to draw from his steady reassuring strength. Fisting her hands in the back of his shirt, she fought to control the effects of the adrenaline coursing through her system.

She pulled in slow, deep breaths until the tremors started to ease. When Luna whined at her feet, Kiya patted her own hip so the dog would stand and hug her paws around Kiya's waist. She curled an arm around the dog's back and stroked her fur but remained tucked into Jake's side.

"What about you? Are you okay?" Kiya's words were muffled against Jake's shirt.

He smoothed a hand down the length of her hair and replied in a raspy, smoke roughened voice, "I'm getting there. The important thing is that we were able to catch it in time. No lives were lost. We can handle the rest."

They turned when more trucks with flashing lights arrived in a cloud of dust. One displayed the sheriff's logo, and the other was a deputy's vehicle. Mitch jumped out of his truck and rapidly assessed the scene in front of him. A head count reassured him that everyone was accounted for. Hillary left Dylan's side to rush into Mitch's waiting arms. He caught her close, breathing a sigh of relief, and pressed his lips against her temple. Over her head, Mitch asked if anyone had been hurt. He took a minute to calm his nerves when he was assured that everyone was uninjured.

Each of them watched in silence as the firefighters continued to work the scene. The acrid smell of burnt wood, hay, and barn supplies mixed with the odor of diesel fuel from the trucks idling nearby. It was a mildly nauseating mix. Before long, the fire chief made his way over to Mitch to let him know that his men were confident the scene was secured, but they would remain on-site a while longer just to be sure and to inspect the barn to see if they could locate a point of origin for the flames.

"Now that the fire is under control and it is safe enough inside to have a look around, why don't we go with the chief here, get a scope of the damage, and hear any ideas he comes up with for what might have happened?" Mitch suggested. "Hilly, you and Kiya should go back to the house and recover for a bit. Maybe get some coffee. There is nothing more you can do here. We'll be in as soon as we take a look around."

"The heck with coffee," Hillary scoffed as she looped her arm through Kiya's and walked toward the house. "I'm breaking out the good stuff."

****

Kiya sipped at the brandy in her snifter glass. The warmth of the amber colored liquid wove its way through her system helping to calm her frayed nerves as she and Hillary waited for news from the barn. The women sat at opposite ends of the table talking in subdued tones while they kept each other company and tried to process the reality of another close call.

"I just don't understand how this could have happened. If the guys are obsessive about anything around here, it's barn and fire safety," Hilly insisted as she frowned down at the glass in her hand. "But if it wasn't an accident, that means someone was not only capable of getting close to the house without being seen but bold enough to sneak right into the very heart of our property and light that fire under our noses."

Kiya shivered at the other woman's words. The thought of someone with malicious intent being able to get so close to the house and the people within was bone chilling. What if they had targeted the house instead of the barn? As it was, all three of the brothers had been in the barn doing chores just before dinner. Kiya herself had been in there alone when she visited Dax with a carrot not long after that. Goose bumps dotted her flesh as she thought about someone watching and waiting without her knowing they were there. Could someone have already been inside, hiding out in the shadows within the barn, waiting for the chance to act when there would be enough time for the fire to take hold? Somehow that scenario was even more disturbing than the previous assaults they had endured. The mental image of being stalked up close and personal by an unseen threat had a totally different feel than the idea of danger striking at you from a distance. It was scary to think that a person could get close enough to reach out and grab you before you even sensed that they were there.

Just when she and Hilly were getting antsy enough to discuss returning to the barn in search of information, the side door opened, and the men trudged into the kitchen. Both women popped up out of their seats anxious for news. The action caused another round of coughing for Kiya.

Cade waved them back into their chairs. "Go ahead and sit. We'll join you." He dropped into the nearest empty seat. He raked a hand through his soot-covered hair and sighed. Dylan circled to the opposite side of the table to sit on Kiya's right. He stopped long enough to lay a hand on Kiya's shoulder as he looked to his sister at the other end of the table.

"You two doing all right?" he asked with obvious concern.

"Other than scratchy throats and feeling like our lungs are still clogged with smoke, we're okay," Hillary responded.

"All that smoke and soot had to be much rougher on you. Your lung is still healing. Are you having any issues with your breathing?" Kiya questioned in return. The irritation to his injured lung was concerning, but Kiya knew that he never could have allowed his family to handle battling that fire without being right there with them. They supported each other and worked as a unit in everything they did. It simply wasn't in his makeup to do anything else.

Dylan shrugged one shoulder as he settled into his chair. "I'm wheezing a bit now and then but nothing alarming," he reassured her.

"So, what did you find out?" Hillary asked the group in general.

"Not enough," Jake supplied with a huff. He sounded worn out. Grabbing a hand towel, he wiped smoke dust and ash from his face and hands. He and Mitch claimed the remaining chairs. As Hilly collected more glasses and placed the brandy bottle at the center of the table for anyone that wanted it, Kiya observed the men gathered around the table. Even when they were tired, covered in grime, and far from their best, they were easy to look at. Mitch didn't share the unmistakable family resemblance the others had, but with his broad shoulders, muscular physique, and chiseled features, he fit right in. Only his flaxen-colored hair set him apart from the rest of the group. It was rather daunting to be surrounded by them when, in her current disheveled state, Kiya felt like Medusa's ugly half-sister.

Dylan laid one arm along the back of Kiya's chair and splashed some brandy into a snifter with his other before telling them that even though the fire was suspicious based on where the blaze started, there didn't seem to be any evidence to prove it was deliberately set.

Hillary's face was pale as she slowly sank back into her chair. Mitch reached over from his position on her left to take her hand in his. His thumb rubbed the inside of her wrist as he elaborated. "The fire started in the hayloft above the tack room. There is nothing in that area that could cause a spark or ignite on its own, but it burnt hot and fast so that by the time Kiya spotted the blaze and you all made it out there, the floor of that side of the loft was collapsing, and the tack room and side walls were engulfed. If it had burned much longer, the fire chief doubted if the building could have been saved."

It was possible that multiple fires had been lit in the same general area to hasten the spread, but no accelerants had been used. Nothing traceable had been left behind. The anger and frustration radiating off the men was almost palpable.

"That blaze didn't start on its own. Not there, it didn't," Cade fumed. "Knowing that some jackass strutted in here like he was untouchable and carried out his plans while we were all present and sharing a meal is enraging."

"Given what Kiya was subjected to at the Billings' place, and the fact that this person was basically able to show up on our doorstep tonight, the situation could have been a lot worse. But Cade is right. This was way too close and the final straw. It's time to bring in added protection. Hire a few guys to help keep an eye on things and the areas closest to the house. Mitch, I'm sure you can give us the names of some men you trust that would be happy to earn some extra cash. The three of us can rustle up some more to rotate through and keep everyone fresh. The local wildlife is no longer our biggest concern, but reinforcing the habit of carrying a weapon when leaving the house is a good idea. We'll make sure a shotgun is near the entrances in here," Jake said.

Dylan agreed that it was time to stop being victims. They were all tired of only reacting to each attack. What they were facing was beyond a doubt interconnected, coordinated attacks. It was time to go on the offensive and bring this to an end. No more being taken by surprise.

"You know I'll be posted outside any chance I get," Mitch assured them. "These attacks are personal for me too. I will do everything I can to make sure everyone in this house stays safe. I will have my guys on alert for anyone or anything suspicious and making regular patrols in the area. I will have people here first thing in the morning to see if we can determine just how they got on the ranch unseen. You might want to consider a security system that includes some outside cameras and lighting."

"Not a bad idea. I'll look into it. And you know you are welcome to crash here anytime you need to in between shifts. Our home is your home, always has been," Jake reminded him.

"Right now, I'm going to head into the office and see who is on the roster for tomorrow and the coming days. I can start on a list of men that could help out here also. I'll be back in the morning. I don't think you will have any other problems tonight, but just in case, I will have Jenkins stop in to do a quick walk through later." He climbed to his feet and looked around at his friends. People he considered family. "Stick together and stay alert. We are going to get to the bottom of this. I promise."

Hillary left to walk out with Mitch. Jake, Dylan, and Cade all agreed to take turns making rounds during the night. Dylan volunteered to stay up for a while first since he was too hyped up to rest anyway. Kiya was feeling drained after all the stress of the evening. The shot of brandy had calmed and softened the edges of her frayed nerves enough to have her dragging and needing to rest.

"I am exhausted. I think I'll head up to my room. A hot bath and some sleep sounds like heaven right about now." After telling them to wake her if they needed her, she said good night and left the room.

"A shower and an early night sound good to me too. Wake me when it's my turn to keep watch outside," Cade instructed his brothers before leaving the room.

Alone in the kitchen, Jake and Dylan remained quiet, each lost in their own thoughts until Dylan was struck with an unpleasant notion. "We need to let

Gretchen know about this before she hears about it from anywhere else. She would be devastated if she hears about this from anyone but us."

"Agreed. But I think we should let Hilly make that call. She and Gretchen have always been close. It might soften the shock of this happening if Hilly was the one to put her mind at ease about being away from the rest of us right now. She will be more likely to remain at home and out of danger that way. Might even be a good idea to have Kiya in on that call too. Those three hit it off and forged a tight bond in a relatively short amount of time. Gretchen will feel much better knowing that Hilly isn't facing this alone; she can rely on Kiya for additional support. If anyone can reassure Gretchen about this, it's those two."

Dylan nodded in agreement. His expression turned thoughtful. "She just fits, doesn't she?"

Jake didn't need his brother to explain the question. He, too, had marveled at how easily Kiya had blended into their tight-knit family. How effortlessly she integrated into their lives. She had become one of them almost instantly with little to no effort. As his brother said…she just fit. The only problem, as he saw it, was how Dylan might perceive Kiya's place within the group differently than he did. Jake felt his gut tighten in response to the idea. He and Dylan had never been at odds over a woman before, but he couldn't change how he felt. Jake sensed rather than saw Dylan's intent gaze on his face.

"You seemed rather invested in her welfare earlier. Not to mention that you always seem to react almost instinctively to her needs."

"Dylan…don't. Now is not the time," Jake warned

in a weary tone.

"Time for what?"

Jake didn't want to hurt his brother, but he couldn't deny how important Kiya had become to him. She captivated him in a way no other woman ever had, made him want things he'd never considered before. He knew Kiya felt just as strongly about Dylan as Dylan did about her. What he didn't know was how she felt about *him*. She enjoyed his company, that much was clear—their shared mornings working together were always a pleasure. It was the highlight of his day. One he looked forward to more with each passing day. It was a hopeless situation that Jake was going to have to learn how to deal with. He just couldn't do it right now when he was already strained to the breaking point. His emotions were just too close to the surface tonight. Jake didn't move anything except his eyes as they shifted up and locked onto his brother's. "I know you care about her. I know she cares about you, okay? Can we leave it at that for now?" Jake asked.

"I don't know. Can we?" Dylan asked with direct interest reflecting in his eyes.

Jake exhaled a forceful breath. "What can I say that isn't going to upset you, Dylan?"

A half smile ticked up one side of Dylan's mouth. "Hilly was right. You think I have a romantic interest in Kiya, and you don't like it at all, do you? You have feelings for her yourself, and you are trying to decide whether you can still back off somewhat gracefully or whether to risk damaging our relationship to fight for her. That's a tough spot to be in." Dylan noted his brother's clenched jaw and tense posture. He knew he was right. "There is something you need to understand,

Jake. Kiya and I have a connection that isn't going away…ever. She was everything I had out in that field, my lifeline, and she has become a lot more. She will always be a part of me."

Jake nodded solemnly. "I know that, Dylan. I wouldn't take that away from either of you even if I could."

"Good, because I love her as much as I love either of our sisters, and that isn't going to change, so if you hurt her, it could get ugly. I can, and will, make your life a living hell if you so much as make her unhappy."

"I would never do anything to…" Jake started defensively, then stopped. "Wait…what?" Jake stuttered in confusion. He was sure he had misunderstood.

"You heard me. If you hurt her in any way, you will answer to me. And most likely the rest of the family too, given how much they all care for her," Dylan informed him adamantly. His smile was smug.

Jake was totally floored. He stared into Dylan's face and saw the truth. Even though his brother had a unique relationship with Kiya, he wasn't in love with her. The realization hit Jake like a truck. Relief coursed through him like a balm to his soul. He wasn't going to have to choose between his brother and the woman he was falling in love with. He could easily live with their relationship if he knew he wasn't fighting for Kiya's heart. A disturbing thought struck him, and he reined himself in. Just because Dylan felt that way, didn't mean Kiya felt the same. What if Kiya wanted Dylan? How would he cope with that?

"Wait a minute. You can't just dismiss Kiya's feelings like that. How do you know *she* isn't hung up on *you*?" Jake demanded indignantly on Kiya's behalf.

Dylan laughed at his brother's obviously divided response. The poor guy didn't know whether to be relieved for himself or offended for Kiya. His brother had it *bad*, and it was rather satisfying to see. "Relax, bro, Kiya isn't hung up on me. She feels as strongly for me as I do her, but she doesn't want a relationship with me. Not a romantic one. Trust me, what the two of us feel for each other is strong and it is real, but it is not physical or romantic on either side. It's up to you to see how she feels about you."

Jake considered the situation for a moment. He loved his brother and wanted the best for him always. "I would never begrudge you anything, Dylan. You know that," he assured his brother earnestly.

"Except for her," Dylan responded easily.

"Except for her," Jake concurred.

"Then take care that you don't screw this up." He was warned.

Chapter 14

"I think we should hire locally and get the repairs underway as quickly as we can," Jake stressed to the others gathered around him. "Winter is approaching fast, and the weather is already changing. If we wait for the insurance people and the investigation results, we will never get everything done in time. We need the repairs done and the security measures installed as fast as possible. We can worry about the financial logistics later."

The siblings all nodded their agreement. Each of them stood quietly surveying the disfigured remains of the barn as people moved about here and there gathering information and taking pictures. The aftermath of last night's fire stood out in stark relief against the morning backdrop of a clear blue sky. The heavy smell of damp, charred wood and hay still lingered in the air. Mitch had already come and gone. He had arrived very early to make sure they all knew the current schedule of rotating men from his office and left a list of possible hires for ranch security. A deputy or two still milled about the scene, but nothing concrete had been found on how the ranch had been infiltrated the night before, or how the fire had started, but Mitch was just as determined as everyone else that it wouldn't happen again.

"I can get on that," Dylan affirmed decisively in

acknowledgment of his brother's comments. He could have a crew hired by as soon as tomorrow if he got after it fast. There were any number of contacts he could tap that would be willing to refer people to him at any given moment. He looked at Kiya as she remained silent and stayed discreetly behind the others, out of the way. "Kiya? Any thoughts?"

Kiya looked startled. She glanced from one person to the next. "Me?" she wondered incredulously.

"Yes, you," Dylan confirmed. "You have been involved in these attacks since the beginning just like the rest of us have been. You are living in the main house with everyone else, and your horse resides in that barn along with ours. What do you think?"

When Kiya saw that the others were waiting patiently for her opinion as well, she decided to answer as honestly as they were willing to ask. "Well, I can't say much toward your family's insurance and financial details, but if it were me, I would do whatever it takes to get the repairs made before the weather sets in. The horses will need the warmth and security sooner rather than later. And I for one wouldn't mind the extra reassurance of having the safety upgrades and security cameras up and running either. The sprinkler system alone would be a game changer."

"It's settled then. We hire ASAP and get this done no matter what the investigation turns up or the insurance gods have to say about the matter. How many men are we talking about?" he wanted to know.

"I think a crew of five could knock this out in a matter of days, maybe a week. Then we can get the security guys in here to set up their stuff in no time," Jake stated. "Cade?"

"I think that should cover it. Five men in addition to us, we can be back to normal operations in no time," the man replied.

"I'll have everything lined up by the end of the day," Dylan assured them.

****

"I still think I should be there," Gretchen worried aloud after both Hilly and Kiya had insisted that everything at the ranch was under control. The elder sister's apprehension could be heard clearly on the other end of the phone.

"We are all safe, and everything is moving forward as quickly as possible," Hilly repeated patiently. She could sympathize with Gretchen's reluctance to remain in Denver while her family was in distress. She would feel the exact same way if the situation were reversed. "We are going to have more security than Fort Knox soon." Hilly looked at Kiya imploringly.

"Gretchen, I know you're worried. That is understandable, but look at it from our point of view. First, you would be risking your job for something you can't fix, and that would make us feel guilty. Secondly, if you were here, even though we would love having you close by, we would worry about your safety too, instead of having the confidence of knowing that you are safer than any of us and far away from this. We want you to remain that way. I promise, I will look out for your sister," Kiya insisted.

Gretchen finally agreed and acknowledged that they were right. There wasn't much she could do other than lend her support and a sympathetic ear. Which she would do, anytime they needed it. "I'm so happy you are there for Hilly," she told Kiya with heart-felt emotion. "Hilly? Give our sister a big hug from me, okay?" Gretchen instructed.

Hillary gave Kiya a thumb's up and silently hugged Kiya's neck while she smiled into the other woman's glistening eyes. As much as Hilly loved her sister, she didn't want Gretchen anywhere near the ranch right now. Kiya understood that completely. The three women chatted for a while longer about everyday things to catch up on each other's lives. Gretchen hooted with laughter when she learned that she had been right all along and that Hilly and Mitch were now an item. She was also quick to point out that she couldn't be happier that the two of them had finally connected. They eventually wrapped things up and promised they would stay in touch often and couldn't wait to get back together.

"I have never hated the fact that Gretchen lives in Denver more than I do right now, but it is also the only time that I have ever hoped that she stays away," Hilly said sadly while wiping at tears as they hung up the phone.

Kiya didn't know what to say to make her friend feel better. Instead, she hugged her tight, professing that everything would be all right.

****

A few nights later, Kiya sat on the porch swing after dinner curled up in a throw blanket to ward off the evening chill. This had become her favorite spot, and she spent time out here almost every evening by herself relaxing and soaking up the calming solitude. Luna dozed on the floor near her feet as Kiya rocked back and forth. The repairs on the barn were underway now that men had been brought in to help with the work.

The entire family was pitching in, and things were starting to progress nicely.

There were also guards moving about the property as added security to watch over the ranch. Pairs of men switched off for day and evening hours. It was an odd way to live she supposed, but Kiya knew that she wasn't the only one that felt better having the extra eyes around.

She rested her head against the back of the swing and drew in a deep breath of cold, crisp air. Luna shifted and rolled onto her belly interested in something nearby. A low growl rumbled in her throat. The sound was so out of character for the dog that Kiya didn't know what to make of it at first. Her senses went on high alert however when the dog rose to a crouched position and her growl intensified.

Kiya stood too, looking for whatever had Luna so agitated. A shadow separated itself from the darkness around it and moved toward the porch. A man Kiya didn't recognize stopped at the edge of the threshold created by the glow cast off from the windows of the house behind her. His features were indistinct in the half shadow where he stood. His choice to remain on the fringes of her field of vision seemed deliberate. It raised the hair on the back of her neck.

"I didn't scare ya, did I?" the man asked in a slightly mocking tone.

"No," Kiya stated defiantly. "But I am wondering why you are lurking around in the dark."

"Lurking?" The man scoffed. He gave the still grumbling Luna a dismissive glance before returning his attention to Kiya. "I was simply getting ready to leave for the night when I spotted you sitting out here. I heard there has been some trouble around this place lately. Are you sure you want to be out here in the dark all alone?"

The question itself was harmless enough, but the way he said it made Kiya uneasy. Maybe she was letting the stress get to her. Everything was making her edgy lately.

"You're Kiya James, right?" the man continued without waiting for a reply. "You took over the Billings' farm a while back. I heard there was trouble over that way recently too. Seems to have followed you, huh? That's rough. Awfully charitable of the McClearys to take you in though. You could do worse as far as hideouts go, but if you ask me, you aren't any safer here."

Surprise that he knew exactly who she was and how she came to be here kept Kiya quiet for a moment. Something about the knowing way he kept watching her made her uncomfortable.

"I'm not hiding," she informed him.

"Is that right? Well either way, you landed in a pretty posh nest."

She was saved from trying to come up with a suitable response to his remarks when another man appeared at the foot of the stairs leading up to the porch.

"Everything all right here, ma'am?" the off-duty officer questioned Kiya in a mild tone while his eyes remained squarely on the man in front of him.

Relief, warranted or not, flowed through Kiya, and she smiled in appreciation of the newly appointed guard's attentiveness.

"Nothing to worry about, my friend. I was just

making sure the lady was okay," the worker replied before Kiya could say anything.

"Exactly why I am here, so you can head on home," the officer informed him in the same deceptively mild tone.

"Sure thing. Not a problem at all. You two have a nice night, now."

They watched as the guy casually made his way back to his vehicle.

Kiya kept her gaze on the back of the retreating man even when the door to the house opened behind her.

Jake took one look at Kiya's tense posture and the officer's presence and felt his pulse rate jump. Luna was pressed up tight to Kiya's leg, still on alert.

"Do we have a problem?" he demanded.

"Ma'am?" the officer asked Kiya, looking at her fully for the first time.

"No. There's no problem, but I really appreciate you checking on me," she told the man with a smile. "I was just startled when that guy appeared out of nowhere. Luna certainly didn't care for him, but he didn't do anything but talk to me. I'm just jumpy I guess."

"Did he say something to upset you?" the officer wanted to know.

"Not really. I simply haven't adjusted to the small-town rumor mill yet. Everybody seems to know everything about everyone out here," she joked lightly.

"Takes some getting used to," he agreed, then shifted his gaze to Jake. "I think I will make one more circuit around the place before my replacement gets here. I want to make sure everything is quiet and everyone has left for the night. I'll be back tomorrow."

Kiya bid the officer good night then reclaimed her seat on the swing. She shivered and pulled the blanket around her again. She wasn't sure if it was the temperature that had her chilled or if it was the lingering effect of her uneasiness from her odd encounter.

Jake sat down next to Kiya on the swing. "Are you sure everything is all right? Anything I should know about?" He playfully nudged her arm with his elbow. "Anyone I need to give a serious dressing down tomorrow?" he asked softly, only half kidding.

Kiya chuckled and nudged him back. "You sound like Dylan, but no, that won't be necessary."

"Why? Did Dylan need to intervene with something?" Jake immediately wanted to know.

"No, he just told me that if any of the new guys hassled me about anything, to let him know and he would put an end to it."

Jake nodded with approval. "As he should. If he doesn't, I will."

Kiya shook her head. She didn't know if she envied or pitied Hillary and Gretchen for always having lived under the watchful eyes of so many protective males. It had to have been both a blessing and a curse.

Thinking that it might be time to test his brother's theory about Kiya's feelings and try to get a better idea about her response to him, Jake extended his arm along the back of the swing behind her shoulders and shifted her blanket-wrapped body closer to his. He was pleased by how easily she accepted the adjustment.

"That's just Dylan's way of letting you know he cares about you. He wants you to feel safe and protected here. To know that he has your back if you need him to. And he will. He cares as strongly for you as he does for Gretchen and Hilly. Next, he will be including you in his game of favorites with those two. It's only a matter of time."

Kiya remained silent long enough to have Jake's heart lodging firmly in his throat. Maybe his brother had things all wrong. Maybe Kiya felt differently about Dylan than he thought. Jake had to clear his throat before he could speak. "Does Dylan feeling that way bother you?" He regretted the question, when it caused her to move away from him so she could face him without looking up.

"Bother me? Does it bother me that he cares so strongly about me?" She shook her head either to answer his question or to show disbelief. Jake wasn't sure which. "Does it bother you?" Kiya questioned back. "That he feels that way about me and wants to include me in his life like family when I'm not? I'm truly sorry if that is the case, but his feelings don't bother me in the slightest way. They make me happy. I didn't have much in the way of a loving family growing up, and it may not make sense to many people, but Dylan has become that for me. He is the brother that I never had. He filled a void I didn't want to acknowledge was there. People without many blood ties tend to say that the family that matters is the family you choose. Dylan and I chose each other. I might have helped to save his life, but he gave me a wonderful gift in return, and I will cherish that forever. In fact, I feel similarly about the rest of your siblings too. They have welcomed me into their lives so freely and completely, and I love them for it. It is an entirely new thing for me to have that, and to want that, but I do."

The last remaining knots that had tangled themselves so deeply inside Jake's gut began to unravel. Hope blossomed where only doubts and fear had resided. She loved his family, and they loved her. In time, he was sure he could convince her to love him too. Only in his case, in an entirely different way than she might expect. They already shared an easy rapport. They worked and meshed well together in almost every aspect of their daily lives. He just needed to show her how much more they could be. In the meantime, he couldn't allow her to even entertain the idea that he didn't like her close connection to his family. He never wanted her to doubt her welcome here.

"I have absolutely no qualms about sharing my family with you. In fact, I couldn't be happier about it. On bad days, I might even beg you to take them off my hands," he teased lightly.

An errant breeze swirled through the porch, setting a stray lock of glossy hair dancing against Kiya's cheek. Jake reached out to capture the soft strand and twirled it around his finger. Kiya was a little taken aback when his intense gaze suddenly locked onto hers.

"I guess that leaves me with just one question," Jake told her.

"And that is…?" Kiya asked cautiously.

"Whether or not you think of me as a brother too?"

Kiya's breath shuttered to a halt. How was she supposed to answer that question? Did he want her to say yes or no? Thinking back to the times he had held her, comforted her, or protected her, she couldn't say that she had ever felt anything remotely brotherly about it. Not like with Dylan. Cade, too, was a friend and a brotherly figure if she needed it. Her feelings for Jake were more complex. She responded to him for the man he was, not because of his connection to Dylan or as part of a whole. Even the times he had argued with her or cajoled her had a different quality to it than with the rest of the family. She acknowledged, at least to herself, that the way she felt about him was entirely different than how she felt about the rest of his family, and there was no denying that she found him attractive, but she was at a total loss as to what to say to him.

"I...ahh." Kiya's brows knit together as she stopped to gather her scattered thoughts.

Jake watched the confusion flicker across her face. That she struggled with her answer was enough to fill him with hope. His lips twitched.

He eased his hand to the nape of her neck. His gaze dropped to her mouth as he drew her closer. Kiya was still trying to think of something rational to say when Jake's lips took possession of hers.

Heat flooded her entire system. Every jumbled thought fled her mind. His kiss was definitely not brotherly, and it felt so achingly right. She leaned into him and opened herself to his searching embrace. A contented hum rumbled through Jake's chest prompting Kiya's hand to trace its path along his taut rib cage. The light caress of her fingers had Jake's muscles tightening in reaction. His free arm twined around Kiya's waist to pull her against his body as he deepened the kiss. In an instant, his exploration of her mouth went from a gentle search for a response to a hungry and insistent demand. The taste and feel of her burned themselves into his senses, ensuring that she would always be a part of him, his thoughts. In that moment, he wasn't thinking about his brother or anyone else for that matter, only Kiya and how it felt to have her in his arms, responding to his touch, his kiss.

This...this is what I want, Jake thought. He wanted her to respond to his every touch and welcome him with open arms. She belonged here with him, just like this, and he was determined to prove that to her. He wanted her in his life regardless of what was happening around them. He needed her to choose to be with him for himself. Not as a side effect of the circumstances. But before Kiya could think to protest his onslaught, Jake curbed his emotions and reluctantly eased her away from him. The last thing he wanted to do was scare her off with his intensity.

Jake ran the pad of his thumb along Kiya's bottom lip. "Just so you know, I'm going to take that as a no."

"No?" Her brows furrowed together.

"No, you don't think of me as a brother," he told her with a soft smile.

Kiya was totally bemused. "Oh."

Jake chuckled and drew her to her feet. "We better get you inside before you freeze."

Freeze? Kiya wondered absently as she allowed him to steer her into the house. *Was it cold?*

Chapter 15

"You're sure she didn't recognize you?" a smooth steely voice demanded across the phone connection.

"I'm telling you; I don't think she is as big of a problem as you had thought. She gave no indication of ever having seen me before. She didn't seem to recognize my voice or question me at all. I doubt that she ever saw us up on that ridge. From the buzz circulating around town, she just came across McCleary during a ride. She probably just stumbled upon him down in that field by sheer dumb luck. Bad luck on our part, but I would bet money that she couldn't place either Seth or me there at all. Things have been quiet since they checked out the cabin. I don't expect them back anytime soon. They are a little preoccupied for now."

"Good. I will send word to get things moving. You just make sure you are prepared to do your part as soon as it arrives."

"Will do, boss."

The man disconnected the call with a jab of his index finger. Bad luck indeed. He had wanted McCleary dead. Maybe that nosy wench wouldn't be a thorn in his side after all. If she was unable to link them to their actions or presence on the ranch, he had little interest in her. It was unfortunate that she had interfered with his plans, but that could be remedied. It might be more advantageous to focus his sights back on McCleary. Thinking back to the very first time he had met the man, his hands tightened into fists. Who did McCleary think he was to brush *him* aside without even a thought? Without consideration. Nobody dismissed him. Nobody. That entire family and their self-important attitudes were about to take a very serious hit.

****

Dylan grabbed the clamoring phone and shoved it between his ear and his shoulder while he continued to shuffle through the papers stacked on the desk. "Five M, this is Dylan."

"Have I caught you at a bad time, Mr. McCleary?" The smooth, overly confident voice seemed to imply that his call would be accepted no matter what.

"Kennedy," Dylan said in a cool tone.

"You have a good memory. I'm impressed."

"What can I do for you, Mr. Kennedy?"

"No need for such formality. You may call me Preston," the man decreed as if bestowing a gift. "I merely called to see if you and your family have reconsidered my offer yet?"

The undercurrent of animosity in the emphasis on the word *yet* had Dylan pausing his search. He could have misinterpreted the way that sounded, or it could have been a simple slip of the tongue, but he didn't think so. "Why would we do that?" Dylan inquired carefully.

"Rumor has it that you have run into some pretty nasty…mishaps. It is worrisome how many close calls your family has endured. With all you have going on lately, I thought you might have had second thoughts about unloading some unutilized acreage for a healthy profit. The extra cash flow might come in handy; you never know when new problems might crop up. And if the word around town is true, you have even taken in some extra tenants during this stressful time. Accepting my offer would ease your burden."

Dylan's fingers tightened around the handset. "Our cash flow is just fine, and we are fully capable of handling any so-called mishaps that come our way. I assure you, we are taking measures to ensure that there are no further incidents. I'm flattered and a little surprised that our business here inspires such *concern* on your part, but in the future, maybe you shouldn't rely so heavily on rumors and hearsay. We are more than capable of taking care of our own. We won't be selling any of our land. Mr. Kennedy, I'm afraid you are wasting your time."

"That's your final word on the matter?" The man's voice was cold and flat.

"It is."

"In that case, I wish you luck, Mr. McCleary. I dare say, you are going to need it."

Dylan stared at the buzzing phone in his hand as the connection was abruptly terminated. He replaced the receiver, shaking his head in disbelief. The man's audacity was astonishing, and his negotiation tactics left a lot to be desired. Dylan dropped down into the chair behind the desk, his previous search forgotten for the moment. He replayed every nuance of the call over in his mind. Something about the whole exchange just didn't sit right. Kennedy seemed positive that recent events would have changed their position on the sale. Was it too much of a coincidence that the man was showing so much interest in their land while they were busy fending off unknown aggressors? He frowned in concentration, and was he overthinking the man's parting words, or had they been offered as a veiled threat? After this newest attempt, it was just too big of a coincidence for comfort in his book. *Something fishy is going on there.*

****

"I'm telling you, I don't know how or why, but that guy is involved in what's been happening around here. He is just way too interested in this ranch and everyone on it for it to be a casual interest in a possible land deal. He seemed to take the refusal very personally, like he was offended by our refusal to deal with him. Everything he said gave the impression of a hidden double meaning. It was unsettling." Dylan glanced around at the people surrounding him. He had called everyone together for a "family meeting" to discuss the new security measures and cameras going in around the house and in the outbuildings, but he also wanted to get their take on this newest development.

"Sounds like it is time for me to do a more thorough investigation into this guy. Take an in-depth look at his known associates, pull apart his business dealings, scour through his financials. See if I can figure out what he is up to. I do find it very interesting that he just happened to show up out of nowhere and is interested in the same tract of land that the hunting cabin is on." Mitch didn't like the implications of this new angle any more than Dylan did.

"I say we need to make another trip up to the cabin and have a closer look around. There is a lot of interest in that land, and it's close to where Dylan was shot. We know there has been some unwelcome and unusual activity up there. Maybe someone wanted to keep him out of the area for some reason. I want to cut off that lock up there and find out what the hell is going on." Jake's eyes gleamed with determination. "We have left that particular development slide long enough. I know we have had other events take priority lately, but now it's time to take a closer look at all the suspicious activity happening up there. There is a reason for all the interest, and it must tie in somehow."

Agreeing that there was greater safety in numbers, it was decided that the men would ride to the cabin as a group while the women chose to remain at the main house. Margaret, who had swung by earlier that morning to check on her *favorite set of siblings*, insisted she stay and help around the house so the girls could get their work projects done. With the added protection of the two men watching the ranch from outside, everyone felt confident that Hillary and Kiya would be well looked after while they themselves set out for the far side of the property.

When Mitch questioned if horses or vehicles would provide the best means of transport, Cade suggested that on the off chance that someone was in the vicinity, horses would offer quiet movement and the element of surprise. They would also allow quick maneuverability through rough and wooded terrain if it was needed.

As they saddled their horses, Jake worried if riding back through the field where he took a bullet would be too much for Dylan. The memories of lying there in the grass, bleeding, struggling for air might still be too fresh. Jake knew the image still haunted his own thoughts. It had to be so much worse for Dylan. "Are you sure you want to do this right now? You don't have to ride along if you're not up for it."

Dylan gazed back at him with a determined look. "This ranch is my home, my life. I can't…I *won't* allow anyone to make me afraid of it or avoid any part of it. I refuse to give them that much power over me."

Jake found his brother's courage and strength of will admirable. Taking him at his word, Jake nodded and swung onto his horse.

"But for the record…" Dylan added with a tentative smile that reminded Jake of the young boy he used to be, "I'm glad the rest of you are along for this ride."

They galloped through fields and wooded areas enjoying the freedom of the ride and the cold, crisp air of the approaching winter. The clouds were gray and heavy when they slowed their mounts to a gentler pace as they neared the location where they would start the ascent to higher ground.

As they crossed through the open land that held so many tumultuous memories for all of them, Dylan pulled his horse to a stop. His expression became strained, his jaw clenched tight. The fingers of one hand rhythmically tightened and released on the reins he held, while the other absently rubbed at the scar that marred the flesh under his clothing. His watchful eyes roamed the surrounding hills as if they would reveal the answers that still eluded him about that day. He consciously tried to control his breathing and slow his racing heartbeat.

This place obviously held a stranglehold on his emotions, but he wouldn't allow it to dominate him. He had survived. He would continue to flourish here as he always had. One evil act would not destroy that. He wouldn't allow it to. He loved this land and the life he had built here. He would overcome this as he had any other trial thrown into his path, with the support of his family and friends. He took one final look at the shadowed hills above him before pulling himself back to the present. Dylan shifted his gaze to the right where his brothers and lifelong friend patiently waited a short distance away. He nudged his horse forward and joined them, grateful that they understood his mood and were more than willing to give him whatever time he needed to come to terms with his experience.

Without a conscious decision, the men closed ranks around Dylan as they continued the journey toward the hunting cabin. Along the way they pointed out signs of unauthorized use of the land they moved through. The tracks leading to and away from the area were still visible although a little more obscure. Once they entered the clearing containing the small structure, the use became more apparent. Fresh, snake-like paths could be seen entering the far side of the clearing leading straight to the ramshackle building.

"What do you make of that?" Cade asked his companions as they surveyed the area. "Last time we were up here, the tracks were newer on this side and leading up here. Now it seems like there is more activity coming into the back side through the woods."

"Maybe whoever is using the place is trying to be a little more inconspicuous," Dylan suggested.

"It's a possibility. They changed vehicles too," Mitch agreed before suggesting that they split up and circle the meadow looking for more signs of activity prior to searching the cabin. Dylan and Cade circled left while Jake and Mitch went right.

"I remember this place as being a quiet hideaway when Dad used it. Is it just me, or does it feel more ominous now?" Cade asked as they moved along the edges of the clearing.

Dylan responded with a mildly derisive laugh. "Look who you're asking, bro. I find everything more ominous now."

They continued checking the area for anything of interest. Shortly before they were to veer off toward the rendezvous point, Cade suddenly pulled his mount to a stop and swung to the ground. He followed a tiny path into the woods. Dylan followed suit. Slightly inside the tree line, the underbrush thinned out enough to reveal a single rutted path winding its way up the hillside to their current location.

"Well, from the looks of this, our mysterious visitor seems to be cutting across state game land to gain access to our property or vice versa. Unlike the other trails though, where there are signs of them using ATVs or trucks, this is strictly a dirt bike path. A well-used one at that."

"Maybe this is nothing more than a case of rebellious joyriders hauling their bikes in to tear around on isolated terrain they aren't supposed to be on," Dylan proposed.

"But why would they make repairs to the cabin and put a padlock on it? We didn't see any evidence of anyone storing supplies or a bike in there," Cade replied.

"Good question. Let's head over there and see if we can find an answer."

When they arrived at the front of the tiny cabin, Jake and Mitch were already waiting. They hadn't found anything that would suggest anyone was doing anything other than passing through the center of the meadow. Cade filled the others in on what he and Dylan had found, and Dylan's suggestion of joyriders.

"Not a bad theory," Jake admitted, "if this was the only thing going on. But if we are assuming this somehow ties into Dylan getting shot and all the other assaults, I doubt illegal joyriding would be the cause."

"It's possible that it's not related at all, and it is just a coincidence that someone is trespassing on the land Preston Kennedy is so eager to buy," Mitch said thoughtfully. "Kennedy could simply be taking advantage of the attacks to procure a sale. It seems unlikely, but again, why on earth would anyone resort to such extreme tactics to gain access to a practically inaccessible tract of land?"

"What are the odds that Preston Kennedy is basically a sociopath that just doesn't like to take 'no' for an answer?" Dylan wondered.

Mitch responded with a hollow laugh. "I have been a lawman most of my life, at this point, I would never rule anything out. People are crazy."

Jake moved to his saddlebag and pulled out a pair of bolt cutters. "Since none of us can argue that sentiment, let's get this show on the road and see if we can find out why someone would take the time to lock us out of a shack."

The padlock gave way easily to the jaws of the tool and the man wielding it. The door swung open without a sound, surprising the assembled group. Whomever had replaced the entryway had done a remarkable job, right down to oiling the hinges. They moved into the structure and scrutinized the empty space.

"You're right, nobody is storing a bike or anything else in this place. Other than the slight remodel, this place looks completely unused," Dylan said to Cade. His forehead wrinkled in puzzlement.

Jake moved across the floor to inspect the farthest reaches of the room. This made absolutely no sense. The cabin was still nothing more than an abandoned shell. They were missing something. They had to be. He heaved out a frustrated sigh and started back toward the others hovering near the door. In the middle of the room, Jake stepped on a loose board. One end lifted under the weight of his foot then fell back into place when it was removed.

"This place is an accident waiting to happen," he muttered as he bent to poke at the offending board. The entire thing came up with little effort. Jake stared into the cavity beneath the floor, then suddenly pulled a few more boards free and tossed them aside. "Holy Hell," he breathed. "We are in serious trouble here." Disbelief showed on his face when he looked up at the others. "They are using the ranch to traffic drugs."

The men crowded around him and peered into the dark recess. Stunned silence gripped each of them as they stared at a substantial number of tightly wrapped cellophane bundles stacked neatly below them. There had to be close to forty pounds of individually secured blocks of marijuana filling that void.

Suddenly, Jake started grabbing the floorboards and shoving them back into place. "We need to leave. We have to get out of here before someone finds us here."

"This is *our* land; we can't just leave that there!" Cade protested gesturing to the floor.

"We can't remove it and risk drug runners showing up on our doorstep trying to retrieve it!" Dylan countered.

The color drained out of Cade's face as he considered that scenario. "Oh my God. What do we do now?"

"Now we call in the Feds," Mitch told them. "This is well beyond the scope of what my department can handle alone."

"We can plan a course of action after we are safely away from here," Jake urged.

Cade was nodding in agreement when a worrisome thought presented itself. "Aren't they going to be suspicious anyway once they discover their shiny new lock is missing?"

Jake swore under his breath.

"With any luck, they will think we checked the place out but when they see that nothing is missing or disturbed, they will assume we didn't find anything," Dylan theorized in a hopeful tone.

They hastily made sure everything was returned to the way they had found it and left the area. They deliberately set a casual pace in case someone noticed their progression. If that happened, they wanted it to appear that nothing was amiss or out of the ordinary. Along the way, they discussed the implications of what they had discovered in low voices. The chances of catastrophic repercussions were very real. They had to safeguard themselves and their property as quickly and thoroughly as possible. As they neared the house, Mitch informed them that he was going to leave them at the barn and head directly to the station to brief his men and start placing calls to the proper agencies. The faster he could get the Feds on the scene, the better.

When the horses were unsaddled and comfortably back in their stalls, the brothers proceeded toward the main house. None of them were looking forward to the discussion they were about to have with the women waiting inside. They may have discovered the root of their troubles, but it didn't help them any. It only highlighted how dangerous their situation was.

Chapter 16

When Jake strolled into the kitchen early the next morning, he was surprised to see that everyone else was already present. He had awoken early, and his troubled mind wouldn't allow him to linger in bed. He thought he would have been one of the first ones up. Instead, Dylan and Cade hovered near the coffee pot while Hillary was seated at the table enjoying a plate of eggs and toast. "It appears that I somehow managed to be the latecomer today," he observed out loud.

The aroma of frying bacon drew his attention to Kiya, who was busy at the stove. She looked content while she folded a veggie filled omelet and flipped sizzling strips of meat. Her hair was knotted at the back of her head, exposing the delicate length of her neck. The homey scene was a very enticing image. He couldn't resist stepping over and placing a light, lingering kiss on the side of her neck where it curved to her shoulder. "Good morning. How did you end up on breakfast duty?" he inquired. His mild tone didn't portray his internal struggle to withstand the intense urge he had to wrap his arms around her waist and draw her against him to kiss her properly. He saw surprise in her eyes when she looked up at him, but her smile was genuine.

"I volunteered. I was up early anyway." She stole a furtive glance at the others to see how they had reacted to his greeting, but they didn't seem to notice.

"Better be careful with how often you volunteer, or these hooligans will try to use it against you," he playfully scolded as he placed a hand against the small of her back and leaned around her to snag a piece of bacon.

"Are you hungry? This is ready to be plated, so I can start a new batch while you get coffee."

"That sounds great, if you don't mind making more."

"I don't mind. I still need to make mine, so I will just make enough for two." She smiled again, and Jake's gaze dipped to her lips. The look on his face suggested that he was considering kissing her again.

Dylan cut in by shoving a mug of fresh coffee under Jake's nose. "Here, take this, and stop distracting the cook. At least until I get my food." He then turned to Kiya and mischievously tapped her on the nose. "You can flirt later."

At a loss on how to respond to him teasing her about his brother's attention, Kiya hurriedly returned to her task. *So much for them not noticing.* She served Cade and Dylan heaping plates of food then quickly prepared more for herself and Jake, who thanked her as she handed him his plate, and sat down next to him with her own.

Dylan leaned back in his seat after he finished his own breakfast and savored a second cup of coffee. "Yes, thank you, and this coffee is top-notch by the way." He raised his cup to her before continuing. "My stomach and I are beyond happy. Please feel free to volunteer to make breakfast anytime. You may resume your flirting now." He grinned magnanimously.

Kiya's jaw went slack, and her eyes widened as she gawked at Dylan. "I wasn't…"

"I was," Jake interrupted smoothly, "but Dylan tends to be impatient."

"What can I say? The woman makes a mean omelet," he responded.

"Can't argue with that," Jake conceded while scooping up another bite.

Cade snickered into his coffee cup, but Hillary laughed outright at Kiya's expression as her gaze shifted between the two men.

"It only gets worse," Hilly warned.

****

As the McCleary family finished their breakfast, Mitch sat watching the obscure old pathway leading onto McCleary land while he mulled over the information he had received from the DEA and his contacts within other departments. He had reached out to some friends trying to collect as much information about Preston Kennedy and his known associates as possible. He wasn't surprised when he was informed that while no charges were ever filed against the man, everywhere he went, whispers and rumors followed. Whenever he was involved in a business deal, strong-arm tactics seemed to be the norm. No one was ever willing to talk about such matters, but the people involved eventually usually ended up doing what Kennedy wanted one way or another. With the amount of drugs these guys seemed to be moving, they were probably willing to do just about anything to keep their supply lines running. His thoughts returned to Dylan lying in a field struggling to breathe with a hole in his chest. *Even attempted murder.*

The DEA, unfortunately, was going to need a few days to get a team together and get them on-site. In the meantime, Mitch was setting up his own surveillance and calling in favors from the locals to make sure his extended family, as he liked to think of them, were safe from Kennedy's goons. He wasn't willing to lose his dream of a life with Hilly because of some drug smuggling narcissist.

His vehicle was almost completely hidden by the surrounding brush and vegetation as he watched the surrounding area. The air was cold enough to make him wish he had stayed at the station. Mitch briefly thought about turning on his engine for added warmth, but instead tugged the zipper on his duty jacket up to his chin. *No sense giving away my hiding place if someone happens to be nearby.* He had been sitting here for a couple of hours going over possible scenarios for the activity on his friends' land and mentally considering strategies on how to take down Kennedy's operation. The DEA would undoubtedly want to run things their own way once they got here, but Mitch couldn't sit around doing nothing when his friends' lives, and livelihood hung in the balance. That was how he ended up sitting out here in the cold watching an empty roadway. It was something proactive to *do* on the off chance that someone might try to use the hunting camp road to access the old cabin. He wasn't sure how or when the drugs were being moved around, but someone knew the drugs were there and would be wanting their product soon. The chances were slim that he would find anyone out here during the day, but he doubted anyone would want their stash sitting under those floorboards for long. Still, not a single vehicle had traveled through this location since he had arrived. *No matter. I'm no worse off mulling over this situation here than I am at the station.*

No sooner than he had thought those words, the sound of an approaching vehicle reverberated through the trees. Mitch sat up straighter in his seat when the sound of the approaching engine slowed as it neared his hiding spot. What were the odds that the only vehicle on this road was operated by someone he would be interested in talking to?

He couldn't believe his eyes when a dirty blue pickup truck rounded the bend and entered his view. He instantly remembered Kiya's description of the truck she saw leaving the area when Dylan was shot. This was a perfect match.

Pulse racing with anticipation, Mitch waited until the truck had crept onto the obscure path leading toward the cabin and had moved away from the road, disappearing into the trees, before he started his vehicle and swung in behind them with lights flashing to block their escape route.

He pulled up to the rear of the stopped vehicle and cautiously climbed out of his truck, then made his way up to the side of the suspect's vehicle. Through the back window, he could see hunting rifles hanging suspended in a gun rack behind the seat. Fortunately, he saw only one occupant inside. Releasing the safety strap with his thumb, Mitch drew his service weapon. He questioned the intelligence of his actions with every step he took in the direction of the waiting vehicle. Even if he wasn't out here without backup, help was a long way off if the driver of that truck decided to try and fight his way out of this situation. Mitch doubted he could count on his own guardian angel coming to his rescue the way Kiya had for Dylan. Truth be told, he hadn't expected to find anyone out here when he decided to stake out the place this morning. Not really. Now he wished he would have done more than tell Joni, his secretary, that he was headed out to the McCleary place. He hoped he would have time to radio this in if it turned out to be anything important. *Better play this by the book and pray that whoever is in that truck isn't a trigger-happy drug runner willing to engage in a gun battle with the local sheriff.*

He warily approached the driver's side window. "Let me see your hands!" he called to the person inside. Two hands appeared out of the driver's window after it was lowered. *So far so good.*

"I'm unarmed," a male voice called out.

"Unarmed? There are at least two weapons in your vehicle, and that's just what I can see from here. I'm going to open the door. Keep your hands up and extended where I can see them." Mitch leaned in and pulled open the door, making sure he stayed out of range of the guy's reach while keeping the door between them. The driver, whom Mitch gauged to be in his early twenties, did as he was told. "Now, exit the vehicle and step back. Place your hands on the side of your truck." When those instructions were also followed without incident, Mitch asked him if he had any weapons or sharp objects on him. The kid denied having anything, so Mitch quickly patted him down. After he was sure he wasn't in immediate danger of getting shot or stabbed, Mitch relaxed slightly and took a good look at the guy in front of him. The man looked vaguely familiar, but he couldn't put a name to the face.

"Want to explain why you're trespassing on private property?" he questioned in a serious tone.

The man swallowed audibly. "I didn't know it was private property."

"Try again," Mitch said in a tight voice and indicated a bright yellow sign decorating a nearby tree. An insolent shrug was the only response he got. "You want to pretend you can't read? That's fine by me, but I'm going to need a name." Once again silence was his answer. Mitch's voice turned cold. "You either answer my questions here or you *will* answer them at the station. Your choice."

"Seth," the man mumbled.

"Seth…?"

"Just Seth."

"Well, just Seth, you hunt?"

The man shifted from one foot to the other. He cast a quick glance at the rifles in the window of the truck. Mitch caught the action and tensed again.

"Yeah, so? Hunting's legal."

"Indeed, it is. If you're not doing it out of season or on private property. What do you have there? Looks like a thirty-ought six and what…a semi-automatic? When was the last time either of those guns were fired?" Mitch asked in a seemingly mild manner.

"I don't have to answer that. I know my rights."

Mitch nodded. "Funny thing, though, the owner of this private property, which you are currently trespassing on, just so happened to get shot recently with a rifle like that. A friend of his had her house shot up too."

"What's that got to do with me?" Seth questioned hotly.

"Probably nothing," Mitch responded casually. "Just doing my job, ya know? I have to cover my bases and answer to the higher-ups like anybody else. Good thing we managed to collect a lot of evidence from the crime scenes. You know, the bullet that was lodged in that guy's chest, and the ones in the walls of the house. Shell casings, things like that. You wouldn't have a problem with us checking your guns and prints against those results, would ya? Just to rule you out as a suspect of course, seeing as how this location isn't used much and a crime was committed here."

"You got a warrant, hot shot? You ain't touching my guns without one."

The younger man grew more agitated with every second. His eyes darted around the immediate area, as if he felt trapped and was looking for a means to escape. He constantly shifted his weight from one foot to the other and tapped his fingers against the side of his leg. Not exactly the usual reaction for your average law-abiding citizen.

"Not a problem. Easy enough to get one," Mitch told him. "I'll just take you in to the station with me then we can have you back on your way in no time." He made a show of reaching for his cuffs.

Faster than Mitch would have thought the kid was capable of, Seth slammed a shoulder into Mitch's chest, causing him to stagger backward, and dashed off in the direction of the partially hidden police vehicle. *Surely the kid isn't stupid enough to add grand theft auto of a government vehicle to his record at this point.* Sure enough, Seth changed direction at the last moment and veered off toward a heavily wooded section of land behind the parked truck. He obviously hoped to use the surrounding terrain to disappear.

Mitch leaped into action and raced after his fleeing subject. He wasn't about to let his first possible lead get away from him. Gritting his teeth, he bore down and willed his legs to move faster. Even with the added weight of his service belt, Mitch was soon closing the distance between himself and his prey. He judged the distance he needed then launched himself at Seth's legs. The tackle brought them both to the ground, and they slid to a halt. Still not ready to give up, the kid bucked and struggled against Mitch's weight.

After an elbow caught him squarely on the jaw, and with his chest heaving from the exertion, Mitch pinned Seth to the ground and slapped cuffs onto his wrists. "What do you say you and I go have a nice long chat huh?" He dragged the man up by his arms and steered him back to the waiting service vehicle where he radioed the station to let them know he was on his way in with a suspect for interrogation.

****

"Why don't you make this easy on yourself and tell us what we want to know?" Mitch growled impatiently at the man across from him. So far, the guy had been mostly uncooperative. He insisted that he was only out scouting around when he had driven onto the ranch this morning and that he couldn't remember his exact whereabouts when Dylan was shot or Kiya's house was attacked.

"Can you remember where *you* were on those days, at those times? It's not like I keep to a set schedule or anything," Seth sneered.

"Look, we know someone is running drugs across the Five M. Things will go a lot better for you if you tell us who it is and how they are doing it. You didn't just stumble onto that old hunting path. You have used it before."

"I don't know what you're talking about, man," was the insolent reply.

"Then why run? If you weren't doing anything, and you have no idea about the stuff going on in that area, why assault an officer and take off?" Seth glared at him but remained silent. "You don't want to talk? That's fine, but here is what's going to happen. We are going to hold you for trespassing and assault on an officer. In the meantime, those weapons of yours will be cross-checked with the evidence we have for potential matches. I will also be putting the word out on the street that you are sitting in here talking to us after being picked up on Five M land and that you are being questioned as a person of interest in drug smuggling and attempted murder. I'm sure nobody will have a problem with that. No one will have any cause to want to keep you silent seeing as how you know nothing about any of it."

The cockiness vanished, and nerves once again had his suspect acting jittery. His leg started to bounce in agitation as he sat in his chair, and his fingers drummed against the tabletop. "You can't hold me here!" he demanded.

"Actually, I can." Mitch rose to his feet and headed for the door but paused before opening it. "Ya know, it is a good thing that you *aren't* involved. It's always the little guy, the low man on the totem pole, that gets hung out to dry and takes the fall for things like this. The people in charge go free to move on to start over somewhere else, while the little guy pays the price. In this case…assault with a deadly weapon, multiple counts of attempted murder, conspiracy to commit murder, drug smuggling, along with a host of other charges, you would be looking at a minimum of a life sentence in a very rough prison. Could even face the death penalty. That is, of course, if they let you live long enough to face those charges. Loose ends are a liability after all." He shrugged and pulled the door open. "I'll let you know when those ballistic reports come back."

Seth was sweating, and his eyes were wide. "Wait!" he blurted urgently, "what if I can help you out? I help you, you help me, right?"

Mitch felt a surge of triumph. *Now we're getting somewhere*. He kept his voice and expression neutral. "Depends on what you know, and if it is useful. Lies and half-truths get you nothing."

"I want an agreement in writing, and you have to agree to protect me."

Mitch played it cool and eyed the man thoughtfully before responding. "Let's hear what you got."

****

"Jake, we need to talk," Mitch exclaimed the instant he heard his friend answer the phone.

Immediately picking up on the serious tone, Jake's reply was just as intense. "Where and when?"

"My office as soon as you can arrange it. I would like everyone present, but at least make sure Kiya is with you."

"Give me an hour. We'll be there." Jake disconnected the call and gave the bay colt he had been working with a final pat then closed the stall door behind him. He called out to Cade who was cleaning out the hooves of a mare in the cross ties. "That was Mitch. Sounds like he might have some new information for us. He wants us to meet him in his office."

Cade lifted his head but didn't release the foot between his knees. "He say what it was about?"

"No, but he sounded fairly hyped up about it."

"Well then, it's a good thing I am finished here." He let go of the horse and rubbed its flank as a reward for good behavior.

Jake nodded. "Let's get cleaned up and gather the troops."

It took two vehicles, but the McCleary clan arrived at the municipal building together and with ten minutes to spare. The drive into town had been quick, with very little traffic. Their small town was usually pretty quiet during the workweek and only became active on the weekends. The doors to Mitch's office and the meeting room were closed when they arrived, but Joni saw them and instructed them to go straight on into the conference room, where Mitch was waiting for them. As they filed into the specified space, Mitch was just wrapping up an official sounding phone call. He waved them into the chairs across from him and told the person on the other end of the line that he would meet them first thing in the morning.

"Busy day, I take it," Cade said as Mitch replaced the phone back on its base and raked a hand through his hair.

"You could say that. Thanks for making the drive here. I would have come to you, but this is more of an official meeting. I want it public and on record." The group shared curious glances as Mitch picked up the

189

phone again and punched the button for the outer office. "Joni, find Jenkins and send him in."

It only took a moment or two before the door opened again and the other officer entered the room with a file folder in his hand. He circled the long table they were gathered around and dropped into a chair near the sheriff.

"Kiya, you might remember Officer Jenkins." Mitch gestured to the man at his side.

"I do," she said, offering the man a small smile. He nodded in return. All this formality was making her nervous. She wished Mitch would just get on with whatever had brought them here. She didn't have to wait long.

"I had a run in with a guy named Seth Myers this morning. Any of you know him?"

"Doesn't sound familiar," Jake said then looked at his siblings for input. They all shook their heads.

Mitch looked over at Jenkins who acknowledged the cue and opened the file in front of him. He pulled out a photo and slid it directly across the table to Cade.

As Cade examined the image and passed it along, Mitch went on, "He is currently sitting over in lockup at the county jail. I ran his name and prints through the system. He is just a local punk with an all too familiar story. Bad home environment leading to problems with authority figures, acting out, and some brushes with law enforcement for petty theft, breaking and entering, the usual rebellious teenage rap sheet but nothing violent."

When Hillary paused over the image looking thoughtful, Mitch stopped. "Hilly?" She glanced up. "You recognize him?"

Her brows drew together in concentration as she

studied the photo. "He looks familiar, but I'm not sure where I've seen him before. Maybe the Watering Hole?" she replied, naming a local bar.

"Not surprising. He is closest to you in age, so maybe he frequented some of the same places." Dylan leaned over to look at the photo in his sister's hand. "I think I've seen him around too, but I can't place him." He slid the image back toward Jenkins.

"This is where the story gets interesting," Mitch told them. "Early this morning, I confronted Mr. Myers for trespassing on your land. On the old trail leading up to the cabin as a matter of fact." Both Dylan and Jake sat up straighter in their seats as he continued. "Driving an older model blue farm truck, no less."

Jenkins pushed the picture of Seth Myers under his folder and pulled out a new image which he placed in front of Kiya. "Can you identify this truck?"

"I can't be absolutely positive since I only saw it from a distance, but it definitely looks like the truck I saw leaving the area after Dylan was shot."

"What about when you were run off the road?" Mitch asked.

Kiya frowned. "I couldn't describe that vehicle to save my soul. All I remember was blinding lights from something big."

Mitch shifted his gaze to Hillary, but she was already shaking her head. "All I can tell you is that it was a full-sized truck, not an SUV."

"Okay," Mitch said then took a moment to gather his thoughts before he went on to tell them how, on a whim, he had decided to drive out to the old road and keep an eye on any activity in the area. He described his subsequent altercation with the driver, and the types of weapons confiscated from the truck. "We started the process of getting ballistics run on those guns to verify that they were the ones used against Dylan and Kiya. After putting up a good front, Mr. Myers knew he was in over his head. He caved to some good old-fashioned police-style coercion and agreed to a plea deal. He had a very interesting story to tell."

According to Seth's sworn statement, he was approached to do some odd jobs by a man he only knows as Slade. Originally, he was told to make some minor repairs to an "old shed." Then to keep an eye on the place after Slade's people started to make trips in and out of that location. Every couple of weeks, a delivery would arrive that was divided between two electric dirt bike riders wearing backpacks. Their haul was brought in and left at the cabin for Slade to retrieve. He didn't know where it was taken after that. Seth quickly realized that they were moving drugs, but the money was too good to pass up, and nobody was being harmed by them using an abandoned shack in the middle of nowhere. Until the day he alerted Slade to the fact that Dylan was in the area and nearing the cabin. After placing a call to someone that was obviously in charge, Slade said that the two of them were going to handle the problem. He told Seth to grab his guns before they set out for the ridge. The kid insisted that he didn't know Slade was going to shoot Dylan. He said he thought they would possibly take a few pot shots to scare the guy off. Seth claims that it was Slade that fired the gun that day. He admitted to being involved with the assault on Kiya's house but denied targeting her directly. Again, he said he thought their actions were to scare her and he randomly strafed the house with gun fire until he was instructed to stop by Slade.

Seth had appeared genuinely clueless when asked about the women being forced off the road or the fire at the ranch. Mitch was inclined to believe that he hadn't been present for those events. His truck showed no signs of impact damage or recent repair, and he certainly didn't come across as being crafty enough to infiltrate a busy ranch without being detected and pulling off an unprovable arson job. No, that was more likely this Slade character that seemed to be enforcing the will of the yet unverified orchestrator of the operation. They had their money on Kennedy. Now all they had to do was prove it.

Mitch gave everyone present a few minutes to process the information he had just given them. As he scanned each of their faces, he saw everything from confusion to shock and anger.

Dylan was clearly frustrated. "So, what do we do now? How do we use this to our advantage? We still have no idea who this Slade character is, and we have nothing even remotely substantial to tie Kennedy to this."

"Now, we keep an eye on those drugs and any movement in the area until the Feds arrive. I have already updated them with this latest information. They will be speeding up their timeline for arrival. First thing tomorrow morning I am bringing in a sketch artist who, with any luck, will be able to give us a good likeness of Slade based on Seth's description. Maybe we will get lucky and be able to find him too. He is our ticket to the top. Whether that is Kennedy or someone else, we will bring them down one way or another. Somebody is bound to start getting antsy with Seth having been picked up, and there is a heck of a lot of drugs just sitting out in that field."

"So how do we keep them from just picking up the drugs and disappearing without ever being held accountable for everything they have done?" Hillary wanted to know.

Mitch reassured her that he wasn't going to let the people responsible for harming them go unpunished. He explained that he had a few men covering the field and cabin. They would know if anyone tried to retrieve the drugs, and they would be stopped unless they were willing to risk a full-blown assault on his department. He would bet that they didn't want to tangle with any members of law enforcement. "With your permission, I will increase that number and keep eyes on that building twenty-four seven."

"You have it of course, but I want in on that," Cade told him. "I will take shifts in whatever rotation you have set up. They are using our place and coming after us. I want to be involved in taking them down."

Jake and Dylan nodded. "Us, too. We will rotate with whoever you have up there and with the guys who help keep an eye on the house. You must be spread pretty thin in manpower. We will help however we can," Dylan agreed.

"We could certainly use the help, along with your knowledge of the woods and the surrounding areas for the best possible vantage spots or access points. In the meantime, I think Hilly and Kiya should stick close to the house. Until we catch the people behind this, it would be safer. That way we can focus our efforts on the cabin and tracking down this Slade guy."

"We can't live like caged rats," Kiya stated

emphatically. "I'm willing to help too. In case you all have forgotten, I was on the receiving end of their depravity more than once. I'm not some shrinking violet that needs to be hidden away."

"No. We won't have you hurt again. You have been sent to the hospital twice already," Jake countered instantly.

"And Dylan was shot, Jake. Nobody is telling him to hide in the house."

Dylan shook his head. "You don't have to be hiding in the house either, just staying out of the direct line of fire and not taking any unnecessary risks, so we don't have to worry about you."

Her laugh was sarcastic and completely without humor. "Yet you want us to sit back and watch while you stake out a pile of drugs and do nothing other than wait at home and worry about the rest of you. If that's not a double standard, I don't know what is."

Mitch held up a hand. "Hold on, hold on. Worrying about each other is inevitable in this situation. There is no way to avoid that, but I need a different kind of help from you and Hillary. You would be the most useful to us by tracking down anything that will help us locate where Kennedy and Slade are right now. They are staying somewhere. They have a system set up. You can make calls to see if anyone has rented out rooms nearby in those names and do online or social media searches for anything that might help. Hilly can search articles on Kennedy's company and their offers to buy land, their history, or any unusual news in the locations they invest in. Talk to the people they made offers to and see if they might be holed up on a different piece of property. Things like that."

Kiya eyed the sheriff suspiciously for a moment wondering if he was just pacifying her with busy work. It was possible of course, but she could see his point. His office didn't have anyone specific assigned to do research or track down information. They certainly didn't have an intelligence officer on staff. Joni handled office business only. He and his deputies were on their own when it came to digging up whatever information they needed. They didn't have direct access to the kinds of databases they needed at the moment.

"Fine," she relented. "But I won't be held captive from my own life indefinitely."

Mitch reassured her that she wouldn't have to. He had every intention of making sure his department, in addition to the team of Feds being assigned to the case, put an end to this group's operation in as little time as possible.

Chapter 17

Kiya sat enjoying her favorite after-dinner location on the porch. The swing under her rocked gently back and forth. A cozy blanket was wrapped around her to ward off the icy chill in the air. Her breath created visible clouds of steam as she exhaled, but she loved the contrast of sitting in the cold, still air while snuggled into the warmth of the blanket. Bright, vibrant stars decorated the dark sky like glittering diamonds. It was a perfect pre-winter evening. Luna rested nearby watching and listening to the night sounds of the ranch. Kiya leaned her head against the back of the swing and allowed her mind to drift.

The door to the house opened casting a soft glow across the porch. Jake appeared holding a steaming mug in his hand. "I thought you might like some tea. Hilly brewed a pot before going upstairs for the night." He handed her the fragrant cup but remained standing near the swing. "Would you like some company?" he asked, "or are you enjoying being alone?"

"Both." Kiya smiled up at him. "I was enjoying my time alone, but I wouldn't mind your company. Thank you for this." She gestured with her cup. "It is just what I need. Have a seat."

Jake joined her on the swing, settling in close while making sure he didn't jostle her tea. They sat quietly for a few minutes just enjoying the night. Kiya sipped at her tea. She had thought that the evening couldn't have gotten any better, but this was lovely. She delighted in the rich aroma and added comfort the tea provided while she nestled in closer to Jake. She appreciated his thoughtfulness and liked the feeling of having him next to her. His presence always seemed to fill her with a sense of well-being. She had never been so at ease with anyone as she was with this man and his family. She was starting to dread the day she would have to leave them and the ranch for her own place. She was content here and with the knowledge that she was accepted for who she was by these people.

"You seem lost in thought; did I disrupt your mood?" Jake inquired softly.

"No, just the opposite. I was thinking how nice this is. How much I enjoy being here. How unexpectedly comfortable I am with all of you. I am going to miss it when things get back to normal."

Jake lifted the cup from her hand and placed it on the railing next to the swing, then tipped her face up with a finger under her chin. "No one here is in any hurry for that to happen. We enjoy you being here just as much as you do. You are a part of our lives now. That isn't going to change no matter what." His gaze held hers intently to convey how earnest his words were. Her soft smile drew his eyes downward. Slowly, he lowered his head to hers. A moment before his lips took hers, he murmured, "I want you here with us…with me."

At first, Jake's kiss was gentle with a hint of promise, but it soon changed as his mouth continued to move over hers with both possessive intensity and enticing seduction. His lips slid over hers in a caress full of persuasive intent. The tender words followed by his strong embrace sparked an immediate response deep within her. Kiya let the blanket fall from her shoulders as she leaned into the solid heat of his body and returned the slow drugging kiss. Her arms slid around his waist when he shifted his position, inviting her closer. Kiya felt lightheaded as one alluring sensation after another coursed through her. Warmth spread like a molten flame from her core to her limbs. Her pulse jumped as the blood rushed through her veins. The hand that had rested lightly on her leg stroked up to her hip. His other hand rose to sift through her hair and settle at the back of her head, increasing the pressure of his lips. When her hands tightened their hold against the muscles of his back, he continued his leisurely journey upward along her rib cage to settle just below the tempting swell of her breast. His breathing ticked up at Kiya's hum of pleasure. She arched toward him as he skimmed his thumb along the underside of the soft mound.

Kiya's movements grew restless. Jake's hands and lips were creating a tension that had her straining for more. Each firm, purposeful stroke of his hand, each murmur of encouragement, every increase in the intensity of his mouth against hers heightened the sensation. Her fingers pressed into the corded muscles at his waist before fanning out over his taut abdomen. She couldn't seem to get close enough. His mouth released hers to explore the soft, smooth skin of her neck. Responding to her silent appeal, and feeling the same desire for more contact, Jake curled a hand around the back of her upper thigh while lifting her with gentle pressure against her opposite side to settle her across his lap. She ended up straddling his thighs as he gazed up at her with longing burning brightly in his eyes.

Jake ran his palms down her outer thighs to her knees and back up again before leaning forward and reclaiming her mouth in a heated sensual assault. He gripped her hips and pulled her tight against his body, allowing her to feel the effect she had on him. Strong fingers edged under the hem of her shirt to glide along the bare skin of her spine. Her head fell back, and a low moan escaped her parted lips when his work-roughened hands grazed along her flesh, circling around to her chest, allowing him to cup her and tease his thumbs over the sensitive buds covered only by a thin layer of lace.

Jake pulled back to watch her. His voice was rough with desire. "Do you have any idea what you do to me? How much I want you?"

Kiya brought her gaze back to his. She let her hands slide over the hard expanse of his chest until her forearms came to rest on his shoulders. "I know what you do to *me*," she said softly, wrapping her arms around his neck. She paused for a moment to glide her tongue enticingly along his lower lip, then kissed him with potent intensity.

Jake's gut tightened reflexively; there was no way to hold back the strained sound that formed in his throat. Without relinquishing her mouth, he shifted to move her shirt out of his way, but Kiya stopped him. Until that moment, she had entirely forgotten about the extra security roaming the property and the people inside. All she had been able to think about was him and the feelings he had awakened in her. She cast a nervous glance at the door to the house. "Jake, your family…"

"You could come upstairs with me," he gently implored her.

"I'm not sure I am ready for that. I don't think I could face anyone again in the morning."

Jake leaned his forehead against hers and groaned. "The downside of living and working with your family. There's not a lot of privacy even when everyone is spread out. I forget that you don't have much experience with that."

"Are you upset?" she asked in a cautious tone.

He eased back so that she could see his face. "Mildly frustrated, yes," he acknowledged. "Upset? No. I never want to put you in a position that you are uncomfortable with. Although, I have to warn you, this is giving me plenty of incentive to steal you away with me. To find somewhere that I can have you all to myself for as long as I want."

Her lips tilted upward. "Warn me? That doesn't sound like much of a threat to me. In fact, I might like the idea."

The cheeky reply pulled a pleased laugh from him. "Ugh, woman, you're killing me here." He gave her a quick, hard kiss and stood up with her still in his arms. He allowed her legs to slide to the floor. "As much as I have enjoyed this, we better head inside. We have a lot to do tomorrow. With any luck, Mitch's sketch artist will come up with something for us to work with."

Kiya collected her abandoned teacup, called to Luna, and followed Jake inside.

****

Early morning sun streamed into Kiya's room filling the space with bright, clear light. It was impossible to ignore, even though she wanted to. She squinted at the offending window with a sour expression. She had forgotten to pull the blinds last night. Mornings were not her favorite time of the day in general. It didn't help that her sleep had been fitful, and she didn't feel at all rested. Instead, she was tired, edgy, and dissatisfied. Her own fault of course. It would have been a more enjoyable, fulfilling night if she had spent it with Jake. With frustrating ease, her mind drifted back to the evening before. A pleasant tingle raced up her spine. The memory of his hands roaming her body, the pull of desire in his kisses, brought a heated blush to her skin.

Enough, she told herself with a shake of her head. *This isn't helping at all.* She threw back her covers and stalked to the bathroom for a shower. The hot water forced sleep from her mind and rejuvenated her body but did little for her mood. *I need coffee,* she decided.

Kiya entered the kitchen and without greeting the others in the room, went straight to the coffee pot already steaming on the counter. She hastily filled a mug and took a large gulp, scalding her tongue in the process. Her hand jerked, sloshing hot coffee down her arm.

Dylan was watching her with concern, and Hillary cocked an eyebrow in question. Kiya just shook her head, set her cup down, and grabbed a towel to wipe at her arm. She finished in time to see Jake stride into the room looking fully rested, cheerful, and raring to go.

He crossed the room and with little regard for their audience, kissed her thoroughly. "Good morning. How did you sleep?" he asked once he released her.

Kiya's eyes narrowed. "Not well," she grumbled.

A knowing gleam glinted in his eyes. One side of his mouth quirked up. "Good." He whistled a tune under his breath while he filled his own cup. He could feel her glaring at his back, and his smile grew larger. He turned to snag an apple from the table. "I assume Cade is already at the barn since he is the only one missing. So whose turn is it for breakfast?"

"Mine, we're having waffles and bacon," Dylan told him.

"In that case, we'll be done with chores in as close to half an hour as I can make it." Jake gave Kiya a flirty wink and left for the barn.

"Well, at least *he's* having a really good morning." Hillary's eyes sparkled with amusement.

"Did I hear something about waffles?" Kiya asked.

"You certainly did. But no changing the subject," Dylan told her.

"Subject? Were we discussing something?"

"Oh, no, you don't get off that easy in this family," Hillary informed her with a gleeful smile. She leaned forward and rested her elbows on the edge of the table. "I don't think I have *ever* seen Jake that happy, and based on that display a couple of minutes ago, I'm guessing you're the reason."

"It *was* a rather interesting display," Dylan agreed.

"That was some kiss. If he wasn't my brother, I think *I* would have swooned." Hillary giggled.

"I think I swooned anyway." Dylan managed to keep a perfectly straight face. He turned toward his sister. "Did it look like I swooned? It sure felt like I did."

"Oh, I definitely saw you swoon."

Dylan looked back at Kiya with an impish grin. "I

definitely swooned."

Kiya couldn't help but laugh. She pitched her towel at his head. "You did not swoon, you moron. You are both being completely ridiculous."

"Come on," Hillary urged, "this means you're together, right?"

Kiya's eyebrows rose. "Together? I don't think I would call it that. Maybe more like exploring a mutual interest."

"I know my brother. That wasn't him showing an interest," Dylan remarked.

"More like head over heels if you ask me." Hillary popped up out of her seat to give Kiya an enthusiastic hug. "I'm so excited. Just wait until Gretchen hears this!" she called over her shoulder as she hurried from the room.

Kiya looked over at Dylan with surprise. "She isn't really…"

He cut her off with a nod. "She is. Hilly can't keep anything to herself."

"So I've been told. Still, I don't want anyone getting the wrong idea."

Dylan frowned. "Are you saying that you don't *want* any kind of serious relationship with Jake? That you would prefer to keep things casual? If that's the case, angel, I'm asking you to tell him now, rather than later."

Kiya felt a chill run through her. "What? No, that's not what I meant at all."

The smile returned to Dylan's face. "Then, like I said, I know my brother. He has already staked his claim, and he's happy about it." He rose to his feet. "You don't strike me as the casual fling type anyway."

When she caught the side of her lip between her teeth, Dylan pulled her in for a quick hug. "Kiya, relax. There's no pressure. We are happy for you both. Now, I better get breakfast going before everyone comes back looking for food that isn't here. How do you feel about being my sous chef?"

Not long after they had started piling fresh waffles onto a serving platter, the troops started making their way back to the kitchen. Heaping mounds of bacon were added to their own serving platter, and they all dug in. Kiya complimented Dylan on the waffles, which he had made from scratch. She was impressed with how light and flavorful they were.

"It was our mother's recipe. She passed down all her favorites and made sure we all knew how to cook them. There was no male versus female division of chores around here. We all chipped in with both barn and household chores, but when it comes to cooking, lemon pepper chicken and waffles are my specialties." He blew on his fingers and rubbed them on his shirt.

"We each found our own styles and likes. Gretchen is a whiz with soups and stews. Cade makes a killer lasagna, and Jake's pot roasts and steaks are to die for. Personally, I prefer to bake," Hillary admitted with a shrug.

"Her sweet tooth is a blessing to us all. Between her and Margaret, we all have to be careful that we don't overindulge, but she has a gift," Cade complimented with a smile for his sister.

Hilly beamed with pleasure. "What a wonderful thing to say. I think you just earned yourself a pie with dinner."

"She is also very smart and a talented writer," Cade

added with a devious grin, then looked at Hillary hopefully.

"Not working."

"Kind-hearted and generous?"

His sister sighed dramatically. "Fine. Two pies, but that's all."

Cade punched a clenched fist into the air in triumph. "Yes!"

"Nice job, bro." Dylan chuckled.

"You can all thank me later," the man replied.

Talk around the table turned to plans for the day and schedule coordinating. It was decided that Jake, Dylan, and Kiya would meet with Mitch later in the day. They planned to bring a copy of the artist's rendering back with them, so they all had an idea of who they needed to keep an eye out for in addition to Kennedy. Cade and Hillary needed to stay at the ranch. Cade would be busy fielding business calls at the home office to complete a cattle sale, and Hillary had a pressing deadline for an article.

Eventually, with breakfast over, they each started to leave the room to get on with their workday. Kiya wanted to finish some work on a current project before Mitch called with the results of the meeting with Seth and the sketch artist. She bid everyone a good day and was heading for the stairs when Jake pulled her aside.

"Have dinner with me tonight."

Kiya's forehead crinkled with confusion. "I have dinner with you every night."

"I meant alone. Just the two of us."

"Aren't we all trying to stay close to the ranch at night for now so that none of us can be singled out as targets? We know from experience that even trips into town can be hazardous, and that was before you found the drugs."

He took her hands in his. "Let me worry about the details. We will be as safe as we can possibly be, I promise. Will you do it?"

"On one condition," she hedged.

"Name it."

Her eyes sparkled with mischief. "Somebody has to save me a piece of Hilly's pie."

Jake smiled and tugged her forward for a light kiss. "Done. Now, get to work. Mitch will be calling in a couple of hours."

Chapter 18

It was barely noon, and Jake, Kiya, and Dylan were back in the conference room at the station seated across the table from Mitch. He had already informed them that the federal agents assigned to their case would be arriving the next day and were eager to speak to them. In the meantime, Mitch was pressing ahead with his own leads.

"I know you said that you didn't actually see the men that shot Dylan or who was driving the truck that ran you off the road, but do you recognize this guy at all?" Mitch asked Kiya as he slid the sketch artist's drawing across the table. "I think the artist did a fine job with the description Seth gave her. Even he said that the resemblance to Slade is remarkable."

Kiya picked up the sketch he put in front of her and froze. Her eyes widened in shock. She studied the image, scanning the man's features to be sure she wasn't mistaken. *It's him. I'm sure of it!*

"Kiya? You know who he is?" Jake asked when he noticed her reaction.

Without taking her eyes off the drawing, she slowly nodded her head. She stared at it for another minute, then her troubled eyes met his.

"And so should you." She included Dylan in her answer. She held the sketch up for them to see. "This is the guy that approached me when I was alone on the porch recently. Just after the crew started working on the barn repairs. He's working on the ranch."

Dylan swore viciously.

"We have to get to the house," Jake declared. He hastily climbed to his feet and addressed Mitch.

"Call your men watching the ranch. Make sure no one is allowed to leave the place until we get there. Dylan can call Cade to tell him what is going on so that he can lock down the house and search it from top to bottom for anything suspicious, and to make sure he doesn't let Hilly out of his sight. We can search the grounds. If he's there, you can haul him in."

"We need to do this by the book, Jake. As of right now, the guy is only wanted for questioning. We have nothing but hearsay from one questionable source that he has anything to do with the drugs or the attacks," Mitch warned him. "Seth could have given us the description of a rival he wants out of the way for all we know."

"Well, I'm damn sure going to find out," Jake stated as he strode to the door.

****

When they arrived at the ranch a short time later, the repair workers were rounded up and asked to remain in the yard with Mitch as he questioned them about any ties they had to or information pertaining to their co-worker. No one was admitting to knowing much about him. According to them, Slade, who was going by the name Trent Michaels, did show up for work that morning but wasn't present with the assembled group. Nobody seemed to know where he was. While Mitch remained with the men to continue his questioning, Jake and Dylan had split up to search the nearby outbuildings.

While Dylan searched the small cabins used for seasonal workers, Jake walked toward a large storage shed located behind the barn. He placed his feet carefully with each step. He didn't want to alert Slade of his approach if the man was inside. As he neared the entrance to the shed, Jake noted that the outside latch was not secured. Someone was or had been inside recently.

Easing the door open, he stepped inside. He paused for a moment to allow his eyes to adjust to the dim interior. His gaze scanned the recesses of the structure. A faint scuffle near the rear of the building drew his attention. Jake vigilantly watched for any signs of movement as he crept in the direction of the sound. Getting ambushed by a desperate or fleeing suspect was not something he wanted to deal with. He would much rather face any threat head on, where he knew what he was up against.

A rattle came from directly ahead at a sliding door that led back outside. Lucky for him, it was chained from the outside. Catching sight of his target, Jake stopped and prepared himself for a confrontation. A figure was bent over, trying to jimmy the door.

"Slade!" he called out.

The man straightened while turning in Jake's direction. He didn't look like a desperate man at all. Quite the opposite in fact. His expression implied that while he would have snuck away if possible, he had in fact been looking forward to a fight. He appeared almost eager. A predatory gleam flashed in his eyes. He smirked with anticipation.

"Well, well, well, look who finally got a clue. I

was starting to think that none of you were very bright. I *would* like to know where you got my name though. You didn't figure that one out all on your own."

"We happened to collect a bit of your trash. You should be careful who you trust. Turns out he was more interested in saving his own ass than covering yours."

"Is that a fact?" Slade sneered.

"I'm here, aren't I?"

"Good thing I can cover my own ass then, isn't it?" He reached into his pocket pulling out a knife and flicking it open. "If you think you have me at a disadvantage just because you know my name, you have another thought coming."

Jake watched the man scrape his thumb over the blade of his knife. "What I think is that you are going to pay for coming after my family. I guarantee it."

Slade laughed. "We'll see won't we." He lunged at Jake with his blade.

With only inches to spare, Jake was able to dodge to the side at the very last second, knocking into a pile of old metal cans. They went clattering in all directions as he tried to regain his balance. His opponent wasn't willing to give him that chance. Arcing his arm wide, Slade swiped again, scoring the knife across Jake's ribs.

Jake sucked in an audible breath, leaning away from the blade, but didn't hesitate. He charged right at Slade before the guy could bring the weapon back around again. Jake grabbed the other man's wrist with an iron grip and twisted hard. At the same time, he threw his entire body weight into Slade's chest. The knife went flying; both men crashed to the ground. It took Jake only seconds to recover enough to pull back, intending to throw a punch, but Slade grabbed a handful of the dirt floor and flung it into Jake's face. Pebbles and dust stung his eyes, clogging his mouth and nose as he breathed in. He squeezed his eyes closed against the onslaught while choking on the cloud of granules in his throat.

Slade took the opportunity to sprint from the building. Coughing and trying to clear his eyes, Jake made his way out of the shed just as Dylan came sliding to a halt in front of him.

"You okay? We heard a bunch of commotion, then Slade came barreling out of here and took off." He gave his brother a once-over, noticing the futile effort to clear his eyes. "Stay here. I'll grab you some water."

It didn't take Dylan long to retrieve a bottle of water. Jake thanked him hoarsely and immediately went to work flushing the worst part of the grit out of his eyes. They would be red and irritated for a while, but as far as injuries went, things could have been a lot worse.

When Jake could see clearly again, he rinsed his mouth then gulped down the rest of the water. "He's gone, I take it?"

"Yeah, hightailed it across the paddock into the woods. At least we know who to watch for now. His days of free roaming are over. Let's get you back to the house, then we can talk."

Once inside, Kiya gently helped Jake remove the last bits of debris from his eyes and cleaned the thin slice along his rib cage while the men exchanged stories of what had transpired.

Mitch had sent all the barn workers home. They were close to finishing the project anyway, and he had felt that it would be safer to complete the finishing touches themselves rather than have any more strangers coming and going from the property. The new sprinkler system was installed and functioning. Security cameras would be active and connected to the ranch office computers by the end of the day. With his men overseeing the last of the installers, Mitch expected the ranch to be buttoned up tight within hours.

"I hope I didn't overstep any bounds by releasing your crew. I wanted to limit your exposure and threat level by only keeping on a few known individuals. After today I'm sure there is nothing remaining that would be a hardship to complete. With my help of course. I wouldn't leave you hanging."

"You didn't overstep. You are trying to protect everyone here, and doing a better job of it than I obviously did." Dylan's voice was full of self-recrimination. He raked a hand through his hair. The action clearly demonstrated his aggravation.

"What are you talking about, Dylan? This wasn't your fault," Cade told him.

"You're kidding, right? I hired that bastard. I gave him access to come and go as he pleased. He could have done a lot more damage or even hurt someone because of me."

"You couldn't have known, Dylan. None of us could have, and he already had access to the ranch, or the fire wouldn't have happened in the first place. We had no idea who the guy was and no reason to suspect him. This is not on you, so don't even think like that. We need your head in the game, not wallowing in misplaced guilt." Jake squeezed his brother's shoulder in solidarity and to take any sting out of his words. He couldn't allow Dylan to feel that he had let them down in any way.

Mitch nodded his agreement. "Everything turned out all right. We will get another shot at him. They aren't leaving without those drugs, and he's far enough up the food chain that he is sticking around. We need to focus on the meeting with the Feds tomorrow, on coming up with a course of action to bring down not only Slade, but the man behind the scenes also."

Everyone agreed to take the rest of the day easy and regroup. They all needed a break to decompress from all the stress. Mitch would arrange for the agents to arrive at the ranch after he brought them up to speed with everything his department was working on and got the interagency logistics out of the way.

Hillary made everyone a light lunch before they all went about with their work and chores. She and Kiya finished their work projects while sharing the large living room. They both simply felt more comfortable with the other close by. They worked and chatted equally, keeping each other company.

When dusk rolled around, Jake called an end to the workday by reminding Kiya that they had a dinner date.

"Oh, I forgot about that," she admitted. "Are you sure you still want to? We can always do it some other time."

He traced the underside of her jaw with his finger. "I want to spend time with you. I refuse to put our lives on hold. We deserve some time to ourselves. Everything else can wait. Our time together should not. Not for them."

Touched by the sentiment, Kiya rose up on her toes to brush her lips over his. "Then I will go get ready for dinner. What should I wear? You haven't told anything about your plans."

His rather cryptic reply was that she didn't need anything too fancy but to wear whatever she would feel comfortable in. "Meet me on the porch in a half an hour."

Five minutes later, Kiya stood in front of her closet nervously contemplating her clothing choices. She was both anxious and excited about her evening with Jake. On one hand, she really wanted to spend time alone with him and not worry about anything else. But on the other hand, it felt odd taking this time for themselves when so much upheaval was taking place around them. *And if I am honest with myself, I am more than a little unnerved at the prospect of starting a relationship with Jake while his entire family is practically looking over our shoulders. What if it doesn't work out and it ends up ruining my friendships with the people I have come to care about the most?* She didn't think she could bear it if her decision to pursue a relationship with Jake ended up severing her ties with the entire family.

A soft rap at the door had her eyes snapping to the clock beside the bed to see if she was running late. She had plenty of time left, so it couldn't be Jake. She went to open the door. As soon as she pulled it open, Hillary stuck her head into the room. "Hot date, huh?" She wiggled her eyebrows. "I'm here to lend some sisterly advice."

The comment and the sentiment behind her presence only heightened the fears that Kiya was battling against regarding what she had to lose. Emotion overwhelmed her, causing tears to gather in her eyes.

Instantly, Hillary's demeanor went from lighthearted to distressed. She took Kiya's hands in hers and kicked the door shut behind her. "Oh, honey, no. What's wrong? What did I say?"

Kiya sniffed, determined not to let the tears fall. "Is this stupid? Am I being selfish? It could ruin everything!"

Struggling to understand the reason behind the outburst, Hillary led Kiya over to the bed and made her sit. "What is going to be ruined?"

"All of this…" Kiya waved a hand at Hilly and the room in general. "You, Dylan, our friendships, everything. If I do this and things end badly with Jake, it will ruin it all. I don't want that to happen. Maybe it would be better to just leave things as they are."

Ah, now Hillary saw the problem. Kiya was afraid that if she opened herself up to Jake, she would not only be risking her friendship with him, but with all of them. "First of all, I think you are borrowing trouble where there isn't any yet and may never be. You and Jake get along great even under stressful circumstances. You're good together. We all see that. There is no reason to think that wouldn't continue and even grow stronger. I can assure you that Jake wouldn't be better off ignoring your feelings for each other, and I don't believe you would either. He really cares about you. Second, you're not only selling yourself short by thinking that you couldn't maintain a friendly relationship if things don't work out between the two of you, but the rest of us as well. Jake is not the kind of person that would ever interfere with you having relationships with us just because it didn't work with him. He wouldn't hurt you or us that way. You shared a bond with Dylan before you started having feelings for Jake, and that isn't going to disappear if either one of you decides a romantic relationship isn't working for you. Dylan is more than capable of caring for both of you, and so am I. I am your friend no matter what happens, okay? And I know I can speak for Gretchen too. We toasted to it, remember? You are stuck with all of us. You don't need to worry. Just focus on how wonderful it could be if things *do* work out." She gave Kiya a tight squeeze. "No more tears, okay?"

Kiya returned the hug. "No more tears…and thank you. This is just what I needed."

"I'll always be glad to lend an ear…and opinion." Hillary laughed. "Now, how about I help you get ready? I know just what you should wear."

****

Twenty minutes later, Kiya emerged onto the porch wearing a long-sleeved, form-fitting, beige cable-knit sweater dress that ended midway down her thighs. She had added buttery soft tights and low-heeled, knee-high boots. Her dark hair fell over her shoulders in soft waves. Hillary had taken great pleasure in being allowed to apply Kiya's artfully subtle makeup. The woman had kept up a happy chatter the entire time. Kiya was still feeling a little anxious, but her talk with Hillary helped put her more at ease. Kiya knew she wanted this chance with Jake. The rest would take care of itself.

Jake turned at the sound of her arrival. His eyes traveled slowly down the entire length of her, then back to her face. He stared at her but remained silent. After a moment or two of continued silence, Kiya started to fidget.

"Is this too much?" she asked, already mentally reviewing her wardrobe for something to change into.

She looked down at the dress and smoothed it down nervously. "I can change."

He moved toward her. "No, don't. You're beautiful." He captured a lock of her hair and twirled it around his finger. "When Hilly came down a little while ago to say that she had made you a few minutes late, the thought had crossed my mind to tease you about women's concept of time, but when you came out of that door looking like this…I forgot everything I was going to say. You take my breath away."

Her remaining doubts faded away with his words. Her face lit up. "I could say the same about you. You look very handsome. I'm used to seeing you in more rugged work clothes."

He, too, had changed for the evening. His dark-gray pants and white button-down shirt looked very stylish. It was an attractive contrast to his hard, muscular physique. The fabric of his shirt hugged the wide expanse of his shoulders and chest. He had his sleeves rolled up to his elbows exposing well-defined forearms and strong hands. Hillary had jokingly said that she should give Jake some "eye candy" this evening, but the same could definitely be said about him. It hadn't escaped her notice that Hillary had made a point to take the blame for Kiya's nerves and tardiness. The woman was a treasure. Mitch was a lucky man.

Jake laced his fingers through hers. "Walk with me."

Somewhat bemused but perfectly willing to just be with him, Kiya fell into step beside him. They strolled around the side of the house and across the yard toward the small cabin Kiya had recently inhabited. When they stopped outside of the door, Kiya looked up at him, not understanding why they were there.

"I promised you both safety and dinner for just the two of us." He leaned around her and pushed the door open. Inside, Kiya stopped and stared in wonder. The main room was bathed in the warm, shimmering glow of at least a dozen candles that were strategically placed around the cozy space in addition to a fire crackling in the fireplace. A small table was beautifully set for an intimate dinner for two. It was draped in a delicate cloth that fluttered in the breeze of the open door. A bottle of wine sat open and waiting at the center of the table. The air was filled with the spicy aroma of pasta sauce and the strains of soft music flowing in the background.

The romantic scene was so inviting that Kiya was utterly dumbfounded. She turned to Jake in amazement. "You did all of this yourself?"

"Do you like it?"

"Like it? Jake, it's wonderful. I love it. It's better than anything I could have imagined."

Delighted with her response, Jake ushered her into the cabin and shut the door. "I thought that after dinner maybe we could relax in front of the fire and watch a movie. I brought a variety down from the house. You can pick anything you like."

Jake guided Kiya to a seat at the table and went about setting out their dinner, which consisted of a colorful salad and savory lasagna. The latter, he informed her, was a frozen dish that Cade had prepared in advance for nights when everyone was too tied up with work to cook from scratch.

"I would have enlisted Margaret's help with the dinner since it was rather last minute and she would have loved the opportunity to fuss over our date menu, but for her safety, we asked her to steer clear of the ranch for a little while."

"That is probably a wise move. The less people at risk right now, the better. Besides, you did a wonderful job on your own. Plus, I get to sample Cade's famous lasagna." She clasped her hands together in anticipation. "There is nothing better than really good comfort food."

They enjoyed their meal at a leisurely pace. The conversation flowed effortlessly through a wide range of topics and interests. The ease of the rapport that they shared made the evening a delightful way to end their stress-filled day.

Kiya leaned back in her seat as she finished the last of her pie. She couldn't remember the last time she had felt this relaxed or happy. "I'm impressed. You certainly came through on your promise, right down to the pie. Which was excellent by the way. I will have to be sure to compliment both Hillary and Cade on their accomplishments, but it was you who made this night perfect. I'm glad we did this."

"The night isn't over yet," he reminded her.

Together, they tidied up the remains of their dinner then settled onto the couch. Kiya browsed through the DVDs Jake had brought over and selected a recently released action film she hadn't seen.

"A woman after my own heart," Jake complimented while he loaded the DVD player.

Kiya pulled off her boots, tucked her feet up beside her, and settled in close to Jake's side once he had returned to the couch. He curled an arm around her shoulders. The feeling of tranquility afforded by the meal, along with the cozy fire and Jake's warm body, lulled Kiya into a state of relaxed drowsiness. She relished in the sense of peace that enveloped her. Being with him like this felt completely right. It felt like home. She slid an arm across the firm muscles of his abdomen, hugging his middle. A contented sigh escaped her. Jake's hand moved rhythmically up her back then down again. The lazy motion seemed to be an unconscious gesture of affection and comfort. She savored the sensation.

Jake loved having her close to him, sharing moments like this with her. If his future could be filled with moments like this, he would be a happy man. "You sound like you're more inclined to take a nap than watch a movie," he teased in an amused voice.

"I'm simply enjoying the moment."

"It doesn't get much better than this, does it?"

Tipping her head back so that she could look at him, she shook her head. "No, I don't think it does."

Jake trailed his fingers along the underside of her jaw. He gazed deep into her eyes before lowering his head to stroke his tongue along the seam of her lips seeking entry. The slow, sensual glide of his lips across hers pulled a murmur of pleasure from her. Kiya's eyes drifted closed; her arm tightened around him. His exploration remained unhurried as he deepened the kiss. The arm around her shoulders cradled her against him. His lips moved tenderly over hers then shifted to follow a path down the smooth column of her throat. Kiya's hand trailed up over the defined contours of his torso to snake behind his neck. She pulled him close, as his mouth returned to hers, becoming bolder and more demanding.

Raw liquid heat coursed through Jake, causing his pulse to surge. A riot of heady sensations left him feeling shaken. Her unrestrained acceptance of his passion heightened his need to discover every touch, every caress that would bring her pleasure. He desperately wanted to feel her whole-hearted surrender to his need for her, for her to want to be with him as much as he wanted her. He allowed his desire to flare only briefly before easing back. He ran his hand down her arm and laced his fingers through hers. "Will you stay with me tonight?"

Kiya's eyes blinked open. "Here?"

Jake nodded. "Here."

She bit the side of her lip. "Don't you think it is rather obvious if we arrange for a date night then don't return to the house?"

Jake raised their intertwined hands to his lips and kissed the back of her hand. "Do you honestly think anyone would have a problem with the fact that we found a way to come together during all the upheaval in our lives?"

Kiya studied the intent expression on his face. She replayed her discussion with Hilly in her mind. "No, I don't."

He cupped her face in his hands and kissed her gently. "Then stay with me."

Her hesitation was brief. Leaning her forehead against his, she whispered, "I'll stay."

Relief and excitement flared simultaneously. Jake nuzzled his face into her neck to place a trail of nibbling kisses down to where her skin disappeared under the fabric at her neckline. "You have no idea how much I wanted to hear you say that."

The corners of Kiya's mouth edged upward. "I'm sure you can show me."

His eyes gleamed with playful warning. "Oh, I intend to."

"Before or after the movie?" Kiya tugged the ends of his shirt free from his waistband to slip her hands under the hem. Her fingers caressed the strong muscles along his spine.

"What movie?" he growled.

"You know, I have to admit, I haven't a clue as to what this show is about. I don't think I caught anything other than the title scene."

"That's okay, I have something much more interesting in mind." He distracted her with a mind-numbing kiss. His hands roamed over her with skillful purpose, stroking over her hip and down her leg. He let his palm glide past the bottom of her dress then tightened his grip around her stocking-covered thigh and retraced his way back up under her clothing. Both his hold and his mouth became more forceful as his thumb raked along her inner thigh.

A thrill of anticipation raced through her. Kiya curled her fingers around the back of his bicep, leaning into him and urging him closer. She breathed his name. With a groan, Jake released his hold on her and stood up. He grabbed the remote off the stand and turned off the TV and DVD player. Turning, he tossed the remote onto the couch then bent to scoop Kiya into his arms and stride toward the bedroom. At the threshold to the room, he stopped to give the bed a dubious once-over.

"I forgot about the smaller beds out here. Hopefully, I don't end up face down on the floor in the middle of the night," he groused.

Amusement danced in Kiya's eyes. "I'll join you if you do," she promised.

"Deal." He crossed the room to the edge of the bed where he set her on her feet. Bending to wrap an arm around her waist, he pulled her close to tease her lips with his. He savored the way her body seemed to mold itself into his. The way they came together felt as if they were made for each other. She fit perfectly in his arms.

Kiya reached between them and slowly released the buttons on his shirt until he was able to strip it off and toss it aside. Her gaze was drawn to the thin red line that scored his side. The set of three white steri-strips holding the edges of the wound together reminded her of his encounter earlier in the day.

"Jake…your ribs. Aren't you sore?"

His reply was tinged with disbelief. "Not nearly enough to make me want to stop. The tip of that knife barely grazed me. It would take a hell of a lot more than an ache in my ribs to keep me from loving you." To prove his point, he tugged her against the hard wall of his bare chest and slanted his mouth across hers in a searing assault that left her breathing labored and her body trembling. She completely forgot about his injured side.

He edged her dress up over her hips until his hands spanned her waist. His palms traced the curve of her hips. Craving the feel of his hands on her bare skin, she helped him pull the fabric over her head. When her dress had joined his shirt on the floor, he lowered her onto the bed. His lips and tongue teased the flesh of her abdomen, drifting lower as he stripped the tights from her body. A tingling sensation of awareness and need rippled along her skin. Fire settled low in her belly causing her to move restlessly against him. His fingers followed a tantalizing path up her body to release the front clasp of her bra and drew it away from her. He dropped the scrap of lace over the side of the bed before taking the exposed mounds into his hands and capturing one sensitive peak with his mouth.

Kiya gasped and tunneled her fingers into his hair to hold him to her. A fevered ache gripped her as he continued an unhurried exploration of her body and the reactions he could entice from her. His every touch had her straining for more. Her hands moved to caress his shoulders and down his back. The muscles tensed and flexed under her palms in reaction to their passage. She wanted the freedom to explore the hard planes and sculpted ridges of his form unencumbered, as he was doing to hers.

"You have me at a slight disadvantage here," she told him in a voice full of longing.

"I have you exactly where I want you," he countered. "But I am more than willing to accommodate you." He made quick work of shedding his remaining clothing and rejoining her. Jake stretched out next to her, drawing her body against his. His hand hooked around the back of her knee, guiding her leg up to curve over his. With slow, purposeful moves, they took pleasure in discovering each other. Soft sighs and low hums of pleasure were the only sounds in the dimly lit room. Passion built quickly until their caresses became urgent, impatient.

Kiya found herself seeking an elusive release to the needy tremors that racked her body. Wanting him to feel the same burning intensity she did, Kiya delighted in discovering new and interesting ways to return the pleasure he was giving her. She savored the knowledge of how easily she could get him to quiver under her touch or groan aloud at her mouth against his skin. She loved the taste of him, the sensation of his powerful body moving against hers.

Jake felt Kiya skim her fingers down his hip to his thigh only to ease her way between them and grip him intimately. His breath caught as a tremor shuddered through him. A low sound of hunger rumbled in his throat; he rolled her under him. The strength and depth of the feelings she aroused in him came as a surprise, but he didn't hide from them. He was in awe of the fact that she was here with him like this. Giving herself to him in the complete and unrestrained way he had imagined. The scent, the feel of her consumed him. She filled his senses until there was no room for anything else. Just her, and his desire to make her his. He should be reveling in this experience, this connection, and he was. But he found himself wanting, needing to know that she was giving him more than her body. That she was offering him more than just a physical connection but an emotional one as well. He wanted this to be a beginning of something more.

"Kiya, look at me," Jake urged, his voice raw. Heavy eyes, laden with desire met his. "Tell me that you're mine. That this is only the beginning."

Kiya's fingertips dug into the flesh at Jake's hips in frustration. Talk wasn't what she wanted at the moment. She rocked her hips toward his to entice him into action rather than answer. "Jake...please."

He remained positioned above her but didn't relent. "Tell me."

His eyes held an uncertainty, a doubt that she felt compelled to dispel. What she felt for him, what they felt for each other, was right. It was genuine and went deeper than she could have ever imagined. She cupped a hand at his jawline, running her thumb over his bottom lip. Holding his gaze, she nodded. "I'm yours, Jake."

He brought his mouth to hers in a caress that was both tender and possessive as he slowly sank into her, finally giving them what they both wanted.

Chapter 19

A shrill intermittent ringing roused Kiya from a deep sleep. Her slumber-clouded mind resisted the intrusion. Jake's weight shifted on the bed as he rolled onto his side, propping himself up on his elbow to reach for his clamoring cell phone. Stretching like a contented cat, Kiya paid little attention to the conversation being held next to her. She was reluctant to let go of the warm, contented cocoon enveloping her. She hadn't slept so soundly in a long time. Her nights tended to be filled with frequent bouts of sleeplessness ever since the day she had discovered Dylan injured and needing help. Scenes of gunfire, smoke, and car crashes dominated her dreams. None of that had plagued her the night before. She had felt safe wrapped in Jake's arms. She wasn't sure how she managed to feel so rested when Jake had repeatedly woken her throughout the night with a soft caress or the tantalizing glide of his lips and tongue on her skin. He was a skilled and demanding lover—her entire being felt sated and well loved.

Kiya turned onto her side, taking advantage of the opportunity to wrap an arm around Jake's waist and place soft kisses against his back. His free hand stroked down her forearm to rest over hers while he spoke into the phone. Fully awake now, she was able to catch more of Jake's side of the conversation. She rested her chin against his back. He must be talking to Mitch about today's schedule. The team of government agents was due to arrive this morning. A sigh rose within her. She wished they could ignore reality for a while longer. She was happy right where she was.

Jake concluded the call then shifted to face Kiya. A tender feeling of fulfillment flowed through him as he studied her. There was quiet joy reflecting in his eyes as he pressed his lips to hers. "Good morning, beautiful."

"Yes, it is. Even with the rather abrupt awakening." Her palms spread over the tempting contours of his torso before inching up to twine around his neck.

"Sorry about that. Mitch wanted to fill me in on what the Feds have in mind for the type of setup they think is needed to watch for signs of movement near the cabin. He is satisfied with the plan for the time being but says he wants our input and suggestions before they get started. The good news is that they won't be showing up out here until later." He ran a lazy hand over her hip. "How do you feel about breakfast?"

Leaning into his hand to capture his lips again, she snuggled closer. "At the moment, I think it is overrated." She trailed a finger along the ridge of his shoulder; her eyes followed the movement with a tantalizing gleam.

"Hmm, sounds like you might have something better in mind." The corners of his mouth edged upward. He liked her lighthearted, carefree side.

She lowered her voice to a mock whisper. "I have devised a plan of my own."

"This I have to hear." He nuzzled the hollow under her ear.

"I say we forget all about whichever three-letter acronym has shown up in Mitch's office, skip breakfast, and spend the rest of the day in bed, pretending the rest of the world doesn't exist." She cocked an eyebrow, giving him a beguiling grin.

"I have to admit, your plan holds a certain appeal," he said as if he was considering her words.

"Does that mean I could talk you into it?" She dragged her fingertips down his arm, then across his rib cage to his navel before she angled her exploration downward.

Jake gave a playful growl, pinning her under him. "At this point I think you could talk me into just about anything."

****

By the time Jake and Kiya arrived in the kitchen, breakfast had been cleared away, but everyone still lingered over coffee before tackling chores.

"About time you two showed up," Cade admonished mildly. "I thought I would end up having to toss all the leftovers to Luna." The dog's ears twitched in his direction when she heard her name, but still happy-danced her way over to Kiya, who bent to ruffle her fur in greeting. The dog didn't appear to be bothered at all by being left to spend time with her housemates.

Kiya focused on Luna while she struggled to settle her nerves. She wouldn't trade her time with Jake for anything, but that didn't alleviate the awkwardness she felt at greeting the entire group of them this morning. Being an only child and a loner hadn't prepared her for situations like this. She gave Luna a final pat and stood.

Jake easily picked up on her discomfort. He curled an arm around her waist from behind and kissed the back of her head. "Want to grab us some coffee?"

Kiya smiled over her shoulder at him. He was giving her something to do to help put her at ease. She moved to the coffee pot and filled a couple of mugs.

Dylan stepped over to tug at a lock of her hair. Holding out his cup, he winked at her. "Mornin', angel, how about a refill?" Kiya topped off his coffee then kissed his cheek. She understood that he was trying to reassure her also, with his show of support.

"Sorry, we were enjoying being lazy until Mitch called," Jake told Cade as he settled into a chair at the table. "But we would be happy to take any leftovers off your hands." He took the coffee mug Kiya offered him and thanked her before he told the others about the arrangements finalized during the early morning call, adding that they had until about eleven thirty before everyone was due to arrive at the ranch.

Cade placed plates of freshly warmed food in front of them while they all discussed the plans for the upcoming day. Despite his teasing, Cade had made sure to save them both a plate. He gave Kiya's shoulder a comforting pat. As she sipped at her cup, Kiya glanced up, catching Hillary watching her with a wicked gleam in her eyes. She raised her brows in question at the other woman's expression.

Hillary's face broke into a huge smile. "Together," she mouthed almost silently, reminding Kiya of their previous discussion on her relationship with Jake.

****

The hours passed quickly as everyone completed their morning chores. Before long, it was time to rendezvous with Mitch and the federal agents assigned to this case. At precisely eleven thirty, a battered, brown crew cab truck pulled to a stop near the main house. The man that stepped out was dressed in jeans with a casual shirt, rather than anything that might identify him as a Fed. He was on the shorter side of average, had a short fade crew cut, and was built like a battle tank. His sturdy frame sported a thick neck and bulging muscles that lent a bullish look to his already intense physical appearance. He didn't look like someone you would want to tangle with. Jake, his brothers, and Kiya were gathered near the entrance to the barn. As the agent approached, he held out a beefy hand to Jake, who was the closest to the newcomer.

"I am Special Agent Kent, DEA. I believe you are expecting me for a ride this morning. You have some unusual squatters that I am extremely interested in meeting. I've heard they have been giving you a pretty rough time of it lately."

Jake returned the man's firm handshake. "Yes, I confirmed your arrival with Mitch, sorry, Sheriff Patterson, this morning. We are happy to have your assistance. The past weeks have been stressful to say the least," he agreed before making introductions all around.

When Jake got to Dylan, the agent paused to study the younger man. "I am glad to see that you are recovering well. I understand you took one hell of a hit."

"One that I probably wouldn't have survived if it wasn't for Kiya," Dylan stated while gesturing in her direction. "It might even things up a bit if we can bring these bastards down, put an end to their operation for good."

"That's what we are here for...to make that happen," the agent assured him before turning to Kiya.

232

"Ms. James, you are a brave woman. You've had more than your fair share of close encounters since you arrived. I wouldn't be surprised if you were rethinking your decision to relocate here. Most people would have already packed up and headed right back where they came from."

Special Agent Jarod Kent led the DEA's team of five and had already been filled in on all the developments in the case along with the events that led up to their discovering the drugs. He was eager to get his people out to the cabin, get a lay of the land. He wanted to get eyes on the shipment that was currently waiting for retrieval. The scale of the operation being moved through this area was remarkable for a recent setup, not to mention well thought out and implemented. It indicated a tried-and-true method of operation that had been previously tested in other settings. Taking down this trafficking group would most likely have a greater impact than on just this one location.

Kent's DEA team would add to the sheriff's current routine by coordinating round the clock surveillance with additional men on-site and with sophisticated electronic equipment. Their goal was to deploy motion activated camera systems that instantly sent high resolution images to the command center and any cell phone indicated, in addition to vibration sensors inside the cabin that would detect human activity, and high-tech drones with night vision and heat sensors that would be launched if any activity was detected in the surrounding area or if tracking a suspect became necessary.

That technology would offer them the option of

both live-feed access and recorded data. The first thing on the agenda for the day was for Jake and his brothers to join the agents in searching the woods and structure for possible cameras or lookout positions already being used by the traffickers to monitor the comings and goings at the site. Since there had been no movement on the drugs since they were discovered, it was possible that they knew when people were in the area. If the surrounding vicinity was clean, they would then help determine the best locations to place their own equipment where it would be the least likely to be detected but still offer a quick response time.

Kent and Mitch decided it would have been far too conspicuous to drive a group of government vehicles onto the ranch then out into the surrounding fields, so before leaving the sheriff's office, the assembled team members had broken into smaller groups that would travel to the drop site, aka the cabin, via different routes. Mitch took a couple of agents with him to the old hunting trail while his deputy, Jenkins, would guide a couple more in from the path Kiya had taken the day she had discovered Dylan. Jake and his brothers would take the most direct route by riding out on horseback cross country with Agent Kent.

It was their hope that if the ranch was being watched, the multiple access points and only one added male figure out on a ride wouldn't draw too much unwanted attention. Everyone involved would keep things as low key as possible. The horses they would use had already been selected and were quickly saddled. As the men prepared to mount up, Jake pulled Kiya aside and gave her a light kiss. "You and Hilly keep an eye on each other. We'll be back as soon as we can."

Agent Kent reached into his pocket and withdrew a card, handing it to Kiya. "Sheriff Patterson informed me that he would still have a man here on the grounds keeping an eye on things around the house, so you and Ms. McCleary won't be totally on your own. My personal cell number is on the back of that card. Keep it handy so you will have another way to contact any one of us if you need to."

Kiya thanked him and waved the men off before returning to the house. Hillary was just disconnecting a call when Kiya walked through the side door.

"They left?" Hillary asked, then continued at Kiya's nod. "I was just talking to Mitch. I meant to go out and meet the new guy, but I guess I will get a chance to do that later. I needed to hear Mitch's voice more. I wish I could have seen him this morning, but I realize that he was needed elsewhere. He has a job to do, but I still would have liked to spend at least a few minutes with him. The arrival of the DEA seems to have upped the stakes, ya know? I mean, the danger was real before, but the government coming in to *take down the bad guys* pushed it to a whole new level for me."

"Yeah, I understand. I never could have imagined being in a situation like this. It is both completely surreal and all *too* real, at the same time. The thought of our guys running around out there like Rambo, hunting down an elusive yet deadly enemy, gives me the chills. Too many things could go wrong. As for Special Agent Kent, I think you will find him to be an interesting guy. He looks like he could wrestle a small rhino to the ground singlehanded, but he seems very pleasant and compassionate."

"Our guys. I like that. It sounds like something Gretchen would say. I talked to her too, by the way. She is having a tough time dealing with being separated from us during all this. She doesn't like hearing about our plans and what is happening through the delay of distance; it is driving her crazy. She suggested that you and I pack a bag, hop on the next flight out, and stay with her for a while." Hillary held up a hand when she saw Kiya shaking her head as she started to protest. "I'm not any more willing than you are to leave right now, but I understand why she suggested it. At least this new agent sounds like a good person to have on our side."

To keep themselves busy doing something productive, the women settled in to do some sleuthing of their own. Hours later, after digging through extensive online sources and making dozens of calls, they gave up in defeat. Hillary snapped her laptop shut in frustration. Neither of them had been able to come up with any further usable information on Kennedy. It was as if the man hadn't existed until about six years ago. It seemed like he had materialized out of nowhere when he started his company. The man had only the most generic of company websites or bios, no education or hometown info listed, no business referrals or associations, and no social media presence. After an exhaustive search, his online presence felt like it was merely a front, a display with nothing to back it up. As Mitch had mentioned before, he had made some purchase inquiries on local land, but no one involved had taken him up on the offers, and no one knew anything about the man himself or what he planned to do with the properties he wanted.

The only thing of value that the women had been able to piece together through phone calls, email, and internet searches was that the tracts of land Kennedy had been interested in were all laid out in a meandering, yet relatively straight line across three counties neighboring the Five M. As far as they could tell, a total of five separate property owners had been contacted with offers to purchase all or pieces of their land. When Kiya suggested that they find each of those locations on a map, a pattern became obvious. The Five M and the neighboring Billings' property made up the majority of the land involved, outside of the state game land areas, but when the other three locations were included, a clear path led across the entire region. Together, they would make the perfect supply chain for a drug running operation.

"This could explain why Kennedy has it out for me, personally," Kiya surmised thoughtfully. "Not only was I a witness when Dylan was shot and intervened to lend aid, but I also took over land he clearly wanted for his operation. The property bordering yours. The attack at my place might not have only been about Dylan. Kennedy might have been trying to scare me out of the area completely. Then he might have been able to coerce the Billings into selling." Her lips turned up in a conspiratorial smile. "It must have *really* annoyed him when his actions accidentally brought us all together instead. Us joining forces because of it must have infuriated him beyond belief."

Hillary grinned in unrepentant agreement. She tapped a spot on the map they had printed. "I know the man that owns this section. He would be more likely to shoot anyone that went near his property rather than not. He is an ornery old codger that dislikes people in general. He wouldn't take too kindly to interference from a nosy outsider, and certainly wouldn't sell to one. He keeps a free-roaming pack of equally disagreeable dogs. I doubt Kennedy would have put much effort into obtaining that land."

"What's this?" Kiya asked after skimming her gaze farther across the map.

Hillary leaned closer. "An old rural airstrip. Nothing more than some privately owned Cessnas and crop dusters ever went in or out of there. It's too small."

Kiya's brow wrinkled in thought. "It's not all that far off the route Kennedy was pursuing, and it's the only thing of interest anywhere out that far. What if that is where the drugs are being transported to? I doubt there would be a lot of official oversight at a place like that. It might be worth mentioning when everyone gets back."

****

Evening was turning the sky dark and the air cold when the men finally returned to the house. They hadn't found anything to indicate how the ranch was being watched, but with the help and equipment brought in by the other groups, they had been able to place their own gadgetry. The entire area around the cabin was now under twenty-four-hour surveillance. Cameras were even deployed at Kiya's place since it was now vacant and a prime area for people to try and cross onto the Five M undetected. A command center was already up and running in the meeting room of the municipal building in town. All of the monitoring feeds were routed directly to that location. Necessary alerts could be sent remotely to both Agent Kent's and Mitch's cell phones.

Shortly after the men had ridden in, Mitch arrived in his truck. Everyone in their respective groups had done as much as they could for the day; everyone was ready for some downtime. After the others had disbanded, Mitch had left for the ranch. He helped take care of the horses, then they all trooped into the kitchen to warm up over coffee. It had been a grueling day despite the lack of hard physical labor. To their delight, not only was hot coffee waiting for them, but a giant pot of beef stew was also ready to be dished out. Kiya and Hillary had anticipated the arrival of cold, hungry men after the long day spent outside and had prepared accordingly. Though some would have found the task tedious or menial, Kiya had enjoyed the feeling of having others to care for while being able to provide comfort with such a small gesture.

As the men helped themselves to the meal, the two women hovered nearby, waiting for everyone to grab what they wanted before peppering them with questions. Agent Kent smiled in gratitude when he was encouraged to join the others.

"Not a bad way to end the day, in my book," the agent commented as he took a place at the table, food in hand. "It is rare to get a decent meal in the evenings when we are on a job like this, let alone a homemade one. You are all lucky to have such a support group. Your family is unique in today's world."

"Family is very important to us. It is central to who we are, and our closest friends become extended family. As you might be able to tell from the assembled group," Cade told the agent as he gave Mitch a brotherly shove when he blocked Cade's path to the table by stopping to wrap Hillary in a hug.

Talk quickly turned to the events and progress of the day. Even though they hadn't discovered how the drug runners knew so much about the ranch's day-to-day operations or its occupants, a lot had been accomplished in a relatively short amount of time. Waiting for the inevitable next encounter would be the hard part.

When the subject turned to how Kiya and Hillary had spent their day, they took turns and sometimes finished each other's sentences as they described their findings, or lack thereof, during the course of their day. "No one using the name Preston Kennedy, or any variation of that name, is registered at any nearby hotels. The man is a ghost. He is seen or heard only when he wants to be, then disappears without a trace," Kiya stated in frustration. "Even the number listed on the card he handed out when he showed up here goes directly to a remote digital voicemail box only. It can be accessed from anywhere by anyone that has the pin number. There is no indication that his company employs any full-time staff or occupies any tangible address or location," Kiya informed them.

"As for the properties he was interested in, there are two remaining pieces of property that we can't rule out as possible locations still of interest to Kennedy. Only one that might be vacant or usable, other than Kiya's, that is," Hillary supplied while retrieving a thin folder containing all the printed information they had been able to piece together. She picked it up off the counter and handed it to Agent Kent. It held maps, land deed information from public records, notes from calls they had made, and a list of the types of searches done and databases they had accessed. They had a duplicate file for Mitch. It wasn't much, but they wanted to contribute anything they could to ending this once and for all. "Kiya discovered an interesting detail, however. Tell them where you think the trail leads," Hillary urged her with a nudge.

Everyone's gaze shifted back to Kiya with interest. "It may turn out to be a coincidence, but if you map out each of the properties Kennedy showed an interest in and plot a course beyond them, it leads to a tiny airstrip basically in the middle of nowhere. If these people crossed the state line via the established route through this area, using remote locations like ours, then transferred the drugs onto a small prop plane at that airfield, they could easily make a much longer, easier jump to just about anywhere for the next leg. Of course, that is assuming Kennedy and his interest in local land are tied to the drugs, which there is no proof of. Maybe Slade is the one responsible for the drugs."

Dylan looked pensive as he considered her comment. "It's possible, of course, but Slade doesn't strike me as an idea man or someone that coordinates an operation of this scale. He seems more like the hired muscle without a conscience type to me. Besides, if Seth is to be believed, there is someone higher up the food chain that Slade is reporting to and taking orders from. I still say Kennedy is our man."

"My agents are delving into the backgrounds of everyone that might be even remotely connected to this case. Sheriff Patterson has already given us quite a bit to go on; with this additional data I should have a better handle on the players involved very shortly. I appreciate everyone's efforts and insight. It is invaluable in a situation like this. We will add the airfield and remaining properties to our list of places to watch for unusual activity. If the amount of drugs in the shipment that was intercepted is an average load, and they make a run every couple of weeks...that is a significant enterprise. I doubt they just bunny hop from property to property endlessly. It's too risky, especially with opposition from the locals. The airport is a good possibility," Agent Kent assured them. "For now, I am going to thank you for this lovely meal and suggest you all relax for the rest of the night. You've earned it." He said his goodbyes, then returned to town.

****

Jake sighed as he settled onto the couch next to Kiya while she browsed through the channel guide on TV. He tucked her in under his arm, letting his head lean back to rest. Time to relax with Kiya was exactly what he needed. He had missed her company today and looked forward to spending time with her now. Even if it was just lounging in front of the TV. The family had drifted away to pursue their own activities for the evening after dinner had been cleared away and barn chores were done. Wanting to spend whatever time she could with him, Hillary had left with Mitch to spend the night in town at his place. If she wasn't safe there, she wasn't safe anywhere, Hillary told them. Mitch would drop her off in the morning before he started his shift. Dylan and Cade were more than happy to retire to their rooms for the night, which left Jake and Kiya alone in the main living room.

Jake rubbed absently at Luna's belly with his foot as she sprawled out at their feet with her legs in the air.

Something Agent Kent said that morning was still niggling at him. "You like it here, don't you?" Kiya glanced up at him in surprise at the question. "I mean, here as in this state, this town. If we weren't wrapped up in this craziness, you would be happy you moved here, right? You aren't considering leaving?"

Thinking back to determine what could have prompted him to ask, Kiya caught on to the reason behind Jake's question. At the time, the comment from Agent Kent had surprised her, even though it shouldn't have. It's true that almost anyone else would have been second-guessing themselves by now, but even with everything they were dealing with, the thought of leaving had never crossed her mind. She loved the land—its rugged natural beauty—and she had found a sense of belonging here that she had never experienced before. She felt at home in this community, with its people. Even if she couldn't return to the pretty little farmhouse she had rented, she would find a way to remain in the area. She wouldn't allow herself to be chased out of the one place she found that she wanted to call home. Which is exactly what she told Jake.

He tightened his arm around her shoulders and placed a kiss above her ear. "I'm glad you feel that way because there is no way I'm letting you go that easy. You are a part of us now, and you *do* belong here. I've never been more certain about anything. In fact, why don't we head upstairs, and I will do my best to prove it to you?" he suggested in invitation.

Kiya wanted nothing more than to join him and spend the night content in his arms, but she hesitated. It was daunting enough starting a new relationship in these circumstances without doing it under the watchful eyes of a house full of his family. "I want that, I really do…but it might not be the best idea. Our lives are so complicated right now, and it is hardly a normal way to start seeing someone. Maybe we should take things slow. We wouldn't even be together like this if it wasn't for what happened to Dylan. I don't want to feel like I'm taking advantage of you or this arrangement. I don't want anyone else thinking that either."

The corners of Jake's mouth quirked up at the thought of her taking advantage of him. Personally, he couldn't find anything wrong with the idea, no matter what the circumstances. Still, he wanted to reassure her. "Anyone that knows you would never think that, and nobody else's opinion matters. It isn't taking advantage to accept something freely offered, especially when it is something that I want too. We all want you here; you know that." He tipped her head up to capture her lips. "For the record, I hereby give you permission to use me to your advantage anytime you wish."

"You're shameless." She laughed, snuggling closer.

"Entirely possible, but I know a good thing when I see it, no matter how it came about. I'm willing to give you some time and space if that is what *you* really want. Not because of what anyone else might think. If you are more comfortable at the cabin for now, I'm okay with that too. As long as I can be there with you."

"I kind of like the idea of having you all to myself at the cabin for a while. I know it's still on the ranch, but it feels different. Like it's just us."

"Just us sounds good." He stood, holding out his hand. "It would be my pleasure to escort you to the cabin."

Smiling, she placed her hand in his.

Chapter 20

Two days later, tensions were running high among the members of the DEA and Mitch's department alike. During the night, alerts had been sent to their phones indicating that someone was approaching the hunting shack. Men positioned near the cabin engaged in a brief but fruitless chase of a single rider on a dirt bike who quickly lost them on the steep hills of the neighboring game lands. Even the drones had been unable to keep the rider in sight when he used the dense cover of evergreens to conceal his retreat.

Mitch's palms slapped against the conference table in front of him with frustration as he processed the details from the night before. Surrounding him were members of Agent Kent's group, a few of his own deputies, and the McCleary brothers. A meeting had been called to discuss their next course of action. He shook his head. "One thing is certain—we have lost the advantage of surprise. After last night, our suspects undoubtedly know that the location is under surveillance, yet we can't even ID the guy on the bike, where he came from or where he went. We are right back where we started with nothing to show for it."

They had spent the last hour reviewing the images taken by various cameras and the drone video. All they had were blurry images of an average-sized rider wearing a helmet with a face shield in addition to a video showing a human-shaped heat signature weaving in and out of view as the drone hovered overhead until the bike disappeared altogether under dense foliage.

"So, what are our options?" Jake wanted to know. "Surely, they aren't going to risk another attempt for a single shipment. Everyone involved is probably already long gone."

"Not necessarily," Agent Kent argued, sliding a folder to the middle of the table. "I believe your assumptions about Preston Kennedy may be correct. I have the results from the search into his background, business dealings, along with any known associates. What we found wasn't conclusive, but it sure is interesting reading. It also lends credence to your theory that he could be involved with an operation like this. I'll cover the highlights for you, but that copy is for your records," Kent said to Mitch. "First off, the ladies were right. Preston Kennedy is an alias.

"The man didn't exist until rather recently. He was born as Peter Kellerman who has a sealed juvie file that we can't access without just cause. In those early years, there were allegations of emotional and physical abuse within the home. We have copies of hospital files showing suspicious injuries, an investigation into his parents citing neglect and endangerment, followed by their subsequent death certificates, things of that nature. He had a few run-ins with law enforcement for underage drinking, minor drug possession, but he almost did jail time for assault with a deadly weapon when he went after someone with a lead pipe, but he got off on a technicality.

"When he was released, he dropped out of sight for years. Then he shows up again out of the blue with a whole new persona, flaunting lots of money no one can account for, expensive clothes, fancy cars, you get the idea. He changes his name, sets up his business, then starts buying and selling properties all across the U.S. His business records are clean and appear legit, but there are rumors of ties to known cartel members with dealings in not only drugs, but human trafficking, murder for hire, and extortion. None of which can be substantiated or proven. Our psychologist at the home office seems to think he fits the profile for something like this. The information she has seen leads her to believe that he likely suffers from delusions of grandeur."

"Meaning he has a massive superiority complex." Dylan sneered. "We have seen some of that ourselves. It's as if he presumes everyone will bow down to his every whim. He expects everyone to do exactly as he wants, just because he wants it."

"Which could play to our favor," Mitch said thoughtfully. "Somebody like that isn't going to want to allow a few local cops and a bunch of ranchers to get the best of him. He may not know about the DEA's involvement yet. That means he won't run; he'll stick around to get what he wants."

"If he spent any of that time away being groomed by a cartel or some other similar organization, and he now has a position of power running drugs here, it would only add to his ideology that he is superior, untouchable. It would make him dangerous. It is no secret that there has even been a rise in legal marijuana growers, with all the appropriate permits, deciding that they aren't generating enough revenue with the intense regulations involving propagation and the limited supply allowed, that is sent to dispensaries. A fair number of them started growing additional, unreported crops to sell on the black market to boost their income. Some gave up the idea of legal production altogether, choosing instead to take their chances with the more lucrative venture of growing for and transporting to states where it is still illegal to either grow or sell. These people can be absolutely ruthless when it comes to protecting their supply chains. Which leads me to a man we *can* track and identify."

Kent flipped open a second folder before pushing it toward the middle of the table. "Meet Tyson Slidell aka 'Slade.' I had a copy of your suspect sketch run through our database. Now, this guy has a rap sheet a mile long. Theft, possession, breaking and entering, assault, smuggling, you name it. Slade is basically a thug for hire. If there is money involved, there isn't much he *wouldn't* do. He is known for being malicious. He enjoys what he does. Where he shows up, mayhem follows. One fact I thought you all might be interested in is that he was the sole suspect in an arson investigation a few years ago involving a fatality. There wasn't enough evidence in the case to file formal charges."

"So, he is the one most likely to have started our fire. No surprise there, question is...how do we stop them now that they know the cabin is compromised?" Cade huffed. The entire situation was exasperating. It was inconceivable that they had found themselves in the middle of a drug operation. What they were dealing with sounded more like a movie plot rather than real life. It was maddening.

Dylan, who had resorted to pacing back and forth

while Kent laid out Slade's history, suddenly pulled up short. A thoughtful look crossed his face before it settled into a devious smile. "We use their pride and ego against them." Nodding as the thought took shape, he continued, "Kennedy believes that he is smarter, more cunning, and more capable than we are. Slade was confident enough to hide under our very noses. Arrogance just might be the 'Achilles heel' of the entire setup. Kennedy called me directly to imply that our recent so-called hardships should have us ready to sell, to relent, and cooperate with his proposal. What if I return the favor? I could call him, leave a message suggesting that his efforts are lackluster, ineffective. I let him know we are on to him and find his attempts at persuasion uninspiring. If he is as self-absorbed as we think he is, taunting him with being unimaginative and insufficient should set him off enough to trigger a response. At the very least, it will tick him off enough to keep him here, keep him engaged in the outcome of the operation. Even if it is just to teach us a lesson."

It didn't take long for the others to start nodding in agreement. It could work. It was risky to antagonize a man like Preston Kennedy, but they had to bring this to a close. They needed to draw him out of hiding. It wasn't enough to just chase them out of town or off the ranch. Kennedy would simply start again in some other unsuspecting town, putting other families at risk. No, it needed to end here. The next half hour was spent discussing the wording that would garner the swiftest reaction. They all concurred that Dylan would be the one to reach out. He had been the first target and had the most interactions with the man. The call would be placed that very evening from the ranch. Then, the only thing left to do would be to wait and see if their plan worked the way they needed it to.

****

Preston Kennedy clutched the cell phone in his hand in a death grip before giving in to the urge to launch it into a nearby wall. He was only mildly mollified by the forceful crack that resulted as it shattered then dropped to the ground. The screen was spiderwebbed with cracks; a few small shards of glass had dislodged to lie next to it on the floor. Chest heaving, he stared at the offending device. *How dare he? Who does McCleary think he is to mock me? He is a nobody! I could buy and sell him a hundred times over. No one can insult me, criticize me like that, and get away with it. I will crush the lot of them under my heel like the insects they are. Compared to me those men are nothing, nothing*! Rage simmered through him as he plotted out his next moves. The message left on his voicemail replayed through his mind, inciting him further. The McClearys and anyone else in this town that stood in his way would feel the wrath and power he had at his disposal. He wouldn't allow some backwoods farm boys to get the best of him. It didn't matter that they had the local law at their beck and call. He would show them all that he would not be trifled with.

****

Jake sat staring at the computer screen in front of him, willing himself to relax, to focus on the task at hand. This was his least favorite part of running the ranch. Paperwork, spreadsheets, and countless hours spent behind a desk to keep everything running smoothly. With all the events that had transpired lately, these mundane things were starting to pile up. He should be grateful for the time to get caught up this morning, but only a couple of hours in, he was already getting restless from the relative inactivity. He would take hard physical labor over this kind of stuff any day. His muscles twitched with the suppressed desire to stretch and move. He shifted enough to relieve his cramped muscles, rolled his stiff neck, and blew out a breath. Frustration rippled through him. In truth, it wasn't just the office work that had him stressed. More than twenty-four hours had passed since Dylan had left a carefully devised yet scathing message on Kennedy's voicemail, but they still hadn't gotten any kind of response. Everyone was getting edgy; they needed to make some headway in this case, and soon.

If Kennedy was as egotistical as they thought he was, that message should have produced some kind of reaction. Maybe they were going about this all wrong and were wasting precious time.

Unable to sit still any longer, Jake pushed to his feet. The house was too quiet. Dylan was in town with Mitch at the station. Kiya and Hillary had work of their own to contend with, and Cade was taking his turn with Agent Kent's men patrolling the woods near the cabin. Everything was business as usual, except that it wasn't.

When the office phone interrupted his pacing, Jake was glad for the distraction. He leaned across the desk to grab the receiver. "Five M, Jake McCleary."

"Not the brother I was hoping for, but you will do for now," a smooth voice responded to his greeting. "Although, you should know that I will take great pleasure in making Dylan pay for his insolence. You all will. In the meantime, it will be your job to make sure there are no further delays in me getting exactly what I want. I'm done playing."

"Kennedy." A burst of adrenaline made Jake's heart rate jump. This was what they had been waiting for. Preston Kennedy was finally showing his hand. The man's voice practically dripped with arrogant disdain. *This man's ego is going to be his downfall. I'm going to make sure of it.* "You sound a little put out, Mr. Kennedy. Business in our little burg not to your liking? As you have already seen, we aren't overly impressed with your antics. We do not respond well to threats either. Neither you nor your so-called *business* are welcome here. This land and everything, everyone on it is ours. So is this town. We protect what is ours. You can go to Hell."

Barely controlled rage echoed loud and clear across the phone line. "Mind your tongue, McCleary, or I will have it removed! It takes only a snap of my fingers to have it done. You have no idea who you are dealing with, but I will be happy to enlighten you. We both know that you have something of mine on that precious land of yours…I want it back."

"Then you are going to have to come get it. If you are man enough to do your own dirty work. So far, sending your lap dog to do your bidding hasn't been all that effective." Jake pressed the button to disconnect the call. He wished he could see the other man's reaction to the abrupt dismissal. A man like Kennedy had to be downright seething at an affront like that. *He is going to make a play for those drugs as soon as he can arrange it. He won't be able to resist.*

It was time to call Agent Kent. The decision had been made early on not to waste resources on trying to tap the phones. They already knew that Kennedy only used phones that were untraceable and disposable. They wouldn't find him that way. They would be better off casting a wide net of surveillance over the ranch and the surrounding area. Mitch had some men in plain clothes keeping an eye on things around town for any unusual activity too, but now, everyone needed to remain vigilant. When Kennedy went after his shipment, they would be ready.

Chapter 21

Mitch tried to tune out the whiny voice of an irate visitor who was recounting every detail of how someone had backed into him at the corner gas station. A deputy listened patiently while the man embellished his story with gestures and at times, using his whole body to demonstrate the cars movements. From what Mitch could discern, no damage had been done to either vehicle, but the guy was adamant that he should file a complaint.

With a sympathetic smile for the officer, he gave the two men a wide berth on his way into the meeting room. He greeted the agent currently manning the computer equipment that took up most of the table. A quick scan of the monitors and feeds showed him that everything was operating as expected and there wasn't anything that needed his attention. Everyone was operating on high alert after Jake received the phone call from Kennedy yesterday. Satisfied that the agent on duty had a handle on everything here at the station, Mitch decided to take some time for a real meal at the diner, rather than the usual sandwich at his desk or in front of the monitors.

He took his time strolling down the block, enjoying the quiet that came with the encroaching darkness. There was little happening in town at this hour. Most of the townsfolk were at home preparing for their own dinner. The streets and sidewalks were almost empty. Pulling in a long, deep breath, Mitch felt himself begin to relax. It felt good to breathe in the cold, clean air. The quiet stillness alleviated some of the tension that had been plaguing him in recent days. All too soon, he arrived at the door to the diner. He chose a vacant seat facing the door and smiled at the waitress when she quickly appeared with hot coffee. He gladly accepted the fragrant brew but refused the laminated menu. He knew the contents by heart. His decision was easy since the special of the day was pot roast. The hearty meal had always been one of his favorites. When his order was placed, he pulled out his phone to check his email. He hadn't been as diligent with keeping his inbox clear lately as he should have been.

Scrolling through numerous lines of unopened mail, Mitch scanned for names and businesses that would indicate a message that needed immediate attention. There wasn't much to hold his interest. His thumb was still casually flicking past nonurgent notifications when a jarring boom reverberated through the air, rattling the utensils on the surrounding tables. Startled glances passed between the patrons of the diner before some, including Mitch, hurried to the door to locate the source of the sound.

It didn't take long to spot the location of the disturbance when a fiery cloud of smoke and debris still billowed upward from an all too familiar building. Shock hit his system like a physical blow, causing him to stumble as he reached the sidewalk outside. His eyes widened in disbelief when he saw flames rising from the roof of the station he had just left. The sight spurred him into action. He instructed the dazed onlookers to remain where they were so that emergency personnel could access the scene as he gingerly maneuvered his way through the stunned crowd. As he shifted people out of his way, he noticed the waitress as she stared at the devastation. He called out a hasty, "Cancel my order," then sprinted down the street.

****

Snow was starting to fall, and the sky was beginning to dim as Kiya and Hillary made their way to the barn. With the guys out patrolling various locations, the evening chores fell to them. As far as work went, it was a pleasant kind of task. The familiar routine of cleaning the stalls and feeding horses passed quickly as they worked and chatted. At the last stall, Kiya filled Dax's hay rack, then lingered to run a hand along his flank, giving him a gentle pat. The animal returned the attention by turning his head to nuzzle her hair, nickering softly. Hillary refilled the water bucket next to the door, watching them. She leaned against the doorframe. "Boy, he's a lover, isn't he?"

Kiya's lips turned up in an indulgent smile as she ruffled the horse's forelock. "He certainly is. There isn't a mean bone in his body, and he is more affectionate than most of the men I've dated."

"I won't tell my brother that you said that. Although I would love to see his reaction to having to live up to the standards of a horse." Her amusement was obvious.

"I appreciate your restraint." Kiya chuckled.

"On second thought..." Hillary's words cut off at a heavy thud against the back side of the barn.

Kiya jumped. She glanced around, confused. The noise hadn't sounded like a horse kicking the wall or something falling over. It had sounded as if something had struck the outside of the building with quite a bit of force. Sharing a look of concern with Hillary, she hastily secured Dax's door. "Maybe it is Deputy Jenkins, or the agent assigned to guard the house." Even to her own ears, the words sounded doubtful.

"We're done here anyway. Maybe we should check it out before we head in." Hillary didn't sound any more confident than Kiya did. Still, Kiya nodded at the tentative suggestion. Together, they left the barn, circling around the outside to the back wall where the noise had originated. They could hear Luna barking from inside the house. Something had the dog on alert. Kiya was relieved when, at first, she didn't see anything out of the ordinary. She released a breath she didn't realize she had been holding. Hillary's startled gasp had it catching again.

Deputy Jenkins was lying, slumped over against the side of the barn, unconscious. He had no obvious wounds, but when they rushed to his side and checked his pulse, they could not bring him around. They eased him onto his back. There was no way that he could have collapsed on his own with enough force to have caused the noise that had gotten their attention. It appeared as if he might have been ambushed from behind.

Kiya ran her hand around the back of the man's neck as carefully as she could. Sure enough, there was a large lump swelling on the base of his skull. Her fingers came away damp with blood. He was going to be disoriented and have one heck of a headache when he woke up. Glancing around nervously for whomever might have caused the man's injuries, Kiya whispered, "We need to get him up and into the house, now. He needs medical attention, and I don't want to run into the person that did this. Once we get inside, you can call Mitch while I make sure the house is locked up tight. Mitch can get both an ambulance en route and more people out here to find out what is going on. We can check the cameras too."

"What about Agent Kent's man? What's his name? Sullivan? He's supposed to be on the ranch today too. Where's he?" Her voice was quiet, but shaky.

"We can worry about that a little later. Right now, I want to get somewhere safe and call in the cavalry." Kiya's heart sank as she watched Hillary's eyes widen while staring past her.

"I can guarantee, the cavalry won't get here in time to save you. They are going to be very busy for a while. A homemade pipe bomb and a bag of accelerant is taking care of that. It's amazing what a person can do with some PVC and a bit of black powder. Not my best work, but it will get the job done. As for *Agent* Sullivan, was it? He won't be coming to the rescue either. I made sure that he couldn't interfere. Now, stand up and turn around."

Kiya slowly rose to her feet and moved to stand next to Hillary. She turned to face the owner of the menacing, yet eerily familiar, voice. She was not at all surprised to find Slade standing behind her with a gun pointed at her head. Hillary clutched at her arm. Kiya placed her own hand over Hillary's to lend support even as she glared at the man in front of her. "You again."

"You remember our little chat. How sweet."

"I remember more than that. I remember hearing you and Seth talking after you shot Dylan, and I remember seeing you leave in his ratty blue truck. You aren't going to get away with any of this."

Slade's jaw tightened, and his lip curled slightly when he realized that she had witnessed more that day than he thought. "I've heard that before. Many times, in fact. But dealing with problems like you, or even McCleary and his band of merry men, is my specialty. I will enjoy proving you wrong. Now, we are going for a ride," Slade informed them. "And you won't give me any trouble, because if you do, I will make you regret it. I am saying that for your benefit, not mine. As far as I'm concerned, I can't think of anything I would like more than to show you exactly what I am capable of. Unfortunately, I have been instructed to deliver you relatively unscathed if possible. It is up to you at this point what *relatively* means. Annoy me, and the decision becomes mine."

****

Kent stared through his binoculars at the tiny airstrip laid out in front of him. The only building in sight was dark and desolate. Weeds crowded the edges of the dilapidated runway and pushed their way out of every available crack crisscrossing the uneven pavement. If this place was being used by anyone, it sure didn't show through appearance alone. Which is exactly why he was still sitting here. If someone wanted to move drugs or perform any other nefarious activity, this was the perfect place to do it from. He couldn't fault Ms. James in her reasoning there. Still, by all appearances, this place hadn't been used in years. The first time he had driven out here, he had been skeptical that anyone would be daring enough to use it. Now, after a couple nighttime visits and some scouting of the property, he felt more confident the place was worth keeping an eye on. No matter what the outward appearance was, the runway was usable, and the interior of the tiny hangar building had been a little too tidy and uncluttered compared to the ruin of outside. It was an ideal spot to hide a small aircraft, or any vehicle, away from prying eyes. *Heck, if I wanted to trade the law for a life of crime, I would be tempted to use it myself.* He settled more comfortably against the back of his seat while reaching for his thermos. A jolt of caffeine might make this endeavor a little more tolerable.

He poured the dark, rich brew into the cup secured under the lid and sighed in appreciation at his first swallow. Dusk was approaching, making it a little harder to see the full landscape surrounding the airfield. Darkness would make the chances of catching any unusual human movements harder, but it would also help conceal his own presence in the area. So far, he hadn't seen any movement of *any* kind. Of course, it was totally possible that the place was exactly as it appeared to be, an abandoned relic of bygone days. His gut was telling him otherwise.

Sipping at his coffee, he dialed the number for the agent he had assigned to watch the security feeds at the station. If there was anything of interest coming in, Kent knew the man would alert him instantly, but it wouldn't hurt to keep the guy on his toes. Mildly surprised when the connection wouldn't go through, he tossed his phone onto the seat next to him. Way out here, he supposed the coverage would often be spotty or intermittent. He made a mental note to try again later.

The muffled thrum of a distant engine drew his attention back to the view outside his window. He sat up straighter to place his cup on the dash of the vehicle, then grabbed the binoculars again. The landscape remained unchanged even after panning back and forth across his field of view twice. The sound grew louder, closer. The outline of a small plane took shape in the sky as it approached, lining itself up for a landing. What appeared to be a single engine Cessna flew in low and dark. As it neared the runway, landing lights alone illuminated the paved strip in front of the plane.

No airplane conducting a normal flight would have come in so low without any beacon or strobe lights. There were no visible markings or numbers identifying the craft that he could see. It was apparent that this individual wanted *no* attention focused on their activities. That meant it was someone he was interested in talking to.

Kent reached overhead and made sure the dome light was switched off so that it wouldn't give away his location, then he grabbed his phone. He exited his vehicle and circled around the derelict hangar to approach the aircraft from behind once it stopped.

The Cessna touched down with a brief squawk of rubber against asphalt, then rapidly slowed. The landing lights switched off while the plane moved toward the building using only the taxi light. It obviously wasn't the pilot's first time completing these maneuvers.

Hunkered down next to the side of the hangar, Kent cursed his phone silently when his call to the station still would not go through. He made sure the device was set to vibrate, as was his habit, before shoving it into his pocket and pulling his weapon. *Guess I'm on my own. That plane better not be carrying a crew of armed men, or this isn't going to go well.*

He waited until the craft stopped moving before he left his hiding spot, slowly edging toward the Cessna and its unknown occupants. To his relief, only the pilot climbed out. A glance inside on his way past the cockpit confirmed that the remaining seats were empty. With any luck, this new development might actually play in his favor.

The pilot walked to the front of the plane, which gave Kent his chance to move in behind the man without being seen. He raised his service weapon. "Unusual flying methods you have."

Visibly startled, the guy whirled around at the sound of Kent's voice, his hand making a quick move toward his waistband.

"That would be a mistake," Kent warned him. "If that's a gun you're reaching for, you better do it real slow, using only your thumb and forefinger."

The man hesitated for a split second, then carefully lifted the weapon into the air in front of him, pinched between his fingertips. His other hand was raised with the palm out.

"There, you have already made your first smart decision of the evening. Let's keep that momentum. Place the gun on the ground and give it a shove so we can have a conversation without any nasty distractions." Once again, the pilot did as he was told with no further signs of aggression. The guy seemed totally willing to do as he was told, and other than his initial reaction to being surprised, showed no signs of wanting any conflict. Of course, as of right now, all he had done wrong was fly without the required navigational lights. He was better off cooperating at this point, and he knew it. *That will make my job easier. Now, I just need to find out exactly what he is involved in and how much he knows.*

****

An icy wind blew across the meadow, gathering speed in the open expanse before penetrating the tree line. Jake tucked his hands into the pockets of his coat and hunched his back against the onslaught. It made standing out in the weather an uncomfortable pastime. The temperature seemed to drop with every passing minute of the dimming sky.

The cell phone in his pocket vibrated. As he reached into the inside pocket of his coat to fish out the device, he was struck with the thought that it was the first time it had gone off in hours. An unusual occurrence lately. He figured that it was probably Mitch checking in, but when he glanced at the screen, the word unknown was prominently displayed. He thought about letting it go to voicemail but decided that with the number of people involved with the current investigation, it would probably be best to see who it was. He answered with his customary method of stating his name.

"I'm glad you were smart enough to take my call. It would have been problematic all around had you declined. You know my voice, yes?"

"I do, but I also thought we had said everything there was to say."

Preston Kennedy's derisive laugh held blatant contempt. The sound had Jake picturing the sneer that he was sure adorned the other man's face. His own jaw clenched in response.

"What do you want, Kennedy? I have no desire to play your games. If you wanted me to be impressed with the fact that you were able to track down this number, you are going to be disappointed…again."

"Finding phone numbers is a trivial thing. The important question is why I bothered at all, and this is where you're going to want to hear every word I say, McCleary." The tone of the other man's voice was so cold and menacing that a foreboding chill ran through Jake. He had a feeling that he wasn't going to like what happened next. "Accept the video for this call," Kennedy instructed. Jake held the phone in front of him and tapped the button. Preston's face filled the screen. "Good, I see you can follow basic directions without too much trouble. That will come in handy for this next part." The phone turned to pan across an open field with an old barn. "Do you know this place?" Kennedy asked.

Jake stared at the scene in front of him trying to recall if he had seen it before. It didn't immediately ring any bells. "It could be anywhere. There are places like that all over."

"Precisely why I liked it. No matter. I will drop you a pin. But for now, this is what I want you to see." The phone's camera shifted again. This time it came to a stop with three people in view. Jake felt as if the ground had suddenly crumbled below his feet, making his knees weak. His heart seemed to stutter, then race.

Slade stood at the center of the frame with a length of rope in each hand that was wrapped around the necks of two women kneeling in the dirt on either side of him. Their hands were tightly bound, and silver tape covered their mouths. Hilly's eyes were wide and shadowed with fear; tearstains marred her cheeks. Kiya's face, on the other hand, showed more anger than fear despite the bruising around one eye. What gave her away was the way her hands trembled against her thighs. The sight tore right through him.

"You son of a bitch! If anything happens to either one of them, there isn't a hole on earth deep enough for you to hide from us. You *will* pay." Jake seethed.

"Shut up!" Kennedy snapped. "I am doing the talking now…you will listen. You are going to retrieve my shipment and bring it to me if you ever want to see these two again. If I catch sight of one person whose last name isn't McCleary, I will put a bullet through one of their skulls and the other will be sold to the highest bidder."

His sister's muffled sob kept him from voicing the sharp retort that sprang to mind. Instead, he made a conscious effort to keep his voice calm. "How am I supposed to accomplish that when you know the cabin is being watched? If I try to remove those drugs, everyone will know."

Kennedy flipped the phone around. His smug smile grated on Jake's nerves. The man truly saw everyone else as beneath him. "Yes, I *do* know. That is why I have taken care of the biggest problem already. Wait for my signal, then bring me my packages. When you get close enough to know where you're going, turn your phone off. We don't want any uninvited guests. Remember, if I see any law enforcement of *any* kind, it will seal these women's fate."

Jake stared at the black screen left behind when the call was terminated. Almost immediately, his phone chimed indicating a new message. He pulled up the pin he had received showing Kennedy's location. It was about a twenty-minute drive, and he still had to get the shipment, get off the ranch without drawing attention, then follow the pin to wherever it led. Cade was keeping watch in the woods somewhere down in the valley that connected to the game lands. There wasn't enough time to try and meet up with him, but Dylan was just across the meadow behind the cabin. He dialed his brother's number even as he moved into a better position to make a run for the structure without being spotted as easily.

When Dylan answered, Jake quickly filled him in on the call he had just received and what had to be done. It took Dylan a couple of minutes to calm down and think through what Jake had just told him. The idea of the women being held by not only Kennedy, but Slade as well, had thrown him for a loop. The man was an unpredictable wild card. "What do you think Kennedy meant when he said that he had taken care of the surveillance problem already, or wait for his signal?" he asked in a tightly controlled voice.

"I have no idea, but we need to get those drugs out of here without the Feds following us. We can't risk them intervening when Hillary and Kiya's lives are on the line. I'll forward the location pin to Cade with a warning, but we can't wait for him. Besides, all of us disappearing at the same time would be way too obvious. You call Mitch. He deserves to at least know what is happening and why. Anything that affects us, or Hillary, affects him. He won't put any of us in jeopardy just to make an arrest. The DEA's focus is this case, those drugs, and Kennedy's operation. Once we know the girls are safe, we can worry about bringing Kennedy down. Stay inside the tree line but meet me halfway between your position and mine. We can decide what to do then."

Jake quickly shot off a text to Cade, then set off to meet Dylan while trying to think of the best way to get the drugs and get out of the clearing. They had to do this soon. Time was ticking.

When Dylan arrived, the first thing he said was that Mitch wasn't answering. "After Kennedy's cryptic message, his being out of touch has me worried. I had to leave a voicemail."

Just then, the buzzing growl of fast approaching dirt bike engines echoed through the trees. The sound grew louder, coming closer. It would draw everyone's attention in that direction. Their sign had just arrived.

****

By the time Mitch reached the steps of the municipal building, his deputy was already struggling to drag the unconscious, injured DEA agent across the threshold of the front door. Mitch ran over to grab the agent's legs, hefting the man's remaining weight off the ground. Together, he and the deputy carried the man out the door and onto the sidewalk where it was safe to lay him down. A quick assessment of the man's injuries showed that he had various burns and shrapnel cuts, but nothing that would immediately jeopardize his life. The man still hadn't come around yet, but the concussive force of the blast was most likely the reason for that since there was no physical evidence of a head wound.

First responders and onlookers alike were arriving in droves. Volunteer firefighters started pulling out hoses and dousing the flames spreading from the back of the building. Smoke rolled out into the street in hot, odorous waves. Two EMTs and a medic took over the agent's care while Mitch helped his shell-shocked deputy to his feet. "You all right?" he asked the dazed officer. His gaze was worried as his friend and colleague coughed and wheezed with practically every breath. "Do you need me to grab another medic?"

"No, let them work on Agent Donner. He was much closer to the blast. I'll be fine once my lungs clear a bit," Deputy Butler assured him.

"What the hell happened? I heard the explosion clear down at the diner."

"All I know is that it wasn't an accident. I'll see if I can find anything on the security cameras in the vicinity, but something was tossed through the back window, then *boom*."

Mitch placed a hand on the other man's shoulder. "Take whatever time you need to catch your breath and recoup. Wait here and find out where Agent Donner is being transported. They might need to transfer him to a burn unit. Then you can see what you can locate on nearby cameras. I am going to coordinate things here and determine what can be salvaged inside. Come find me if you come up with anything." At the deputy's nod, Mitch turned, purposefully striding toward the building. He ignored the buzzing of his personal cell that was tucked away in his pocket. The scene in front of him was chaotic enough. He would deal with all the calls and questions from locals asking what happened later. Right now, his hands were full.

****

While the DEA agents were converging on the hillside in an effort to either capture or track the unknown riders, Jake and Dylan plotted their own course of action. Jake insisted that he be the one to make his way to the cabin to retrieve the supply inside, while Dylan went straight for the truck they had left hidden on the old hunting trail at the far side of the clearing when they arrived tonight. He could be at the vehicle ready to drive them out the second Jake arrived.

Dylan objected at first, stating that he was faster, but his brother argued that he would have an easier time of getting to the old shack, getting the drugs ready to move, then sprinting to the truck carrying all that extra weight. Jake was adamant about Dylan not putting his body through that much physical stress on top of an already nerve-racking set of circumstances.

Dylan relented. He couldn't argue with his brother's reasoning. Even though he felt good, and his physical recovery was almost complete, he still found himself getting winded and tired much easier than before. He was not operating at one hundred percent. He nodded his assent, then reached out to give his brother's shoulder a light squeeze of reassurance, before hurrying off in the direction of the truck.

Jake watched long enough to see his brother disappear into the shadow of the trees before taking one final steadying breath, crouching low and taking off for the cabin. Getting there wasn't a problem. Nobody was paying much attention to his movements, and if he was seen, it didn't raise any red flags since he and Dylan were the ones positioned to keep an eye on the building. The cameras would pick up his actions, but with any luck, there wouldn't be enough time for anyone to try and stop him before he and Dylan were in the clear. All other resources would be focused on the two riders.

He reached the door to the small structure, only to stop short, cursing under his breath. *I forgot about the damn padlock.* The one they previously cut off had been replaced to keep the stash inside secure. Now, its presence was yet another obstacle he needed to overcome. A hurried search of the ground next to the cabin for a rock heavy enough to break the offending thing off produced one he hoped was capable of the task. The noise would alert anyone nearby, but he had no other choice. He positioned himself in front of the door and took aim. It took three solid hits before the metal lock gave way. *One hurdle down.*

Knowing time was running short for a clean getaway, Jake hurried inside, tossing aside the floorboards covering the neatly stacked bundles. *Now, how do I carry these things out of here?* The packs were too large, too awkward to simply pick them up and carry them. He didn't want to be dropping bricks of marijuana all over the clearing on his way to the truck. Unfortunately, there was nothing lying about that would make the job easier.

Despite the cold outside, sweat was beginning to collect between Jake's shoulder blades. He felt the passage of time weighing on him. Mentally scolding himself for the oversight, he shrugged out of his coat. After loading the bundled drugs onto it, he fashioned the entire mass into a makeshift sling, which he tossed over his shoulder.

So far, so good. Dylan must have made it to the truck by now. All I have to do is get there, and we can be on our way.

A little over a half mile away, Dylan sat behind the wheel of an old work truck, his fingers nervously tapping against the steering wheel. With nothing to do but wait in the oppressive silence, his nerves were stretched thin. He shifted his weight on the seat and checked the mirror again for movement. He didn't want to start the engine until the very last minute. No sense in alerting everyone that they were taking off. Each minute that ticked by felt like an eternity. He couldn't stop thinking about how terrified Hillary and Kiya must be. His own fear was almost overwhelming. He had to believe that they would come out of this safely. Working together, he and Jake would find a way to get them back. Anything else was unacceptable. It would destroy his family.

The passenger side door was wrenched open a second before Jake heaved himself and his cargo inside. Dylan felt his pulse skyrocket at the sudden intrusion. He swore his heart skipped a beat or two. "Damn, man, a little warning would have been nice. You almost gave me a heart attack."

Jake glared in his direction, trying to suck air into his heaving lungs. "If I could breathe, I would have told you I was coming," he panted. "Get us out of here before someone catches on to what we are doing."

Dylan cranked the engine, deliberately leaving the lights off. He made his way to the road at a rate that had Jake clutching the dashboard in front of him, but he didn't say a word. Time was of the essence.

****

Cade was frustrated, leaning toward frantic. He had received one disturbing text from Jake, and now he couldn't reach anyone. He had abandoned his pursuit of a dirt bike rider after receiving that text. It was obvious that he was needed elsewhere, but both Jake and Dylan's phones kept going straight to voicemail as if their phones were turned off. Mitch's phone would at least ring but was never picked up before it, too, was directed to voicemail. The landline at the station only produced an endless busy signal. Jake had made a point of saying not to alert the Feds, so he was running out of options. He needed Mitch's help. Determined to get some answers, he resolved to keep hitting redial until Mitch finally answered.

"Holy hell, man, this is not the time to go dark. Where the hell are you? We have an emergency." He practically shouted when Mitch finally answered the phone with something close to a growl.

"No kidding. Why the hell do you think I am too busy for phone calls? The whole damn town is in an uproar, and we only *just* cleared all the surrounding buildings."

"Buildings? You're still in town? Why aren't you going after Hillary? Jake and Dylan can't handle this alone; we need to get out there!"

"Whoa, wait a minute…out where, and what about Hillary? Is she okay? What are you talking about?" Mitch demanded. He was having a hard time following the conversation.

"I'm talking about Kennedy and Slade ambushing Hillary and Kiya to use them as hostages to lure Dylan and Jake to some godforsaken piece of land in the middle of nowhere. What are *you* talking about?"

Dread flowed through Mitch as he realized that the chaos he was currently dealing with was just a diversion, while the main attraction was happening elsewhere. "I'm talking about some kind of explosive device being thrown through a window at the station and taking out half the building." He cursed viciously. *I should have known. Dammit! I should have known, or at least suspected there was more to this! A random*

273

attack on the station doesn't make sense. Now, the woman I love and her family...no, my family, is in jeopardy.

"How many are hurt?" Cade asked.

"I have one deputy suffering from smoke inhalation and minor injuries and one DEA agent at the hospital having his burns and injuries evaluated. Our side of the building will probably be a total loss, but the fire didn't spread much farther than that. We lost all connections or feeds from the ranch, or anywhere else for that matter. The equipment is toast." He switched mental gears, focusing on the new circumstances. "I can delegate everything here. Where the hell is Kent?"

"I don't know, but Kennedy threatened to kill Hillary and Kiya if he saw any kind of law enforcement. We can't involve him at this point. The most important thing is to make sure they are safe first. Which means *we* can't be seen either." He described the location of the pin that Jake had forwarded to his phone.

"Sounds like they are meeting up at, or near, one of the properties Kennedy had shown an interest in. I remember Kiya pointing it out on the map. It isn't all that far from that old airfield."

"Then that's where we are headed," Cade told him. They coordinated their routes to meet up and prayed they could make it in time.

****

Agent Kent was feeling optimistic. The pilot he had in custody, and currently handcuffed to the grab bar in the back of his vehicle, divulged that a shipment was due to arrive here sometime tonight. The man stated that he had been instructed to wait for the items to be delivered, then transport everything to another facility close to the state border. He was unaware of who had hired him, or exactly what he would be transporting, only that he was paid in advance via an online transaction, and if his drop-offs were made without questions or complications, the amount was then doubled automatically.

Kennedy is making a play for those drugs, and he is doing it tonight, Kent thought. The only problem was that he was unable to reach his agent at the station or Sheriff Patterson. Not willing to lose the advantage, he dialed the number for one of the agents on duty at the McCleary ranch.

What he didn't expect was to hear that during an encounter with dirt bike riders near the cabin, the entire McCleary family seemed to have disappeared into thin air. No one knew where they were or how to contact them. A search of the immediate vicinity revealed damage to the door of the cabin and that the drugs were also missing. His agents needed new orders on how to proceed.

Things were rapidly careening downhill. If the drugs were missing, they might be on the way here. On the other hand, if the McClearys were MIA, there had to be more going on than met the eye. He considered his options, then barked out a string of commands. If he covered enough bases, he might get lucky.

Chapter 22

Jake and Dylan cautiously climbed out of the vehicle and glanced around. The old homestead looked deserted, but they knew they were in the right location. Jake recognized the big barn as the one he had seen in the video call. It had taken them longer to get here than they would have liked. It felt like they were running on borrowed time. There had been no further contact from Kennedy either. Still, they needed to buy enough time for Cade and Mitch to get their messages. Maybe one of them would somehow be able to provide some assistance if things got out of hand.

Dylan pressed the button to lock the coat loaded with drugs into the cab of the truck for safe keeping. The first thing they needed to do was locate Kennedy. It would be getting dark soon. He followed Jake past an old corncrib toward the front of the barn.

They cautiously approached the ancient structure, watching and listening for any signs of trouble. When they were about a hundred feet away, Kennedy stepped into view from inside. Once again, the man was impeccably dressed, as if he'd spent the day in a boardroom. "That's far enough," he called out. "Show me that your phones are off, then toss them." The brothers exchanged a look then did as they were told. Jake held up his phone with the screen facing Kennedy and tapped the display. When the device stayed dark and unresponsive, he tossed it frisbee style, into the overgrown weeds. Dylan followed suit.

Once that was done, they were instructed to lift their shirts to reveal their waistbands and turn in a circle, proving they weren't carrying weapons. That, too, was done without complaint.

"We're here, we followed your rules, but you don't get anything until we see that both Hillary and Kiya are unharmed." Jake's eyes were hard and unyielding. A muscle in his jaw pulsed rhythmically while his eyes searched for any indication that the women were still on the property.

"You are in no position to be making demands," Kennedy stated in a haughty tone. "Where is my merchandise?"

"Merchandise? That's what you call piles of illegal contraband?" Dylan asked scornfully.

"That is exactly what it is. They are goods to be sold. I supply a product that is in extremely high demand. That is what commerce is all about. You have interfered with my business, my livelihood, disrupted my supply line, and placed me in the center of an investigation that puts me at a disadvantage. What is stopping me from killing you outright for your interference?"

Jake couldn't believe what he was hearing. The man was trying to make it sound like they were at fault. That they were the ones in the wrong for protecting their home and family. It was beyond ridiculous, unbelievable. The man was mentally unstable. "You are the one who came into our town, onto our land uninvited, and threatened our family. You don't get to act like you are the one who got wronged. You have no business being here at all, let alone transporting your merchandise across land that you *invaded* for your own means. You attacked people that had done nothing wrong, and if you kill us, it will be obvious to everyone that you are responsible."

Kennedy snorted disdainfully. "I can easily disappear. I have done it many times. I can do it again. It is an inconvenience, nothing more. I gave you the opportunity to avoid all these unpleasantries…multiple times. I tried quietly working around you at first. I even offered you a way to profit from my presence. I was very generous with my offers. I did not need to be. You impeded me at every turn. You did not heed warnings that should have made you steer clear of my business. That was your mistake, then and now. It will not be tolerated. You and everyone you have involved in my affairs will pay for it."

"You're completely delusional. We can't avoid something we don't know about," Dylan said in amazement, shaking his head.

Anger flooded Kennedy's face with bright color. "Enough," he snapped. "Bring them!"

Seconds later, Slade appeared in the doorway to the old barn. He tugged Kiya and Hillary along beside him with rough, tattered ropes, which were tied around their throats like leashes. Ugly red rope burns circled each of their necks. Jake felt his blood start to boil at the sight of them, but he grabbed Dylan's arm to stop him from charging at the other man. "Don't do anything that will make them think they are justified in hurting them further," he breathed in warning. He couldn't fault his brother for his reaction though. He was seething with the exact same fury.

"I see you don't care for the condition of my little pets. Too bad this all could have been avoided if you had been reasonable."

"Reasonable? Do you think that kind of thing is reasonable?" Dylan fumed, indicating the women.

"What I think, is that you had better produce my property before I make you decide which one lives and which one dies." Kennedy pointed at Dylan. "Who would you choose? Your sister or the woman that saved your life? As unfortunate as that occurrence was. Or you…" His gaze swung to Jake. "Who do you save? Sister or lover?" He stroked a finger down Kiya's cheek, laughing when she immediately jerked away from his touch, glaring at him with fire in her eyes. "She's a feisty one. I know many people who would enjoy breaking her."

This time, it was Dylan that placed a restraining hand on his brother's chest. "Not yet. You were right. He is looking for an excuse to hurt them. Don't give him one. We need to be smart here."

It took conscious effort for Jake to suppress his anger. There was no choosing one over the other, for either him or Dylan. They would be leaving here with both women, or they would die trying. "You can have your drugs, the minute you let them go."

It only took a glance from Kennedy to have Slade forcing the women to the ground. He stepped on the rope tied to Hillary to restrain her and pulled a knife from his pocket. He jerked Kiya's head back and pressed the knife against her throat. "You will bring us what we want, right now, or I will cut her throat." The depravity in his smile turned Jake's blood to ice. Fear flashed clearly in his eyes and was mirrored in Dylan's.

"It's in the truck. I'll go. You don't need to hurt her," Dylan immediately responded. He held his hand out in a staying motion as he started to inch backward in the direction of the vehicle.

"You had better make it quick," Kennedy demanded. "Slade here enjoys honing his knife skills." Dylan turned and jogged to the truck, praying with every step that they could find a way out of this mess without dire consequences.

Jake eyed Slade in infuriated silence while they waited for Dylan to return. The man gradually increased the pressure of the blade against Kiya's throat. The razor-sharp edge was angled so that it could slide along her skin with little resistance. His grin turned taunting. Hillary whimpered as she watched in horror from her position on the ground next to her friend. A thin line of blood was forming under the blade of the knife as it cut into Kiya's neck. She sucked in an audible breath, trying in vain to pull back to relieve the pressure. Jake's eyes locked with hers, his own breath hitched. Abject fear was not an emotion he was used to, but it was threatening to consume him now. His hands clenched in impotent rage. If he reacted, he knew it was Kiya who would suffer the effects. He had never felt so helpless in his entire life. Maybe it had been a mistake to follow Kennedy's instructions about not involving cops. They were about to lose their only leverage for keeping Kiya and Hillary alive. If they had informed Kent's team, there might have been some hope of making Kennedy keep his word to let the women go. As it was, he was terrified of what came next.

Dylan came back and dropped the bundled coat at his feet. His chest constricted, as he watched Kiya shift under the force of the knife blade. Blood was starting to run down the side of her neck in little rivulets. He could not allow this situation to deteriorate any further. He owed the woman in front of him his life. She owned a very special piece of his heart, and now she was the one at the mercy of a madman that had none. He would do anything to protect her. She wasn't only important to him, but to every member of his extended family as well, and it was obvious that Jake was in love with her. He tried to make his expression one of reassurance when he met her gaze. His mind raced through one scenario after another searching for a feasible way to get both her and Hilly away from here safely. Unfortunately, there were far too many ways that one or both could be harmed or even killed if he or Jake made a move against Kennedy. He could think of only one thing that might work.

"I have what you want. Let Jake take the women and go. You don't need them. I'll stay," Dylan offered.

"The hell you will." Jake's words were a deep-throated growl.

Dylan focused directly on Kennedy. "This started with me; it can end with me. You've had it out for me since the first day we met in town. You failed in your first attempt against me. Here's your second chance. You get your revenge, your drugs, then disappear just like you planned. Let them go. You might get away with killing me. You won't get away with killing all of us. The Feds know who you are. They wouldn't stop hunting you." He ignored Slade when the man scoffed. He was just another pawn in this game. A dangerous pawn for sure, but a pawn, nonetheless. Kennedy called the shots.

Kiya made a desperate sound of denial behind the tape covering her mouth and started to struggle, but Dylan shook his head. "It's my turn, angel." He bent to snag the drugs then stepped closer to Kennedy. "Let them go. Take me."

Kennedy didn't even blink. In fact, he laughed outright. "An interesting idea to be sure, and your death *will* bring me great satisfaction, but I am not dumb enough to trade three for one. Why do that when I already have all four of you exactly where I want you? I am the one holding all the cards here."

Cade stepped out around the left side of the barn, with a rifle pressed to his shoulder. "I would have to disagree with that assumption."

From his position slightly behind the two men and their hostages, he must have parked farther up on the old dirt road that they had all come in on and diagonally cut across the field past their small group while everyone was distracted. A mixture of hope and relief surged through Dylan at the sight of his brother. Maybe they had a shot at surviving this after all. Jake, too, felt some of his desperation fade. He prepared himself to take any opportunity that presented itself.

Kennedy's head whirled to face the new arrival. With one hand he reached down to grab Hillary and haul her up in front of him. The other pulled a small handgun from under his coat. He pressed the barrel tight against Hilly's temple. "Well, well. We have ourselves a real old-fashioned standoff, now, don't we?" Unbelievably, his voice sounded amused. "What are the odds that you can get a shot off before I put a bullet in her brain?"

Cade cursed silently. His grip tightened on the

rifle, even though he no longer had a shot. There was no way he could risk hitting his sister.

Behind Kennedy, Slade dragged Kiya to her feet to use as a shield also. He looped his fingers through the rope at her throat, twisting to pull it tight.

Kiya's ability to breathe was immediately clamped off. The rough material ground into her windpipe like a vise. With her mouth taped shut, she couldn't get enough air. Her fingers dug at the rope trying to loosen it, but Slade's grip was too strong. She had no leverage with her wrists bound. She felt lightheaded. Bright, shiny glimmers of dancing lights flashed in her vision. It didn't take long for that to fade and darkness to rim her field of view. Her chest burned with the need for oxygen. She fought to stay conscious. She had to do something before it was too late.

Just then, Mitch emerged from behind the corncrib. His face was a mask of focused determination. "If you want to get out of this alive, you will let them go, right now."

It was all the distraction Kiya needed. She slammed her head backward into Slade's nose as hard as she could. There was a gratifying crunch, and his grip loosened. The watering of his eyes and the blood running down his face didn't stop him from shoving Kiya aside so he could hurl his knife at Mitch with remarkable strength. Sprawled in the dirt, Kiya couldn't even call out a warning.

As the blade left Slade's fingers, a single gunshot exploded from somewhere beyond Mitch. Slade collapsed to the ground, unmoving. Instantly, Dylan and Jake launched themselves forward to tackle Kennedy. Dylan seized the wrist that was holding the weapon and violently rotated it backward, wresting the gun away from Hillary's head an instant before a shot rang out. The bullet penetrated the barn wall with a heavy thud.

Jake's full body weight impacted the man's side with bruising force. They both went down hard. Jake wasted no time once he hit the ground. Pushing himself up with one hand, he plowed his fist into Kennedy's face with all the force he could muster while pinning the man's other hand to the ground. How he had been able to hold onto the gun after Dylan twisted his wrist to the breaking point was a mystery. Kennedy thrashed and bucked, trying to dislodge Jake's weight. Jake drew back and threw a second jab while Cade hurried to remove a frantic Hillary from the action. Fire ignited along Jake's upper arm when Kennedy managed to brace his left forearm against Jake's collarbone and angle the gun in his right hand in Jake's direction, before pulling the trigger. The searing pain only incited Jake further as he battled to gain the upper hand. Fortunately, Kennedy was no match for him physically. Jake was bigger and stronger. The added surge of adrenaline coursing through him from the all-consuming desire to protect his family and his way of life made it easier to lift the other man off the ground and plow a fist into his jaw with bone-shattering ferocity. Ready to strike again, Jake realized that the man under him was out cold. He shoved Kennedy's limp form away from him in disgust and climbed to his feet. His eyes searched until they landed on Kiya. Dylan knelt nearby with her held against him protectively. Jake closed the distance between them in a heartbeat. Carefully pulling her to her feet, his arms wrapped around her in a tight embrace. His breathing was harsh and uneven as she clung to him. Unsteady fingers tangled in her hair.

"Are you okay?" He panted without relinquishing his hold. "I have never been so scared in my entire life as I was when I found out you and Hilly had been taken. Then when Slade held that knife to your throat, I thought he would end us both with one action." Shifting slightly, he looked deep into her eyes. "I can't lose you…ever. The thought of you being in their hands had me going crazy. I was ready to do absolutely anything to get you back."

"I know. All I could think of was being able to get back to you. I was so afraid of what would happen once he got you here, but there was no way I was giving up without one heck of a fight."

His gaze moved over her face like a caress. He was both proud and amazed at her strength and resilience. He tilted her head up to get a look at the cut on her neck. The blood was starting to congeal. The crimson trails were starting to dry, and the cut was only oozing. His gut clenched at the thought of what could have happened.

She took the hand under her chin in hers. "I'm okay."

Jake's thumb traced the dark color forming around her eye. "He hit you?"

Kiya shrugged. "Slade didn't like it when I wouldn't go quietly, but I'm fine, I promise." Her gaze dropped to the gouge in his arm. "Looks like we are going to have matching scars."

An anguished cry drew Kiya's attention to Hillary who called out to her.

"We need your help!" she pleaded.

Kiya hurried over and dropped to her knees beside Mitch. Blood stained his thigh in a rapidly expanding pool of red.

"There's so much blood." Hilly sobbed. Her hands hovered over the injury, unsure of what to do. Jake attempted to draw her away to give Kiya some room to work, but Hilly wouldn't budge. She couldn't leave Mitch's side.

Mitch tried to calm her with soothing words as he stroked a hand down her back despite the pain radiating from his wound. The blade was embedded deep. It tore at the surrounding flesh with every movement. Calming her helped settle his own frayed nerves.

Agent Kent strode up and crouched beside them in the patchy grass. He gave Mitch a sympathetic look. His attempt to stop Slade had been just a fraction too late. He arrived in time to see Slade's assault on Kiya and him pitching her to the ground to confront the sheriff, but by the time he could get close enough and draw his weapon to fire, the knife was already in the air.

"Kent. Where the hell did you come from?" Mitch asked through gritted teeth. "Not that I'm complaining that you showed up."

"I was in the neighborhood. Thought I would stop by and see if any of you were around," came his cryptic reply. He would explain later when things weren't quite so hectic.

Mitch eyed him curiously but sucked in a ragged breath at the mild pressure Kiya applied to his leg. "Ow, damn it, I can still feel that, ya know. The leg is still attached," he groused with mild gruffness.

"Quit whining and give me your shirt," she tossed back. He wasn't actually upset with her, and she knew it. He was trying to dispel some of the tension. He had to be in a great deal of pain. The depth and placement of his injury was very concerning.

His chuckle was strained but encouraging as he stripped out of his work shirt, leaving only the T-shirt underneath. "Now she's wanting to steal my clothes. Must be the uniform. It does weird things to the ladies."

"This isn't funny," Hilly huffed. "Besides, you're already taken. No matter what the ladies think." Her heated look dared him to disagree.

"That I am, honey." He pushed some loose strands of hair behind her ear with a smile. "Always have been." He handed his shirt to Kiya.

"This is going to hurt," she warned him as she looped the shirt around the hilt of the knife where it protruded from his thigh. His breath caught when she pressed down gently on the cloth while being careful not to shift the knife. When the blood kept coming, she bunched the fabric up tighter and pushed a bit harder to stanch the flow. She made sure not to cause any more damage or press too hard. She only wanted to slow the loss of blood. It was entirely possible that the blade had hit an artery. That is why the blade needed to stay exactly where it was. It could be the only thing saving him from bleeding out. If it was removed or even dislodged, the one thing slowing or blocking the flow at all would be lost. She brought her eyes up to his. Apprehension was written all over her face. "Do you have a phone?"

Agent Kent answered first. "I'll handle it. As soon as I get EMS en route, I'll make sure Kennedy is secure and ready for transport." He glanced over to where Cade was standing guard over the unconscious man in case he came around. "Time to call in the troops. You keep doing what you're doing," he told her.

Kiya swore under her breath. *This isn't working. He is still losing too much blood. I have to make this stop, or EMS won't get here in time.* Mitch was already starting to show signs of going into shock from blood loss. His breathing was becoming fast and shallow, his skin was looking pale and clammy, and she could tell that his energy was rapidly fading. "I need a belt or a stick…now!" Her eyes searched everyone around her. She wasn't surprised when no one was wearing a belt. They weren't exactly the norm anymore.

"I'll find you a stick." Dylan unbuttoned his shirt and shrugged out of it, tossing it to Kiya. He knew she was planning on creating a tourniquet. That meant things were not going in Mitch's favor. *I need to do this fast. I'm not losing one of my best friends to the actions of an egocentric drug smuggler.* The first couple of prospects he found were not sturdy enough to do what was needed, but the third one could get the job done. *Third time's the charm*, he thought.

Kiya gratefully accepted the offering and spun his shirt in rapid circles between her blood-soaked hands to wind the fabric into a tighter strand, which she wrapped around Mitch's thigh above the wound. After crossing the ends and tucking one side underneath the other, she gently pulled it snug. She then placed the stick onto the top of the first crossover before securing a knot on top of the stick. She gradually started to rotate the piece of wood clockwise to tighten it against the leg.

Kiya held her breath while she waited to see if her

makeshift tourniquet would work. The breath left her lungs in a whoosh when the amount of blood drastically diminished. She continued to hold the tension on the stick. "This will work for now. I'll relieve the pressure occasionally to make sure he still gets circulation to his foot, but he needs an ambulance. I'm not a miracle worker." She hated the fact that there wasn't anything more she could do.

Dylan's palm came to rest on her shoulder. "I disagree. You are doing everything you can, and I know for a fact that if anyone can make this work, you can."

Mitch agreed. "I can't think of one other person I would rather have here right now."

Kiya's eyes misted over at the unwavering support. It bolstered her own flagging confidence. She nodded, taking a deep breath. "Okay, you're right. We can do this." She gave Hilly a reassuring smile.

When they eventually heard the wail of sirens in the distance, there was a collective cry of gratitude.

Chapter 23

The surgical team spent approximately three and a half hours repairing the damage to the artery, muscle, and nerves in Mitch's leg. During that time, Kiya and the McCleary siblings waited anxiously in a small lounge designated for the loved ones of trauma patients. For Jake, Cade, and Hillary, it was the second time in a matter of months that they had found themselves pacing its floors.

Kent was busy coordinating the investigations and actions of both his agents and Mitch's deputies until the sheriff was capable of appointing someone to temporarily replace him during his recovery. For now, the agent was fielding calls and delegating tasks from the hospital. Deputy Jenkins and Agent Sullivan had both been treated and released after being knocked unconscious during Kiya and Hillary's abduction at the ranch. Neither one had been willing to stay overnight for observation. The news of the bombing at the station had been a surprise to everyone except Cade. He confessed, somewhat sheepishly, that in the turmoil of the girls being taken and the confrontation with Kennedy, he had forgotten about the chaos happening in town. The news had only come to light after Mitch had been wheeled into the operating room.

It took time for Kent to catch up on everything that had transpired since then. Deputy Butler had stepped in to handle things in town. He was able to pull video surveillance from the bank next door to the municipal building. Apparently, he had grainy footage of a pickup truck turning into the small alley behind the station with one guy driving and another in the bed of the vehicle. They slowed down just long enough for the guy in the back to chuck a backpack through the window before peeling off. The camera lost sight of them once they turned out of the alley.

Butler said that they found evidence indicating that the bag had been loaded with a couple bricks, probably just to break through the window glass, a homemade pipe bomb, and enough accelerant to make sure they were distracted for a while.

"Give whatever footage you collected to one of my agents and tell them to send it in to the lab and see if they can get it cleaned up enough to be put through a facial recognition database or at least enough to be able to locate the truck used. It's only a matter of time until we track down the men responsible. In the meantime, I will get the drugs transported to a DEA facility. They will be able to track its origins." Kent concluded the call after making sure Kennedy and his hapless pilot had made it to their temporary cells in a nearby town. He was eager to start the interrogation process. "I will stick around until we know Sheriff Patterson is in the clear, then I'll head into town to finalize plans for our withdrawal. The remainder of the investigation can be done from headquarters."

"Well, now we know what Kennedy meant when he said he had taken care of the surveillance issue at the cabin. I still can't wrap my head around the fact that he arranged an attack on a police station." Jake's voice was tinged with disbelief.

"No kidding. The paperwork on the destruction of all that equipment alone is going to take weeks," Kent complained in a dry tone. "At least your involvement in this case is over for the time being and you can get back to the life you had before Kennedy showed up. You may need to testify later down the road, but for now, I hope you all can move past this."

"I don't know about any of you, but it is going to take me a long while before I stop looking over my shoulder all the time, or second-guessing everything I do." A shiver moved up Hillary's spine at the thought. There was something she didn't understand though. "How *did* you end up finding us when you didn't even know what was happening?"

Kent's lips turned up in a half smile. "That's an interesting story." He went on to describe his run-in with Kennedy's pilot who was waiting to fly the drugs, and maybe even Kiya and Hillary themselves, to a so far undisclosed location. "When everyone went dark at the same time, I knew something was happening. I dispatched my people to check every location associated with Kennedy's land deals. The only thing they found at Kiya's place was a couple of sets of dirt bike tracks in the barn. They must have launched the distraction at the cabin from there once they knew the cameras were out of operation. Since I was at the airfield that Kiya had pointed out, I was the closest one to the property you were taken to. I was glad I found you all there and could lend assistance. I just didn't get there quite fast enough." His voice took on a hollow note thinking about the sheriff's injury.

Dylan shook his head. "Things would have gotten a

lot worse if you hadn't shown up when you did and taken Slade out of the equation. He was willing to kill anyone and everyone that got in his way."

"Which reminds me…" Kiya cut in as she punched Dylan's arm lightly. "Just what the hell were you thinking when you offered yourself up like some kind of sacrificial lamb? You could have gotten yourself killed!"

"I was thinking that it was the only thing that might have worked to stop them from hurting either of you."

"Well, it was dumb, and you will *never* do anything like that ever again. I didn't patch you up just so you could surrender yourself to the people who shot you in the first place," she scolded tearfully.

Dylan grinned and tugged her in for a hug. "Yeah, I love you too. And for the record, I don't plan on ever being in that kind of situation again."

A doctor wearing surgical scrubs entered the room, bringing all conversation to a halt. Hillary took a tentative step forward. "You have news about Mitch…Sheriff Patterson?"

The doctor nodded while pulling the cap off his head. "The surgery went well. We were able to repair the damage to his artery and nerves. We gave him a couple units of blood to replace what he lost. General weakness for the first couple of days is expected. He will need rehab and may walk with a bit of a limp for a while, but I see no medical reason that would limit his ability to continue in his current position as sheriff. At this time, he is in the recovery room but will be moved to a regular bed soon. You can see him then, but I prefer that you do so one at a time for now. He needs to remain still and get some rest."

Hillary clasped the doctor's hand in between her trembling ones. Overwhelming relief swept through her. She had been so scared of losing him when they had only recently truly found one another. "Thank you. You have saved more than one life today." The others joined in, offering their thanks before the doctor quietly left the room. The atmosphere in the room was completely different than when he had walked in. There were backslaps and hugs as they celebrated the news.

When the time finally came that Mitch was allowed visitors, Hillary, of course, was the first to enter his room. It was agreed that the others would follow one at a time for a brief visit before they left the two of them alone for the rest of the night. Hilly had already decided that she would remain at the hospital whether they let her stay with Mitch in his room or not.

She nervously eased open the door to the room she had been directed to, but when she saw Mitch lying in the bed with all his monitors, it brought back the anguish, the fear she had felt when her brother was in the same situation, and she rushed to the side of the bed to take his hand in hers. She needed to see for herself that he was in fact safe and doing well. Only he could dispel the anxiety lodged inside her.

His fingers immediately tightened around hers. Drowsy eyes opened to skim over her face. He gave her a weak but heartfelt smile. "I was hoping that your face would be the first thing I saw when I woke up, and here you are."

Hillary's own eyes glistened with tears. "Of course, I'm here. This is where I belong…with you. It may have taken me a while to realize it, but I love you. I could never leave you, especially not at a time like this.

I'm here until you make me leave."

His smile grew larger. "Then you are going to be around for an awfully long time. I have loved you forever, and I think it's about time that you married me."

Shock left her speechless. She stared at him wondering if his pain meds might be too strong. *He isn't serious…is he?*

"Hilly? Honey, grab the bag of my belongings on the chair."

Dazed, she moved to retrieve the bag. He rummaged through it for a minute before pulling out a small black velvet box. He flipped the top open to reveal a beautifully crafted diamond engagement ring.

"Will you? Marry me?"

Her breath caught. "You bought a ring? You kept it with you?"

"I bought it a little while ago. I kept it with me in case I found the right time to ask you."

"And you waited until now?" she asked incredulously.

"Well, at least I have your undivided attention," he said with a crooked grin.

"That's not funny." She stared at the ring he was still holding. It really was one of the most beautiful rings she had ever seen.

Mitch cleared his throat. "Ah, Hilly? You're making me nervous here. You haven't answered my question." His expression became hesitant.

"What? Oh…*yes*!" She giggled. "My answer is yes!" She grabbed his face and gave him an enthusiastic kiss.

"Thank God! I thought I was going to have to beg."

He pulled her in for another, more lingering kiss, then removed the ring from its box and slid it onto her finger. It was a perfect fit.

"I guess the nurses have to let me stay here with you now. They can't refuse to let me care for my future husband."

"I like the sound of that." His voice was tired but happy.

When Hillary walked into the waiting room a few minutes later, Kiya was alarmed by the look on her face. It was obvious that she had been crying again, and she seemed almost shell-shocked. Kiya sprang to her feet.

"Oh Hilly, what's wrong? Is Mitch all right? What happened?" Her concern seized everyone's attention. They all instantly focused in on Hillary.

A brilliant smile spread across her face. "Nothing's wrong. Everything is...very right. Mitch asked me to marry him."

"What?" Kiya asked, just to make sure she had heard her friend correctly.

Hillary held up her left hand, displaying her ring. "We're engaged!"

There was a brief moment of astonished silence, then the room exploded into a chorus of cheers and congratulations.

****

Three days later, the McCleary family was gathered in the kitchen at the ranch. Even Margaret was back and bustling around the kitchen making sure that every member of her chosen family was cared for. The table was covered with baked goods and tasty treats that were a testament to how much she had missed doting on them.

They had just finished a call with Agent Kent on the progress of the investigation. The DEA task force had been able to track down the two men responsible for the explosion at the municipal building, and they were now in custody. In addition to Seth, who was present when Dylan was shot, others involved in Kennedy's activities were now scrambling to make deals to lighten their sentences. As was usually the case, the low level "expendables" were practically tripping over themselves in their efforts to point fingers and name names to save their own skins. Kent was quickly tidying up loose ends and building an airtight case against the entire crew. The DEA now had a blueprint on how some of these types of trafficking routes were set up. It gave them a pattern to look for in rural areas. Agent Kent had thanked them for their help and promised to keep them updated.

The atmosphere in the room was lighthearted and upbeat. They were simply enjoying spending the morning together. Life was starting to return to normal. It was a wonderful feeling to know that their ordeal was finally over, and they could look forward to the future without fear or uncertainty looming over them.

With the business with the DEA out of the way, Hillary was happy to move on to more pleasant topics. Gretchen would soon be home for an extended visit now that the threat from Kennedy was gone. Her sister had been the first call Hillary made from the hospital. They were all excited for the upcoming reunion. Until then, Hilly was only home long enough to pack a small suitcase. She planned on accompanying Mitch to his place later that night when he was discharged from the hospital. She was overjoyed with his recovery and was looking forward to personally overseeing the continued recuperation of her fiancé.

"I should probably start thinking about moving back home too," Kiya said during a lull in the conversation about Gretchen's arrival.

She blinked when Jake and Dylan stated, "You *are* home," at the exact same time. The others nodded in agreement. Dylan walked over to her and wrapped an arm around her shoulders. "I'm sure that under the circumstances, Bill and Edna will be more than happy to release you from your rental agreement. We are your family, and *this* is your home."

Jake shook his head, exasperated that Dylan got to Kiya first even though he wholeheartedly seconded the sentiment behind his statement. He heaved an exaggerated sigh as he watched his younger brother. Folding his arms across his chest, he asked, "Must I remind you to keep your paws off my woman?" He tried to sound imposing, but it didn't faze Dylan at all.

Completely unrepentant, his brother just grinned and planted a smacking kiss against Kiya's temple. "Nope, wouldn't do you any good anyway." He winked at Hillary when she tried to stifle a laugh.

"Looks like I'm going to have to make things official in order to keep you in your place, bro." Jake's response had Kiya looking confused, but Hilly's mouth dropped open.

"Does that mean what I think it means?" his sister asked.

Jake's eyes never left Kiya. He reached for her hand and drew her close. "I know we haven't been together for very long and most of that time was overshadowed with tension, but I know that we are good for each other, we make a great team. I know what I want, and I know that I love you. I want us to make a life together. So, yes, it means I'm asking her to marry me." He gazed into her eyes with a hopeful expression. "If she'll have me."

Joy flooded through Kiya with a force that amazed her. She couldn't describe how much she wanted what he was offering. She had never been more sure of anything in her life as she was of the fact that she wanted a life with him. She wanted him, and she wanted this family. "Oh…she'll have you." She laughed through happy tears.

Jake's hands gripped her waist. "That's a yes?"

Kiya nodded, love shining in her eyes. "That's a yes."

He picked her up and spun her in a circle. "That's a yes!" He lowered her back to her feet and captured her lips in a searing kiss.

When he finally released her, Cade and Dylan wasted no time congratulating their beaming brother. Hilly squealed her delight and hurried over to envelop Kiya in an enthusiastic hug. "Now you really are my sister," she gushed happily while rocking Kiya from side to side. She stopped suddenly when a thought struck her. She held Kiya at arm's length. "We need to call Gretchen! I can't wait to tell her. We have weddings to plan!"

A word about the author…

C.D. Bennett strives to write adventurous tales that make you feel as though you are part of the story. She enjoys leaving everyday life behind for a world of romance and intrigue. Be sure to follow her and her writing adventures on her author pages at Amazon, on Facebook, Goodreads, and Instagram @readcdbennett. https://readcdbennett.wixsite.com/readcdbennett